The Eternal Gateway:

Sentinel

By SB Jones

The Eternal Gateway: Sentinel

Cover by: JR Fleming, www.jrfleming.com
Fonts by: KC Fonts, www.kcfonts.com, kcfonts@gmail.com
Edited by: Carolyn Johnson

ISBN: 978-0-9836818-5-4
Visit us on Facebook at Facebook.com/SBJonesPublishing
Want to find out about new releases? Join the mailing club at sbjonespublishing@gmail.com

Contents

"I've seen that look before."
-Xavier Ross-

"They killed her."
-Camden Arland-

"You're lying."
-Suki Leigh-

"I held her in my arms!
I saw the life drain from her eyes."
-Camden Arland-

"She is not coming.
She has to go back and save Uncle Camden."
-Alyssa Atagi-

"Was it worth it?"
-Camden Arland-

"I don't know."
-Mr. Eleazar-

Chapter 1

SILVERTON

Suki Leigh stood in the flickering light on a deserted street corner of Silverton. The hell she had been living in since that fateful night in Courduff had finally spilled into the reality around her. The night sky glowed with a faint orange hue on the northern horizon. Fires dotted the land, caused by everything from intentional arson, crashed airships, battles, and even lightning strikes. The world itself seemed desperate to burn away everything involved with the war. It was war now. No illusions anymore that it wasn't.

Therion's control had expanded to the western shores with the help of the city of Cahir and far into the southern edge of the continent where The Eternal Gateway stood in the jungles of Canyamar. Only the great cities of the east still held out together against Courduff's army. Smaller pockets of resistance still existed, like Silverton, but the destruction of their flagship the *Snow Break* and the scattering of their leaders, Silverton was no longer a threat. In fact, Silverton had not been targeted for a while, and rumor had it was being saved for a later razing in case morale for Therion's army from Courduff needed lifted.

Most cities were now under martial law, and the governments had prioritized resources into production needed for the war effort. Weapon platforms were now manufactured in every city. It was only a matter of time before Therion crushed everything.

Time.

Suki looked at her hands. Grime had found a place to live under her fingernails, and the palms were sore and cracked. All the windows and buildings around her were blackened out during the night. No reason to give an air raid an easy target. Using one dirty fingernail to clean another, she looked at the dirt and remembered a better time.

"Damn it," Camden cursed, pulling the empty fishing line out of the lake. "That was the last of my bait too."

"Maybe I could just blast a few fish out of the water," Kail offered, pointing his finger at the water like a gun.

"And where is the sport in that?" Camden retorted, inspecting the empty hook. "There is tradition that must be followed in the grand art of angling. You can't just point your finger, spray some magic around and call yourself a fisherman."

"You would do it in a heartbeat if you could."

"True," Camden said quickly, "but I can't so we're doing it this way."

Kail shrugged with a smile. "At least you have mastered the art of finding bait."

Camden's smile faded, and he shook his head. "Don't go there."

"You're the best at it, and I'm sure Suki and Angela will agree that there isn't a better master-."

"Stop!" Camden interrupted.

"Fine, but if you don't master-fish us up some dinner, I'm going to boil the lake and to hell with your traditions," Kail said, leaving the shoreline to return to the camp.

"Have you figured out that device yet?" Angela asked Suki as Kail approached.

"I think so," Suki said, taking a look through the viewfinder of the camera and centering it on Kail.

"How much ammunition does it hold?" the red-head asked.

Suki gave her a funny glare. "Pictures, and it's film, not ammunition," she finished with a click, taking a picture of Kail.

"You said you shoot with it," Angela repeated, watching Suki slide the next frame into place.

Kail could see the pleading for help in Suki's eyes. "Here," he said, holding his hands out to his wife Angela, helping her up off the ground. Kissing her he asked, "Where are the twins?"

As if on cue, a high pitched squeal sounded from just out of view. Everyone shifted their focus in the direction of the sound as Amaya burst into sight. Her red hair matched her mother's, and she continued to shriek as her dark haired twin followed triumphantly, holding something up in her hand.

"What is going on?" Kail asked as Amaya hid behind his legs, putting him between herself and her sister.

Alyssa made a move towards Amaya with what she had found. Shrieking again, Amaya bolted for the protection of her mother.

"What have you got there?" Kail asked as Alyssa tilted her head and smiled.

Holding her hand out, Kail could see the two ends of a large worm struggling to escape her grip.

"A worm," Alyssa said a matter-of-factly.

"A big one too," Kail said.

"A yucky worm," Amaya said, peeking out bravely from behind Angela.

"It is not something to be afraid of," Angela reassured Amaya as Alyssa showed the worm to her. "You should find one of your own to defend yourself with."

"Or you could just team up to go after Uncle Camden," Kail said. "I know he's fresh out of yucky worms."

"Look this way girls," Suki said, holding up the camera. Both twins smiled, and Alyssa brandished the worm in her direction as she snapped a photograph of them.

Alyssa handed the worm to her sister. Tentatively Amaya took the worm but relaxed when it turned out to not be as yucky as she had feared. United, the twins set off to find another worm before planning the best attack against Uncle Camden once both of them were armed.

"I pity anyone who goes up against the two of them," Suki said. "One Keratin is formidable." She looked at Angela. "But twins," she finished, looking towards Camden on the edge of the lake who had no idea of the impending attack being planned on him.

"Natural warriors," Angela agreed.

"Kids," Kail said with a smile.

The street light above Suki gave a faint sizzle as the light dimmed and flickered, pulling her back from her memory. With a sigh she looked down at her hands remembering.

Camden growled like a dog protecting its master as he pushed his hands into the concrete that supported the locked door that stood between them and Alyssa.

Suki watched speechless as he tore the door from the wall of the prison and sent it flying down the hallway with a crash. She knew he could change his body into whatever material he wanted. It was easier for him if he was in contact with that material, but she had never seen him use his magic like this before. The concrete wall had literally turned into sand.

"So help me. I will kill every single one of them," Camden promised.

"You're safe now," she reassured Alyssa, picking her up from the corner of the cell she had been cowering in.

"Take her and go now," Camden said. "I will find Amaya and meet you at the pickup spot," he finished, rushing back into the hall.

"The burned man took her," Suki remembered Amaya telling her. "She is not coming. She has to go back and save Uncle Camden."

"She is not coming," Suki's mind repeated.

Then the stranger appeared. The one Alyssa called grandpa.

"Good bye Aunt Suki."

The light flickered above Suki growing dimmer.

"You're lying," she screamed back at him. She knew he was telling the truth, he had never raised his voice or yelled at her. A dead man had killed Amaya, she winced through the memory. Xavier the same man who had killed everyone in the jungle all those years ago. He would have even killed her if it had not been for Camden saving her and for Kail getting her to safety.

The *Snow Break* had been destroyed in front of them as they stood helplessly. Destroyed by her own brother who had earlier risked everything to tell them where they could find Kail and Angela's twins. The crazed look in Camden's eyes as he tore off into the night, abandoning her while part of the city burned from the wreckage of the airship.

Losing both of the twins had crushed her heart, but facing Kail and Angela a week later had killed her soul. The way Angela had screamed and cried as she was told the story of what had happened haunted Suki every night, as did the look from Kail as he left to find her.

Suki wiped away the tears from her cheeks and looked at her dirty hands one last time as the street light hissed and popped before going out, casting her into darkness.

Chapter 2

SOMEWHERE ALONG THE WESTERN COAST

The photo had grown rough around the edges, and a large crease had found its way across the left half. Kail looked at the smiling faces of his twin daughters. Amaya with red hair like her mother and Alyssa with dark hair like her father. One dead, and the other taken. Both gone.

Kail quickly put the photograph back into his vest when he heard Angela arrive behind him. The sound of her landing from flight was one he hadn't heard in a while. "I'm glad your back," he said. Even as he stood and turned towards her, Kail could sense the depression flowing from Angela, an atmosphere of gloom that he had no way to cast aside. He had his own nightmares about what had happened, but so far he had managed to keep them buried as best he could. It had been over six months now chasing after his wife. Keeping his distance when she wanted to be alone, and comforting her in the moments of complete breakdown.

Angela looked at him through glassy eyes. "How?" she asked.

Carefully Kail waited for more, not wanting Angela to bolt to the skies again.

"How do you make the pain stop?"

He moved to her, holding out his hand. When she took it, he suddenly caught her in his embrace. "I don't think the pain will ever stop," he whispered into her ear.

"He said it would be hell," Angela said, her voice on the edge of tears.

"Who?"

Angela drew back and looked into his eyes. "The Time Walker. I could choose death a thousand years ago, or go to a future that would be a living hell."

Kail understood. He wanted to blame Mr. Eleazar for everything. "There was another part to that offer."

Angela glanced at his chest where he kept the photo of their girls. "Yes, if I survived long enough, there would be something worth living for," she added. "I thought I was passed that, with you and Amaya and Alyssa, but this is the hell he spoke of."

Kail rubbed his thumb across the line of runes on her left arm, a reminder of how close he had come to losing her once before. "He manipulated all of us. He will answer for it."

Returning her eyes to him Angela spoke. "I want out of this hell."

"I know, so do I," he answered. "There is one way."

Angela looked at him questioningly.

"The Eternal Gateway," Kail said. He quickly added before she could say anything, "I know Therion controls it now. That would explain why we haven't seen Mr. Eleazar and why everything has gone to hell. But maybe, just maybe we can get it back." He had tried several times to have this conversation with her before but failed. "Then we use it ourselves."

Angela shook her head. "If it were so easy, none of this would be necessary," she said, reminding him that everyone had been gathered by Mr. Eleazar years ago.

"I thought of that," Kail admitted. "Even if it's not possible, I would happily die knowing I tried."

Angela pulled her Keratin war blade out of its sheath. The runes that made it impossible for it to break or become dull glinted a faint silvery color. Once there had been two of them. Now just the one remained, its twin lost in battle above the Canyons of Cahir. "Can we do it alone?"

Kail shook his head. "I don't think so."

Taking a few agile swipes with her blade through the air, Angela nodded. "Will they come with us?"

"Yes, maybe," he said. "I don't know. We need to find them."

"Where do we start?" Angela asked, returning the lone blade back to its resting spot.

Not wanting to lose her now that she seemed to be ready to try something other than running from their pain. "We start where we left, from Silverton. Find out if anyone is still there and where the Mastersons, Suki, and Camden are." Kail had had plenty of time to plan.

Chapter 3

OUTSIDE SILVERTON

Hours later Kail and Angela stood on the outskirts of Silverton. The light forest area that had surrounded the city had intentionally been burned away. Kail guessed to increase visibility around the city. Behind them, the tear in reality that he had created with his magic for them to travel through snapped shut. Soon after arriving, Kail could feel the heat of the sun through the grey-brown haze of smoke that made midday feel like dusk. The black Imaera hide armor soaked up the warmth causing it to be deceptively present.

"I expected it to be burned to the ground," Angela said, looking at the city that had been their home for many years. Several trails of smoke floated into the air from fires that had been recently put out but still smoldered.

"It is not as bad as I feared, but worse in other ways. It seems quiet though, dead like," Kail added his assessment. He felt it first from his Divination magic, a faint warning that they were not alone and were being watched.

"What?" Angela asked, picking up on his nervousness.

"Not dead," he answered, pushing his magic out around them. Several sets of eyes were on them from the edge of the city, and several dozen people were scattered around them, aware of their presence, but staying hidden from view. "Be ready," he warned, heading down one of the main roads leading into Silverton.

They were only a hundred yards from the city before Kail motioned with his hand for them to stop. One of the people Kail had sensed stepped into view, a man with a sergeant's insignia on his uniform. He came to a stop several yards away from Kail and Angela and held his rifle at the ready. Three more soldiers joined the sergeant.

"Identify yourselves," the sergeant ordered.

Kail could feel Angela stiffen behind him. Holding his hands out in front of him as a gesture of peace, he said. "Kail Falconcrest." Not wanting the man to accidently shoot at them Kail asked. "Who is in charge here?"

"I am, Sergeant Erickson," he quipped and shifted his focus on Angela. "Who's the dame?"

Kail brought his magic to the ready, just in case things got out of control.

"Dame?" Angela repeated, coming to face the sergeant. "I am Angela Atagi of House Atagi. Insult me again, and I will turn you into a dame."

Two of the men behind Erickson took a few steps backwards, clearly having recognized their names if not Kail or Angela themselves. Kail also took a step away from the sergeant, putting himself a safe distance from Erickson who was perilously close to receiving one of Angela's famous head thumps.

Sergeant Erickson, having realized his mistake, refused to back down and committed with his strong arm tactics. "Threats like that will see you in the stockades," he said, his voice beginning to betray some of his fading confidence.

"You did threaten the sergeant," Kail said to Angela, holding back his smirk.

Slowly, deliberately and deadly, Angela turned her head to look at Kail.

Having deflected her ire away from the Erickson, Kail was satisfied that she wasn't going to split the man in two. However, he hadn't given any thought to how he was going to save himself from the same fate. His luck seemed to be in good supply today because an additional group of soldiers from Silverton were quickly approaching and drawing everyone's attention.

"Thank you sergeant," one of the newcomers said, taking control of the situation. "Kail, Angela, it's been a while. Welcome back," he finished, removing a helmet and pair of goggles from his face.

"Duncan?" Kail asked, barely recognizing the Silverton Infantry General.

Duncan Deline nodded his head. "Let's move this reunion to a more secure location. Don't want to be standing out in the open, making easy targets of ourselves," he finished, scanning the open area outside of the city for emphasis before turning back towards the city.

Reluctantly but not without an air of relief, Erickson stepped aside allowing Kail and Angela to follow the general.

SILVERTON ARMY HEADQUARTERS

Duncan lead Kail and Angela to a bunkered building several hundred yards into the city. Soldiers from Silverton, along with volunteers from other cities or perhaps refugees, he wasn't sure, hustled by. A few of them stopped to watch them pass, only to hurry off to share the knowledge that Kail and Angela, heroes or deserters depending on what stories you believed, had returned.

"Wait here please," Duncan said, holding the door open to a conference room. After Kail and Angela entered the room he added, "I will be with you shortly," before closing the door and leaving them alone in the room.

A noticeable amount of time passed. Kail wasn't sure how long it had been, but Angela was ready to climb the walls. Something her natural-born ability to fly would actually allow her to do, having witnessed it on more than one occasion. The show became unnecessary when Duncan returned with an arm load of papers, and Randal Wood followed close behind, a little out of breath.

"Sorry to keep you waiting this long," Duncan apologized. "I wanted Randal to be here."

"Understood," Kail said, having stood from his chair when the men had entered.

"There's more coming, but we can start now," Duncan said, taking a seat across the table from them. Randal quickly joined them.

"Are we prisoners?" Angela asked the two men.

Duncan looked at her and then to Kail. "No."

Kail returned to his seat and motioned for Angela to join him. Reluctantly she took her seat.

Duncan wasted no time in getting to the current state of affairs. "Since your last check-in, over three months ago, there have been some developments."

"Check in?" Angela asked Kail.

"When I could, I would return home. Keep an eye on things as much as I could. I slipped these last few months," he admitted.

"Intelligence reports confirmed that Silverton was no longer considered a target of value while its *gifted* leaders were absent," Randal continued, sliding a folder of reports to the center of the table.

"However, the same reports confirm what we already know. Silverton is riddled with spies," Duncan added.

Kail nodded his head. "But that's about to change."

"We're about as fortified as we can be with what's left. Only three airships remain. The *Sky Hawk*, *Renegade*, and the *Seraph*. The *Seraph* is grounded though. She took quite a bit of damage fifteen days ago from ground fire while patrolling the perimeter," Duncan said.

"Where is the *Odyssey* and the Mastersons?" Angela wanted to know.

Kail answered her question. "They left soon after the news regarding the loss of the *Snow Break*."

"I do not believe they would abandon us," Angela countered.

"They didn't. I think it has more to do with Mr. Eleazar," Kail said.

"The Time Walker?"

"He arranged for them to be there to rescue us in Courduff all those years ago, and they didn't come out and say it, but when he showed up again, something changed. My guess is more deals or favors he was calling in."

"You did all this while staying with me?" Angela asked.

Kail gave her a small nod.

The door to the conference room opened revealing Suki. The medic and former nanny of Kail and Angela's twins looked far worse for wear. She entered, closing the door shut behind her. "General, Sir," she respectfully greeted Duncan and Randal, then took her seat quietly, unable to look at Kail and Angela.

The tension in the room suffocated the debriefing, and Duncan paused until the three of them cleared the air.

Kail had kept an eye on Suki each time he had found time to return to Silverton, but like Angela, he had left her alone with her grief. He hoped that hadn't been a mistake, but he had his hands full with Angela's grief and wasn't able to deal with Suki's as well. He wished that Camden hadn't left. Several times he considered divining the big man's location and teleporting himself there to find out what else had happened that night. Still, Suki's presence reminded him that his daughters were gone, and the sharp pain of that loss would always resurface.

Angela pushed her chair back and rose. "Suki Leigh of the House Leigh, without thought to yourself, you risked and lost your home, comrades, family and everything you held dear to protect and save House Atagi. That debt can never be repaid."

Kail readied himself for anything. He caught sight of Duncan and Randal both leaning away from the women.

Angela continued. "I offer a blood bond between our houses." Angela took her war blade and slid the cutting edge across her palm. "A bond stronger than friendship," she said as a line of blood formed. "A combining of houses," she finished, holding her cut hand towards Suki.

After more than six years with Angela, Kail continually was surprised by some of the customs of the Keratin people. Angela's insistence that any girls born to them would have her last or house name of Atagi, and if any sons were born they would bear his surname of Falconcrest was one of the more mild oddities.

Suki winced at the injured hand in front of her. Taking the offered blade, she mirrored the cut Angela had made. Grasping Angela's hand Suki said. "I accept the offer of House Atagi."

"Our houses are one," Angela finished, releasing Suki's hand from the ceremony.

Kail watched as Suki looked at the blood on her hand as Angela's rigid pose slipped back to the more relaxed state it was during Duncan's debriefing. Clearly for Angela, any and all hard feelings were no more.

"I can't heal anymore," Suki whispered, closing her fingers over the cut in her palm.

Chapter 4

ABANDONED BUILDING, SILVERTON

Treylane Armstrong stepped away from the dirty window. Whatever commotion there had been on the edge of the city, it was over now. He lowered the binoculars from his eyes and set them on the table with the other tools of his trade.

His goal was simple. Spy on Silverton and if a target of value made itself available, eliminate it. His list of targets was short, and he had seen none of them. It was also a list that only a select few would even attempt to assassinate. Kail Falconcrest topped the list along with his freak of a wife who could fly. Camden Arland, Rhonin Masterson and Rayne Masterson were on the list as well, all airship captains who had become some of the most famous names in recent history. The attack on Cahir that resulted in the destruction of the Hyperion Tower had made them collectively enemy number one. Even though the *Snow Break* had been brought down in a failed sneak attack on Courduff, something that he had the pleasure of witnessing himself, her captain, Camden Arland had been reported as having survived the encounter.

The Silverton forces were pathetic. Therion had been right to have killed the Falconcrest kid. It was a blow from which they hadn't recovered. Who knew that one death would send them scattered and broken. It had allowed Courduff and Therion's forces to concentrate the war effort against the great cities in the east. Still when your enemy is a group of magic users, the same type of people who nearly destroyed everything in the last war, one didn't simply dismiss them as defeated until their corpses were lying at your feet. So it was that he remained in Silverton. If they came back, he would send the alarm.

He heard the lock on the door to the room click. Quickly and quietly he retreated to a darkened corner and waited with his pistol. Deceptively the door opened without a sound, and a man stepped inside before closing it and resetting the lock.

"Sir?" the man spoke.

Treylane returned his gun to its holster, he knew the man. "Report," he said, stepping back to the edge of the window. Something was different; there was more movement than usual in the street below. "Did anyone see you?" he added.

"No sir," the man said. "They are here."

Treylane looked at his spy to continue.

"Kail Falconcrest and the woman who can fly."

HYPERION HOSPITAL, CAHIR

The hospital built by Hyperion Industries in Cahir was a complete state of the art facility. Private recovery rooms, therapy wards, and even sealed rooms that brought in outside air through graphite lined copper vents for the exceptionally sensitive patients. It employed a group of scouts whose only job was to search the world for the sharpest minds and the most skilled doctors. But even the best that money could buy had not resolved one dark-skinned woman's problem.

Vincent watched through a large window from an adjacent room. Vials of fluids, rich with nourishment hung above Bastiana. Tiny tubes fed the mage and sustained her still body. Her condition had not baffled the finest doctors, but the fact that she was still alive had. Burns and a fall that should have killed any living person had left his darling in a coma they were unable to heal. Months had come and passed. The doctors had slowly run out of procedures to try and now simply checked her a few times a day.

One of the hospital's staff entered the room. "The specialist you requested has arrived."

Vincent turned away from the window looking into Bastiana's room and nodded at the man. "Thank you. See that she has everything she needs, and I would like to speak with her as soon as possible."

The man nodded and left the room.

HYPERION HOSPITAL ROOFTOP, CAHIR

"Right this way ma'am," the man shouted over the noise from the four spinning blades of the personal air transport.

Ari Bailon kept her head down and followed the man who had come to greet her. She had flown a few times on large airships, but this had been the first time she had been on one of the newer small airships that carried only a few people. She made a mental note to never do it again. Unlike the large airships, these individual transports were shaky, bumpy and downright scary.

The man led her to the edge of the roof to a set of stairs. She looked back as the small airship's engines roared, returning it to the air, to head back to the airfield where she had just arrived. Once inside the hospital, she could let her heart rate slow down after the recent transport. Ari had been told about the new hospital in Cahir. After the destruction of Hyperion Tower, the hospital was built in its place. The request that she had received had been hand written by Vincent, the ruler of Cahir. Her husband, Admiral Wilhelm Bailon, could offer very little insight on the man, but it had been her own reputation as a maverick in the world of medicine that had spurred Vincent to request her help.

She was led through a series of long clean corridors, and past several sets of security checkpoints before the man escorting her stopped at a closed door. "Everything you will require will be provided for you."

"Thank you," Ari replied, entering the room.

Inside stood one lean older gentleman, looking through a glass viewing window into an adjacent room.

Vincent his voice gravelly but firm, spoke with clinical detachment. "She has been like this for six months," he said without turning around. "There have been over a dozen doctors of the highest caliber looking into her condition, yet they remain unable to provide a solution."

Ari stepped up to the window to look at the young woman lying in the other room. She was unlike anyone she had seen before; dark-skinned with wild black hair on one side of her head and snow white hair on the other. What shocked her the most was the number of tattoos that covered the woman's body.

Vincent handed her a folder with the current diagnosis of Bastiana. "You have had success, I am told, when all others had given up."

"Her vital signs are normal, at least as normal as someone consistent with this state of injury," Ari said, flipping through the charts. "These are injuries from a fall?" she asked, stopping on one of the summaries.

"Combat injuries are more accurate," Vincent corrected, "magical combat."

Ari sighed at the last revelation. Magical injuries, however rarely she had encountered them, were nearly impossible to treat. She had heard the most successful treatment of injuries of this type was by another magic user. "I'm not sure what I can do, and I don't want you to have the wrong expectations."

Vincent interrupted her. "I am well aware of the difficulties in treating patients injured by magical means."

Trying to keep an open mind about the problem, she went back to the charts. "This part here," she pointed out, "the tattoos on her body are runes of protection?"

"Yes, the results of a protective staff that has been lost."

"Lost," she repeated. It would have been nice to have been able to examine the magical device. Her first hunch was simply to return the staff. If Bastiana was fine with it and comatose without, it wasn't that unreasonable to assume if it was brought back, everything would be fine. "Lost or destroyed?"

"Unrecoverable," Vincent stated.

Ari shook her head and closed the folder with Bastiana's charts. "You know far more about magic and the nature of her injuries than I do." She glanced at Vincent. "Why am I really here?"

A soft glow reflected in the window as Vincent looked away from Bastiana for the first time since Ari had arrived. "You are here to do what others have failed to do. Born and raised in Aldervale, a town with more magical background than anyone realizes, you have already succeeded where others have not." He pointed towards Bastiana on the bed.

Ari looked into the room to see what had caught Vincent's attention. Bastiana's face had changed from oblivious sleep to a deep scowl.

ARMY HEADQUARTERS, SILVERTON

Angela decided that living underground in a bunker was borderline torture. Access to the open sky was where she belonged, and a home in the sky was sorely missed with the loss of the *Snow Break*. The room that had been assigned to Kail and her was a small grey hole, and it was better suited for the storage of turnips. The desire to escape the room and fly was becoming so overwhelming that even her skin began to itch from the need.

"Fly for me my little bird."

Angela spun, her war blade instantly in her hand, looking for the source of the voice. She caught a shimmer in the corner of the room just before a flash of light knocked her off of her feet and sent her into the back wall.

The shimmer began to take shape as it moved towards her. Angela felt a stab of panic and quickly suppressed the emotion. Launching at the ghost, the war blade sliced through the center of her attacker with no effect.

Shrill laughter filled the room as the ghost condensed into the hazy form of Bastiana. "Now you die my pretty angel," Bastiana's voice sang.

This was magic on a level that Angela had never seen nor heard of before. There was only one course of action she could take. Flee. The cramped room was a death sentence if she remained. "You have failed at every attempt," Angela taunted, slamming open the door and bolting down the hallway leaving Bastiana's wild screams behind her.

Angela wasted no time running through the corridors of the army headquarters. She needed to find Kail if there was going to be any hope of defeating Bastiana. The attack had caught her unprepared, but given the nature of the attack, she did not think there could have been any way to have been ready short of spending every moment of every day fully armed in the company of mages. Fortunately, that just happened to be the norm these days. However unfortunately, she did not know where Kail was at the moment, but there was one way to hopefully get his attention. She slammed the hilt of her war blade into a fire alarm box and pulled the release valve open. Pressurized gas rushed through the series of pipes and the shrill whistle of the alarm sounded throughout the building.

Sprinting down the hallway she saw people starting to file out of the various rooms. Angela hoped she had not made a mistake with the alarm by putting additional people in danger. It was something to worry about later as a blast of magical energy filled the air behind her. The shouts and commotion caused by the blast ended any doubts anyone had about the alarm being real.

"You cannot escape me this time!" Bastiana's voice promised.

"Everyone out," Angela commanded after bursting into the common area of the headquarters. A second blast filled the hallway emphasizing the importance of her order. Her only chance at this point was to hold out as long as possible until Bastiana's magic attracted Kail, or someone managed to get word to him that she was under attack. One thing she promised herself was that in the future she was never going to be without her Imaera hide armor. Its protection would be most valuable right now. Still, the indestructible blade in her hand was more than capable of deflecting a blow or two.

"Such beauty," the misty form of Bastiana said as it glided into the room.

"Such single mindedness," Angela answered, bringing her war blade between the two of them.

Bastiana looked at the weapon Angela brandished at her and came forward until the tip of it passed through her body as she stood face to face with Angela. "Not going to help."

The attack was fast, but Angela was faster and managed to spin out of the path of the deadly blast of magic as it carved a line of destruction across the room. Reflexively and without effort, Angela brought the war blade up and across the apparition. A practiced move that would have left a normal opponent disemboweled. Bastiana had never been a normal opponent, and the blade whistled through the air, barely curling a wisp away from her misty body.

Angela caught the second magical attack with the flat of her war blade. The silvery runes of indestructibility began to shine as the ancient magics trumped everything Bastiana threw at her. The blade could take the blow, however Angela could not. The force of the magic and the energy surrounding it tore the blade from her hand, sending it to the far side of the room with a resounding clatter.

Bastiana halted her attack once Angela was disarmed. After taking a deep shuddering breath of pleasure she said. "Delicious."

Help, Angela wished. *Please help.*

The room flared with an intense blinding light followed by a crack of thunder. Even the transparent form of Bastiana was taken aback by the surge of magical power. Tendrils of ethereal energy floated off of the runic staff of protection that Angela now held in her hands.

Rage crossed over the face of Bastiana as she screamed, "That is mine!" Sparks of energy lanced from the staff at Bastiana as she tried to grab it, forcing her to back away. "Impossible," she screamed.

Angela was just as shocked to see the staff as Bastiana. The artifact that Bastiana used to carry had clearly chosen a new master. She wondered if maybe it was tied to the last person it had healed, remembering the fatal wound it had healed those many months ago. Now was not the time to theorize. One thing was for sure, she had gotten her wish, and the staff had already proven its effect on Bastiana, ghost or not.

Angela leapt about four feet through the air towards Bastiana and brought the staff around. She could feel it connect as the end of the staff slammed into the insane mage's shoulder and through her left arm.

Bastiana screamed as the misty form of her arm disintegrated in a swirl of disrupted magic.

Angela pressed the attack. The staff was effective, but its abilities other than to protect its user were unfamiliar to her. Swinging the edge of the staff around, it passed through empty air as Bastiana's apparition vanished, just a split second before she could deliver another blow.

HYPERION HOSPTIAL, CAHIR

"I don't know what is going on." Ari said, leaning over the body of Bastiana. "We need more help in here," she shouted.

Bastiana's bed shook as her body convulsed.

"Hold her down," Ari ordered Vincent who had stood puzzled by the strange looks of anger, excitement, fear, and ecstasy that passed over his Bastiana's face in the last few minutes.

"I cannot," he said. "She is using magic."

"What?"

"I cannot interfere," was his only explanation as he remained still, refusing to help.

Ari pulled her hands back while stepping away from the girl on the bed. The black tattoos that covered the dark-skinned girl's arm slowly changed to a ruddy bruised color. The healthy skin also changed to a dull grey color. "What the hell?" she whispered, looking to Vincent for an answer who offered nothing but a shake of his head. "It's dead," Ari whispered, "the arm." She had seen this color of flesh before, on corpses and on the aged meats hanging in butcher shops.

Bastiana sat upright in her bed with a scream that shook the entire room. Both Ari and Vincent were forced to cover their ears. Bastiana's crazed eyes took in the room. She scowled at Vincent before looking at her lifeless arm. A look of intense pain and effort crossed over her face before she collapsed back onto the bed.

Ari stepped forward to the side of the bed. "Stay calm," she said, resting her hand on Bastiana's chest to keep her from getting up again.

Ari remained unaware of what caught Bastiana's attention. As the necklace carved from a stone that she had found years ago on the edge of a lake in Aldervale softly glowed. The same stone that Therion had used to focus and amplify his own magical powers to remove the binding runes from Kail's flesh.

Bastiana instantly recognized the stones for what they were. With her working arm, she swiftly grabbed the necklace from Ari. A blast of magic tore through the hospital room, sending Ari to the floor. Vincent stood watching unaffected by the magical outburst.

Again the look of intense pain and concentration filled Bastiana's features. The dead arm began to move as she poured magical energy into it. More energy channeled through the focusing stones than she had ever commanded before.

"Stop this," Vincent said, taking a step towards Bastiana.

"Never," she hissed as the dead skin began to roil and blister. The old runes of protection on the arm began to glow as it fought against the magic.

"I said stop!" Vincent ordered, moving towards the focusing stones.

Bastiana threw magic at the unconscious form of Ari, pushing her body across the floor, pinning the doctor against the wall. "Stop me, and she dies," Bastiana threatened.

Vincent halted his steps.

Grunting through the effort she let out another scream as the dead skin on her arm began to split and tear. Blue energy poured through as the dead arm disintegrated. The runic tattoos remained as did a new arm, one made of pure magical energy.

Chapter 5

ARMY HEADQUARTERS, SILVERTON

The door clicked shut behind Suki, closing the former medic of the *Snow Break* into her room, and she sighed a breath of relief that she didn't realize she had been holding.

She was finally alone after a long day of questions that no one had the answers for. No one had been seriously injured in Bastiana's attack... this time. The leaders of Silverton were busy writing up new protocols and countermeasures in case she tried to attack again. Kail could place some enchantments and wards around the headquarters, but he was reluctant to do so. Each bit of magic he left behind weakened him, and as he pointed out, Angela was her target, not Silverton.

She pulled at the band holding her hair back and shook it out. It was still damp from trapped moisture from her morning shower. That was how hectic the day had been. Turning to the mirror she began to comb it out before it became any worse. Sadly, *worse* seemed to be the running theme of her life. She sat there for a moment, eyes closed, breathing deep deliberate breaths. She could feel the wave of despair creep up inside of her as it had so often lately.

The knock at her door startled her.

"Just a moment," she said, settling herself as best she could. Checking herself in the mirror again, she looked cool and composed, but she knew that it was a lie, and anyone with half a sense would see otherwise; the dark circles around her eyes, a smile that looked forced and tired. She wasn't fooling anyone. Hollow, that was what she was on the inside.

She opened the door, revealing Angela standing in the cement corridor. Angela had on her Imaera hide combat uniform, not unexpected, and she was armed. She could see the ancient war blade strapped to Angela's back. Once there had been two of them, twin blades, but one was lost. The symbolism wasn't lost on her. One twin blade gone. One twin daughter dead. One twin daughter lost.

Suki wasn't ready to trust her voice with words so she stepped aside, motioning for Angela to enter.

"Suki," Angela said, stepping inside the room. "Thank you."

"For what?" she asked, leaving the door half open. She couldn't think of any reason that would have Angela thanking her.

"For being here."

Suki frowned, still not understanding Angela's comment.

"I ran. I ran for a long time, but you did not."

"Angela stop," she tried to interrupt.

"No, you need to hear this. I wish every night it had been me and Kail instead of you in Courduff. I played out a thousand different outcomes in my head." Angela continued. "But finally I realized."

Suki swallowed hard.

"I realized that you were the warrior I wished I was."

Suki coughed, choking back tears. "You don't want to be me, and I am no warrior." She held up her hands for Angela to see. "What little use I had is gone," she said, wiggling her fingers that would no longer let healing magic flow through them.

"That is not true. If I could not fly, I would still fight, still push forward, and still do what I think is right. Even if all of my weapons were taken away, I would still be Angela Atagi."

"You're not making me feel any better."

"I admit the warrior code I try to live by has not prepared me for battles that use emotions."

"I'm leaving," Suki said bluntly.

"I know," Kail's voice said from the half opened doorway.

Suki looked dejected. "Is there anything you two don't know?"

Angela walked over to stand next to Kail. "Where are you planning to go?" she answered.

How they had found out about her choice to leave was a question she couldn't answer. She hadn't told anyone. Maybe she had unconsciously been giving signals or more likely a new subtle use of Kail's magical heritage. "I think," she hesitated, "I think I am going to look for him."

"Camden," Angela stated.

"It's foolish, I know. It's been so long, I wouldn't even know where to start," Suki said with a shake of her head.

It was Kail who offered her some insight. "I won't pretend to understand Camden's thinking, and the fact that Xavier Ross has somehow managed to come back from the dead makes it even more insane. He was there when Xavier died. I remember how he was that day in the jungle when he found you stabbed and dying on the *Snow Break*, and when he found everyone else dead."

Suki nodded. The whole memory was a bit blurry for her, but on that day she had lost everyone she considered a friend or family: Ellenore Black, Harris McAllister, Montoy DeSantos, and Pyron Redstone. Only she had survived Xavier's murderous rampage. Survived only because of Camden.

"He had become very single minded, but he cared more about his crew and the people around him than anyone else I have known," Kail continued.

Angela nodded. "We all have not acted as we should have. It is time to fix that."

Suki moved off towards the center of the room. "I think finding him is something I have to do... alone."

Kail looked at Angela who held up her hand, stopping what he was going to say.

"I agree," Angela said, to Kail's obvious disapproval.

Suki turned back to the pair. Part of her wanted Angela and Kail to come with her, but a larger part wanted to go alone. There were her own inner demons she still needed to deal with, and that same part told her that finding Xavier wasn't only Camden's responsibility. She harbored her own grudge against the man, not just for trying to kill her and destroying her life, but for Amaya's young life as well. "Besides, I'm not doing any good here. Silverton needs you two, and there is still Bastiana and figuring out what to do about Therion. I feel like we all are pressed against the wall with a razor at our throats."

Involuntarily Kail rubbed his throat. "I have a few ideas about that."

"When are you planning on leaving?" Angela asked her.

"Soon, but don't think badly of me when I am gone. I don't want any long goodbyes."

"That will never happen," Angela promised.

"I have something for you," Kail added. "I have been thinking about it for a long time. Everything we have been through, everything I have seen, even the prophecy that started all of this."

Suki felt a stab of guilt. A gift was the last thing she felt she deserved.

"I won't take no for an answer, but I want you to have these," Kail said, revealing the magical bindings that

Therion had pulled from his body then later retrieved from Vincent and Bastiana in Cahir.

Suki couldn't fathom why Kail would want to give the bindings to her. "Why? We risked and lost so much for you to get these. What will you use against Therion if I have these?"

"That's for me to worry about," Kail said. "Besides, twice I have seen the final battle, and twice I am not there. I've even been told by Mr. Eleazar it is not my fight."

Slowly she accepted the gift. The three circles of runes were cool to her touch. She didn't feel the numbing sensation that Kail had spoke of when he touched them. Of course she wouldn't have now that her healing abilities were gone. There was no magic left in her for them to block.

"And you must have dinner with us before you go," Angela spoke. "Tradition demands a clean start."

Chapter 6

SILVER DOLLAR SALOON, MINING CAMP
300 MILES SOUTH OF COURDUFF

As far as saloons went, Camden thought, this was easily on his top ten list of absolute worst dives he'd ever been in. Part of it was how hastily it had been constructed when the mining camp population exploded once a rich vein of titanium had been discovered. The demand for the metal by war factories had made several people instantly rich. It helped explain the rush of people trying to cash in at the camp.

As close as he could tell the walls looked like they were welded together from rusted train cars. The rest of the décor looked just as cobbled together. The glass, if it could even be called a glass, that the server had given him he suspected had come from an old light fixture. He considered himself lucky to even have a glass given the amount of brawls and fights that broke out here on payday. With nothing else for the miners to spend their earnings on, it was inevitable. Bullet holes in the walls confirmed just how bad it could get. But fine dining and stimulating conversation partners were not the reason he was here.

He felt someone press behind him, and a grime covered man pushed his way onto the chair next to him.

"Finally," the man huffed as he flagged down the server. "Two of the good stuff, and he's buying," the man said, thumbing at Camden.

The server looked to Camden for approval, and he gave a small nod. The server set down a drink in front of each of them and left them to their business. The man next to him reached over and set Camden's drink in front of him, correcting the server's mistake. Both drinks he ordered were for himself.

"What-" Camden said before the man interrupted him.

"Nope, not yet," he said, taking a long drink, emptying more than half the glass before sighing with satisfaction. "Money first."

"Half, if what you have to say is worth it, you can have the rest."

He didn't care about the money. A deal with the Guardian years ago had seen to that. An empty deal he later came to realize. He had always assumed what little Alteration magic he could command was limited to turning his skin into the same material as something he touched. He knew now that it extended much further than that. He had used his power to change the walls of a prison once. It was the first time he had changed something other than himself, and he hated himself for not knowing earlier. Hated himself for doing nothing while a little girl died.

Reaching into his pocket, he found a few pieces of useless metal. With a quick pulse of magic he produced a couple of ounces of gold and tossed them onto the counter in front of the man.

"Now that's a problem," the man said, picking up the gold. "While I've been digging up information for you, I found out some things about you that I don't like. Price has doubled."

"What do you mean?" Camden asked.

"You're a wanted man for starters, and you're light on my money."

"We're through here," Camden said.

"Not so fast," the man said, snapping his fingers.

Camden froze halfway to his feet. Behind him two men who appeared to have been minding their own business now held pistols, not surprisingly, pointed at him.

"Sit down," the man ordered.

Slowly, Camden returned back to his chair. "You're making a mistake," he said mildly.

"Is that so?" the man said, sitting taller now that his friends had shown themselves. "Now, it's going to be a big hassle trying to cash in on you. So we figure if you pony up the reward money yourself, then we won't have to."

"Please tell me you have the information I hired you for," Camden said. "Because if you don't, and you have wasted my time. I will have to hurt you."

The man turned to his friends as all three of them laughed. "You just don't get it do you-."

Camden was already in motion. His backhand had smashed into the mouth of the grimy man with a clank, sending him backwards to the floor. He hoped he hadn't broken the man's jaw so he could still talk when he was finished with his friends.

"Don't move," one of the men said, cocking the pistol.

Camden paid him no mind. He caught sight of the bartender ducking behind the counter. This wasn't the first time guns were about to be fired in the saloon. With two quick steps he was almost to the men. A second before he got to them, the man shot. He felt the bullet hit him square in the chest.

Everyone stopped.

"What the hell?" cussed the man who had fired.

Camden pulled free the bullet that was stuck to his chest. He had turned his body into the same iron as the walls. Dropping the spent bullet to the floor, he reached up to the two men and knocked their heads together with a sickening crunch. The pair fell into a pile on the floor. Behind him, a groan came from the first man he had hit.

"Ready to talk?" Camden asked.

"You broke my tooth!" the man whined through his split lip and holding up the tooth in question in front of him.

"You broke our deal." Camden reached down, hauled the man to his feet and shoved him back onto his stool. "Here, this will help." Camden took the other drink he had paid for and poured some of it onto the man's face.

"Stop it. What's the matter with you?" the man cursed as the alcohol stung into his wounds.

"Now, tell me what you know about the man with the melted face. Xavier Ross."

"It hurts," the grimy man continued.

Camden sighed as he gripped the man's shoulder and squeezed until things began to pop. "Pay attention or even more is going to hurt. Now, what do you know about Xavier Ross?"

"Ok, ok," the man insisted as Camden eased up. "He was here, about a month ago. Right when things around here exploded."

"What do you mean?"

"The town was nothing but dirt and broken dreams, then one day in he walks. Convinces a handful of people to go with him and just like that," the man snapped his fingers. "The largest strike ever of titanium."

Camden gave the man a curious look. Why would Xavier suddenly get into the mining business?

"Don't you get it man? It was like the man knew it was there before he got here."

None of it made any sense to him. "Where is he now?" Camden asked.

"Cashed out for all I know. No one has seen him since. Took a bunch of money, bought enough supplies for a dozen people and headed south."

"South is the jungle of Canyamar."

"Maybe he's expanding," the man offered. "That's all I know man."

Camden tossed several more chunks of gold onto the counter. "Sorry for the mess," he told the bartender as he turned to leave. *Like he knew it was there*, he repeated to himself. None of it made any sense, but there was a nagging feeling he couldn't shake. First, a man he saw torn to bits over five years ago was walking around. This same man seemed to know things he shouldn't. Looking back through his memories of when Xavier had been part of his crew, odd behavior that he had paid little mind to now seemed to have some logic behind it. One thing was for certain. Xavier was familiar with The Eternal Gateway, and now he was headed there. There would be no other reason he could come up with for him to head into the jungle.

"What am I missing?" he mumbled out loud as he walked through the mining town. The last time he had seen Xavier, he stood at Therion's side. If he had wanted to go to the gateway, why not stay with Therion? Therion was now in control of it. Mr. Eleazar had taken them there the first time, or maybe Xavier didn't know where it was, or perhaps he did and just couldn't find it without the Guardian. Still, he couldn't shake the nagging feeling that there was more, and he just hadn't put all the pieces together. There were more questions than he had answers.

Chapter 7

TRAINING ROOM, SILVERTON

"Try it again," Kail instructed.

The runic staff of protection remained against the wall where they had placed it, and Angela shook her head in frustration. "I have," she said. "I do not know how I summoned the staff. I do not even know *if* I summoned it to begin with."

Kail raised his hand and without warning fired a blast of magical energy at her. Angela's side flip was as perfect as it was reactionary. She came down in a crouch with her war blade in her hand. "What was that for?" she demanded from her husband.

Kail shrugged. "Maybe you needed to be threatened for it to work."

She stood slowly, suppressing her anger and rising frustration with the whole exercise. "This is a waste of time. We should not be relying on this weapon."

"Relying?" Kail questioned. "It saved your life more than once. This isn't some game of honor and rules. We're not living a thousand years ago with spears and bows anymore either."

Slowly, deliberately she turned her back to him. "Do you think there has been a day that has gone by when I am not reminded of that fact?"

She heard him exhale behind her. "Ten years ago, my biggest worry in life was the survival of a turnip cart against the abuse of an old lady who liked to kick it. Then everything changed. First a time traveling guardian stepped into my life followed by powerful mages that few people even remembered existed. All of them hell bent on taking their revenge out on me. Even more impossible there was you. The most beautiful sight I had ever seen."

Angela fought back the rising pain of emotion in the back of her throat, then turning she looked back across the room at Kail. Nothing more than a naïve farmer when she first met him, now a powerful mage, leader against the darkness foretold in a prophecy, father of her children, and her husband.

"There is a woman out there who wants you dead. An enemy that has survived the impossible that has proven she can get to us any time, any place," he said. "I don't care, and I don't need to understand how it works. If it can be used to protect what I love, then I'll take it."

She walked over to the staff against the wall and ran her fingers across the runes. Some of them were dark while others shone with the same silvery glow as the ones on her war blade. Healing wounds, appearing out of thin air, what else was it capable of? Who had constructed it and for what purpose? Had it been created for the same reasons that Kail spoke of now? Was it created by powerful mages who wanted nothing more than to protect the ones they loved?

It was a strange sensation. She knew how to use a staff in combat, it was part of the basic suite of weapons training every Keratin underwent to become a warrior. This went beyond that. Picking up the staff she spun it through her hand with practiced ease. It felt right to use the staff, as if it wanted her to use it.

Stepping forward with her left foot, she spun the staff end over end in a windmill pattern. She recalled the training with ease and passed the staff to her other hand behind her back. The metal bands on each end of the staff whistled as it cut through the air. She rolled forward and planted the end of the staff on the floor and with a small hop, locked her leg around it and spun, kicking through the air with her other leg.

Once through the spin, she let herself fall into another roll, flourishing the staff out in front of her and slapping the far end of it onto the floor. Magic from the staff thudded through the impact, sending a tremor through the building. A third roll across the top of the staff placed it across the back of her shoulders. Using the same momentum she circled the room through a series of leaping round kicks.

Stopping half way across the room from Kail, the staff shot forward from her extended arm. Then as true as any arrow she released the staff. The end of the staff slammed into the far wall, ricocheting once across the floor and returned to her hand. Her war blade was now free from its sheath, and she spun through the air in a dizzying display that was made possible only by her ability to fly. Blade and staff each sung through the air around her as did precision kicks to imaginary foes.

Kail watched in awe as Angela finished her routine. "It's like the staff is an extension of you."

"A worthy weapon," she huffed through heavy breaths.

Angela saw Kail flinch. "What is it?"

"I'm not sure. Magic," he whispered with a look of concentration on his face.

That was the only warning they had before the ground began to violently shake. Using her ability to fly, Angela floated a few feet above the floor as the building started to groan. "Kail!" she called out as part of a support beam in the ceiling broke free. With a flash of light Kail teleported out of the way. He appeared next to her and in a second flash, pulled the both of them though a tear in reality as more of the room collapsed.

MAGE COUNCIL TOWER, COURDUFF

Admiral Wilhelm Bailon, former captain of the airship the *Lotus* and now the Commander in Chief and reigning figurehead of Therion's forces in Courduff, sat in his chair and considered ordering an all out siege against Cahir.

"I don't care," Bailon said harshly. "Assault is assault. I don't care how you spin it. Get out of my sight!"

Word of the incident, no attack, on Ari in Cahir had reached him a day earlier. It was all his advisors and his most trusted council, Cid Daltry, could do to keep him from single handedly taking the *Lotus* to Cahir and putting Vincent and his pet mage in their place.

Cid nodded to the ambassador from Cahir. "This way sir." He held his hand out to the open door for the poor man who had the unlucky position of taking responsibility for the attack.

Trusting in that Cid knew his anger was not focused at him, Bailon got up and stepped away from his desk to look out over the city of Courduff and at the same skyhook and landing platform that he had assaulted while secretly leading a rescue of the same people he now considered the enemy. Though in recent months, they had pretty much all but dropped off the map, and the city states in the east had become the greatest threat. "It's only a matter of time."

"Sir?" Cid asked.

"Cahir. It doesn't take a military genius to see the writing is on the wall."

"I can understand your position regarding your wife, but I fail to see how that justifies starting another warfront."

"The order will come. Once Therion is finished amusing himself with The Eternal Gateway, there will be no place left that isn't under his control." Bailon turned away from the windows. The giant map embedded into the floor shifted and centered on the jungles of Canyamar. Its magic allowing anyone to observe any place on the planet just as it was at that moment. To the east, a large shadow was inching its way across the map. Night was less than an hour away. "What are the latest reports?"

Cid produced a clipboard and reviewed it quickly. "Supply shipments are holding steady, and we are running about three weeks ahead of schedule in platform production for the year thanks to the new ore discoveries. The resistance in the eastern cities remains high. Zythomit and Yunuan in particular. Our forces have yet to even establish a beachhead and with what little information we are able to gather suggests that their air force is as advanced as our own."

Bailon's focus shifted the map to the east. It was the middle of the night for the eastern city states, but he could clearly see the illuminated outline of the great cities. "Increase the number of operatives in both cities."

"Noted," Cid replied, marking down the order. He hesitated before continuing his report. "There is an alpha priority report regarding Silverton."

Bailon nodded, and the map shifted to the besieged town. "They have returned then," he said as a statement, not a question. The leaders of Silverton, specifically Kail and his deadly wife Angela were so dangerous by themselves that a special task force had been created just to keep watch on them.

"It appears so," Cid confirmed.

"How long until the report reaches Therion?"

"They should be receiving it anytime now if they don't have it already."

A red light on Bailon's desk lit up, accompanied by a quiet buzz. Cid halted his report as the Admiral responded to the call.

Pressing a button on the intercom Bailon said. "Go ahead, Bethany."

"Sir, your wife has arrived," Bethany's voice said.

"Send her on in please," Bailon said while nodding to Cid, indicating that the rest of the reports could wait until later.

His secretary, Bethany, opened the door to the map room and escorted Ari into the room. She smiled and gave a polite bow before returning to her station, shutting the three of them in the room.

"I am so glad you're alright," he said, crossing the room to hug his wife.

"I'm fine," Ari said with a smile, brushing back strands of his hair to tuck them behind his ear in a bid for neatness.

Bailon held her hand against his face. "I was ready to start a war for you." He kissed her hand before letting go. "They said you had been hurt."

Ari moved forward and reassured Bailon that she was alright. "Actually I feel like one of those spies in those novels you like to read."

Cid gave the two of them a curious look. "You learned something?" he asked.

Ari nodded at Cid and turned back to her husband. "Witnessed is more accurate. You remember Vincent's companion? The mage girl Bastiana?"

"Of course," Bailon said. "She was the reason for your trip to Cahir in the first place. The doctors there were unable to help with her condition."

"Injuries," Cid corrected. "From the same assault from Silverton that saw the Hyperion Tower destroyed. We were there."

Bailon nodded, remembering when he captained the *Lotus* to Cahir to aid against the attack. "The report contained nothing of her condition. What did you see? Is she dead?" he guessed.

"Oh no, far from it," Ari said, shaking her head. "As soon as I got there her condition started to change. I wasn't even through reading her charts."

"You hadn't even done anything yet?" Bailon asked.

Ari shook her head again. "I've never seen nor heard anything like it before. She was in a coma and then it was like she was having some sort of fit."

"Caused by your arrival?" Cid asked, confused.

"That's not the half of it, let me finish. The whole time this is going on, the necklace I had on was glowing. I didn't notice it at first."

"Wait, the one you had made?" Bailon interrupted.

"Yes, now quit interrupting me. This is the part that gets strange. She's weird to begin with; all covered in tattoos her hair white on one side and not on the other." Air said, moving her hands over her arms and hair. "Her arm, the one covered in tattoos, it just, I don't know how to explain it. It just turns all grey and dies."

Bailon lifted an eyebrow in disbelief. "Her arm? It dies?"

The floor of the map room shifted its perspective and centered over the jungle of Canyamar as it started to zoom in over the gateway outpost.

"If this is boring you Cid, there is plenty of other work I can assign to you," Bailon said angrily over the interruption.

Cid blinked, totally surprised at the accusation. "I assure you sir. I did not move the map."

Bailon looked back to Ari who also shook her head. "Magic, as untrustworthy and unpredictable as a deserter," he mumbled.

"Sir," Cid said bravely, pointing to the map on the floor.

Together the three of them came to stand over the gateway outpost. Clearly there was a commotion of some sort going on there when the whole room lit up in a bright flash. A ring of distortion was expanding through the jungle away from the outpost. The map zoomed out on its own as they watched.

"What the devil is that?" Bailon whispered, watching the distortion expand past the jungle north of the outpost. Part of it had reached the western seas and continued unhindered across.

Cid glanced away from the map towards the large windows overlooking the city of Courduff. "I don't know, but it's not stopping, and it will be here in a minute, maybe less."

The distortion passed over the eastern cities, and the night time lights winked out as it passed. Silverton and Cahir were next and seconds later, Ari's hometown, Aldervale to the south of them.

Cid glanced back at the map on the floor one last time before focusing on the view outside. "Here it comes."

Bailon and Ari grabbed each other. "I love you," he heard her whisper as the magical energy from The Eternal Gateway swept over the city.

Everyone lost their footing as the building shook violently beneath them.

Chapter 8

CAMPUS DINER
ACROSS FROM THE MAGE TOWER, COURDUFF

The frightened screams and commotion from the various patrons finally began to settle down. The earthquake had lasted only a few moments, but its effects on everyone who experienced it would not be forgotten so quickly, except for one table.

"You by far have the absolute worst sense of timing, you know that," the woman said to the man across the table from her. The hood of her cloak pulled back and a pair of high performance anti-keratitis goggles hung from her neck. Her long dark hair was pulled into a braid and had several red streaks through it, in honor of her twin sister. "How you managed to become the Guardian I'll never understand."

"I assure you my dear Alyssa Atagi; you are not the first to arrive early to this very table," Mr. Eleazar said, dismissing her reason to be angry at him as nothing more than the results of her own actions.

"Six months Mr. Eleazar, six months. Don't you dare try to pin this on me," she chastised him.

Tiny blue eyes also frowned at him. The blue wisp stuck its tongue out at him from its hiding spot inside the folds of the cloak.

Unfortunately, he knew she was right. He had lied to her when he had told her about when to travel back to this time, however there was no other choice. The window of opportunity was limited. Therion was about to control The Eternal Gateway. Once that happened, Alyssa wouldn't have been able to arrive in time.

For everyone present, it had been a little over six months ago, but for him, it had been just shy of forty-five years ago when he had last dealt with this time period. He, along with the Duke's son, Kail, had traveled to The Eternal Gateway to reset it. He only had enough time to set a loop that would allow himself the ability to reach this specific time. It was also a one way trip until Therion could be dealt with. The energy that had erupted from The Eternal Gateway was a result of forcing that paradox. Time quakes as they were known, were extremely dangerous and frowned upon.

"What is done is done and in the past. We must look forward," he assured her.

Alyssa shook her head. "Everyone knows that's not true. Do you have any idea how hard it has been?"

"You didn't reveal yourself to them did you?" Mr. Eleazar asked quickly, fearing that his plans might already be unraveled.

Alyssa sighed, sitting back into the booth and looking out the window across the campus towards the Mage Tower. "No, I didn't. But they're not doing well. None of them are," she said referring to her parents who believed that she and her sister were killed and kidnapped. Even Suki and Camden were broken and scattered.

The wisp mimicked her and looked dejected as well, but it perked up when Alyssa broke the edge off of the sweet crust on her plate to hand it to the wisp. The wisp grabbed the food with both little hands and eagerly chomped down with content.

"It is always the coldest and darkest before the light of dawn," he said, pouring himself a cup of coffee. He brought the coffee up to his nose to inhale deeply. "My favorite part of the day, I might add."

Alyssa looked at him with a frown. "It's almost night time Mr. Eleazar."

"Somewhere the sun is about to rise," he countered, taking a tentative sip of the coffee to test its temperature.

He watched as Alyssa looked around the diner. Almost every conversation was focused on the recent earthquake. Several people had left, and just as many had come in. All with the same look of disbelief as they asked each other if they had felt the earthquake. None of them mentioned the magical wave that had created it. Magic was becoming so rare that it was now almost invisible to normal people. One day it would all be gone, replaced by technology and science. The few people still attuned to it will have their belief in magic dismissed. That was for another Guardian to worry about.

"We only get one shot at this," she said.

"I know, it makes what we are about to do all that more important."

"Despite what you say, he cares for her first over everything else. Just keep that in mind. I don't care what promises were made to my grandfather."

"He has kept his promise so far. I see no reason for him to stop doing so now," he said, taking out his pocket watch to look at the time. Two times were recorded into history: six twenty and twelve fifteen. The third time however was fuzzy. It was supposed to be eight minutes past five, but that had come and passed. *Nothing I can do about it now*, he thought, closing the watch with a click. "Grab your belongings. The train to Cahir is leaving in twenty minutes."

MASTERSON GEARWORKS, SCABLANDS

Rayne Masterson looked through the glass of the front viewport of the *Odyssey*. In her hand was a small gold pocket watch that had been given to her and her husband, Rhonin, by the Guardian. She noted the time and closed the watch with a soft click. The private gearworks had been built when she and Rhonin had been young just after they left their studies in Courduff. Political shifts in the wind and more than a little pushing by Mr. Eleazar had them taking their families' fortunes and striking out on their own. The *Odyssey* had been built here and so had Camden's airship the *Snow Break*.

Workers crawled over the massive unfinished hulk in front of her, and just as many more were moving about the *Odyssey*. An entire overhaul of the *Odyssey* was near completion. Prior to this the most extensive repair they have ever done was a fresh coat of paint, and she hoped it would be enough. The final battles of the war would soon be fought and if they had any hope of surviving, they needed every advantage they could get.

The new airship in front of her however was another story. She doubted it would ever fly. Although it was nearly finished except for cosmetics, it lacked one important piece. There wasn't a power source for the engine, and it didn't look like they would be getting one anytime soon either. Exotic fuel sources were in short supply, and their last attempt at getting some had been intercepted by Courduff. However, they did get a report that the *Seraph* was out of action. They might be able to salvage her core for the new ship.

Rayne decided to find her husband and let him know about the signal from the Guardian. Keeping to the safety of the catwalks, she moved through the complex. Large mechanical welders were throwing shards of superheated metal as they affixed new armor plating to the *Odyssey*. At the far end, standing above the work floor stood Rhonin and Conrad Black. Both were supervising and shouting orders to the workers below them.

"I do have experience with this Black," she could hear Rhonin argue. "It wasn't all skirt chasing and partying. I did learn how to design and build an airship."

"And I have spent my entire life in the gearworks," Conrad retorted. "Face reality, not every ship built gets to have magical rune forges, mystical balls of energy, and fancy time traveling wizards to make them work!"

Rhonin shook his head in frustration.

"Steam powered turbines, fueled by standard kerosene burners is what this army needs. And they need to be mass produced. That's what Courduff and Cahir are doing. Not this," Conrad said, waving his hand over the unfinished airship, "experimental impossibility."

"It will fly, and it will be the greatest airship in history," Rhonin countered.

"Yeah, if you can find something that lifts eighty five tons and runs on wishful thinking."

"That might be all we have left," Rhonin said as Rayne approached. "Is it time?" he asked.

She nodded her head. "It activated after the earthquake."

"What do you want to do Masterson?" Conrad asked.

Rayne looked at the older gentleman. He was a valuable addition to the gearworks as he brought a life time of experience with him. It was a rather sad story. He and his sons ran a metal works shop. When Courduff started to go to war, they were stripped of all their belongings and forced to work in the clockwork factories of Courduff building airships and other war machines.   Eventually word had reached him of Ellenore Black's death, his daughter. Conrad, his sons, along with a number of other workers eventually escaped.   He came looking for Camden Arland to find answers about Ellenore.   Camden was captain of the *Snow Break,* and Ellenore was her pilot when she had been killed by Xavier Ross.   After learning the details of her death, he and his sons as well as many of the others decided to stay. Camden's offer of employment as well as the chance to work against those responsible for her death gave them a new sense of purpose.

"We're not ready," Rhonin concluded, sharing a frustrated look with her.   "Ask for volunteers to work extra shifts," he said to Conrad.

Conrad nodded as he headed off to cobble together additional work shifts to aid in the construction of the new ship and to finish the refit of the *Odyssey.*

"What do you think?" Rhonin asked her.

"I think a lot of things.   I think we have been extremely lucky so far that the gearworks has remained under the radar for this long. I think the Guardian knows what he is doing and already knows that we are not ready for him. I think in the end, everything that matters is already beyond our control. So why not focus on what we can control, like getting the *Odyssey* back into the sky, then put everyone on the other ship."

Rhonin considered her words and said, "I agree we need a functioning ship now, not two that might be ready after it's too late."

"What about the others? Kail, Angela and Camden."

"Par for the course. Mr. Eleazar tells them just enough to point them in the direction they need to go."

"I don't like his games, and I don't like this form of blackmail he holds over us. We live our lives, but when he needs something, we drop everything. We're just waiting around for his next order."

Rhonin placed his hand in hers. "I don't like it either, but if it wasn't for him, we wouldn't be alive. He's a pain in the ass, I agree, but I will take a pain in the ass any day over not being able to do this," he said, moving in closer to kiss her lips.

Chapter 9

PASSENGER CAR, EAST OF CAHIR

Alyssa made her way through the jostling train. It was a constant effort of diligence to keep the food and drinks from spilling. The diner car was located near the front of the train, and the private cabin she and Mr. Eleazar had rented was near the end. The train was nearly overflowing in the regular seating areas. Travelers, workers, refugees from the war and people fleeing from populated areas after the earthquake all eyed her and the food she carried.

She finally managed to slide the privacy door behind her without losing too much food. Who was she kidding? This was her third trip to the diner car before she managed to make it all the way back with food.

"You can't save everyone," Mr. Eleazar said, looking at his pocket watch, noting how long she had been gone.

"I don't have to," she said, tossing him a sack of food. "But I'm not going to stand by and watch children suffer or go hungry."

Mr. Eleazar took out half a sandwich then shook the empty bag upside down. "Yes, well do remember that *we* also need saving from starvation too."

"Don't give me the 'save ourselves first' speech again."

"Yes, yes. You have informed me of that a million times," Mr. Eleazar said, unimpressed with the reminder while taking a bite from what remained of his lunch.

"With Hyperion Tower gone, where will we find Vincent?" she asked, taking her seat and examining what she had left of her own lunch.

"There is a residence, but I doubt he will be there now. He will have moved to the *Colossus* I imagine. The signs are there, he knows the final battles will soon be upon us."

HYPERION AIRFIELD, CAHIR

Vincent paused before entering his private quarters aboard the *Colossus*. He had to prepare himself for dealing with Bastiana. He had lived for a very long time, much longer than any normal man, but even his ability that made him immune to magical attacks and energy, it did not make him immune to physical violence or emotional blackmail.

However, Vincent was experienced as suggested by the grey in his hair. He assumed his normal indifference with practiced ease and stepped toward the door. The locking leaver slid open without protest, and he made a mental note that the crew was to be commended for keeping the ship in top order.

Sitting on his desk, with her back to the door, was Bastiana. The dark-skinned mage did not react as he entered the room and secured the door behind him.

Vincent circled past and took his seat behind the desk, facing Bastiana. "I have received word that we will be having guests aboard the *Colossus*. I must emphasize that they are to be treated with respect." He looked at Bastiana to make sure she understood.

Bastiana's eyes were closed, her breathing was normal, and he could tell that she was using her magical ability of Divination. Whom or where she was looking he didn't know.

Bastiana slowly opened her eyes. She smiled, amused, but there was something else in her eye. *Arousal maybe?* He considered repeating himself, but he knew that she had heard what he said even if she acted like she hadn't. She had on an unfamiliar outfit; a thin white blouse leotard and red leather corset that laced up the front. The corset also flared at her hips ending with a pair of long tails just above the back of her exposed knees. Matching red leather high heeled boots completed the outfit. *It covers more than the black dress*, he conceded.

Her arm still unnerved him though. Blue magical flame rippled underneath the constraints of the protective tattoos from the staff. In all his years, he had never encountered nor heard of anyone who had replaced a lost limb with pure magic. Also she had kept the necklace that Ari Bailon had worn to the hospital. He had insisted she return it to its owner, but she had refused.

"So I can play with them but not kill them."

"I don't think that word means the same to them as it does you. I recommend you don't test them. If something were to accidentally happen to the *Colossus*, I would be very displeased."

"Fine, but I won't make any promises." Bastiana squinted at him suspiciously. "There is more to this than simply asking me to behave."

"You and I both understand what is happening to the world right now. Therion is fulfilling the prophecy."

"What do I care?" Bastiana leaned forward until she was just an inch away from his face. "Magic users first, remember?" she whispered.

"Of course," he replied, not backing away as she invaded his personal space.

Slowly and deliberately she got up off of the desk and stood in front of him, one leg on either side of his chair. When she failed to get a reaction from him, she slowly stepped over his legs and walked to the front of the desk. "You're not much fun anymore."

Vincent shrugged.

A light on the wall lit up, and he rose from his chair. Bastiana playfully watched him as he crossed the room to press the call button. "Captain, there two people outside requesting permission to come aboard. They claim you are expecting them," a voice crackled over the intercom.

"Bring them up to the outer deck. We will see to our guests shortly," he replied, shutting off the intercom. Vincent opened the door for her. "Shall we my dear?"

Alyssa ran through a series of mental exercises while the guards outside of the *Colossus* waited for Mr. Eleazar's and her story to be checked out. Mr. Eleazar had found time to buy an apple and casually sliced one piece after another. He had offered the guards a slice, but they sternly refused.

She took a moment and frowned when Mr. Eleazar teased the wisp with a slice from the apple as well. She didn't like exposing or showing off the wisp, and held firm to the belief that the fewer people who knew about the wisp, the better. It was a protective reflex she knew, but considering the wisp's origins, no one would blame her.

"They check out," a uniformed officer said, approaching the group. "This way. The captain has instructed me to escort you to the outer deck," he finished, holding his hand out for them to proceed.

"Thank you," Alyssa said, taking the lead.

Mr. Eleazar asked about a trash can for the apple core, but the officer ignored his request, clearly unimpressed with the two of them. However that changed when Mr. Eleazar decided to use his magic to incinerate the apple core in a burst of flame.

Before she knew it, they were standing on the outer deck of the *Colossus* surrounded by soldiers with their weapons drawn. "Way to go," she mumbled, keeping her hands raised in front of her.

"It would have been rude to just toss it on the floor," he said, unconcerned with the amount of potential violence pointed at them.

"What is going on here?" Vincent's voice said from behind the line of soldiers.

Alyssa and Mr. Eleazar turned as the soldiers parted, and Vincent along with Bastiana stepped through the gap.

"Sir, I brought them to the outer deck as ordered. However, he," the officer pointed at Mr. Eleazar, "is a magic user. We were not aware of that when you were contacted."

"Stand down," Vincent ordered. "I am well aware of their capabilities."

The officer nodded and looked to his men as they lowered their rifles and backed away, but remained at the ready in case they started any trouble.

Alyssa kept her face neutral as Bastiana sauntered up to her to look her over. "Well, if it isn't the old," she sneered at Mr. Eleazar, "and the beautiful. I absolutely love your hair," she said giving her a second look.

"Thank you young lady, but I assure you she isn't that old." Mr. Eleazar accepted the compliment backwards.

A sharp look passed over Bastiana's face. "Aren't you supposed to be dead?"

"Probably," Mr. Eleazar answered with a shrug.

"Enough," Vincent said, ending the banter. "Why have you come Guardian?"

Mr. Eleazar looked at Alyssa to answer.

"I'm calling in a favor," she said.

Vincent focused on her. "Black hair, chemical highlights, pistols of advanced design, twin Keratin war blades with indestructible runes, and you reek of magic and other abilities not seen in a thousand years," he summarized. "Clearly the offspring of Kail and his exotic wife Angela. And I owe *you* no favors."

"Kail?" Bastiana interrupted. "You're Kail's daughter, and the woman who can fly?" Bastiana finished with a look of predatory hunger in her eyes.

Alyssa ignored the mage. "You owe me a debt-"

"I owe you no such thing!" Vincent said angrily. Even Bastiana stepped back, not having seen Vincent react with such emotion. "How arrogant you Falconcrest's are. You know absolutely nothing." He turned to Mr. Eleazar. "Clearly whatever he has told or shown you was nothing more than what it took to convince you of his delusional scheme to save the world. You are not the first, nor will you be the last."

"The Guardian didn't show me anything. My grandfather, Duke Falconcrest, did," she said, stepping forward to counter his challenging tone. The wisp hidden inside the hood of her cloak also peeked its head out and scowled at him.

Several of the soldiers closest to the confrontation took several steps back, and a few even raised their rifles.

Vincent took several deep breaths while keeping an eye on the wisp as he calmed down. "Commander, if your men cannot follow simple orders, remove them from my presence."

Angry at having been chastised more than once today, the commander quickly ordered several of the soldiers to report downstairs for extra duty assignments.

Bastiana, however, was infatuated with the tiny creature. "Where did you get that?" she asked breathlessly. "I want one."

"You don't" Alyssa said, returning to Vincent.

The wisp circled Bastiana, focusing on the reddish runes that floated on the magic that Bastiana now used for an arm. Finally the wisp settled onto Bastiana's shoulder above the missing arm and leaned its head against her neck with sullen and sorrow filled eyes.

Alyssa glared at the wisp.

"I do apparently," Bastiana said with a smile, clearly smug that she had won some sort of competition between the two of them.

"She bites," Alyssa retorted before returning to Vincent. "I know exactly who you are Vincent, and you knew this day was coming."

"Wrong child. I have already fulfilled the promise made to Duke and Catherine, several times in fact. I even saved your mother and father on more than one occasion. I do offer my condolences regarding your twin sister," he offered, glancing at Bastiana playing with the wisp, "but we already know how that ended," he finished with his eyes on Mr. Eleazar.

Mr. Eleazar frowned, clearly having underestimated Vincent's knowledge.

Alyssa was becoming more frustrated with each passing moment.

"I suggest the two of you rethink your strategies and your faith in a self-fulfilling prophecy," Vincent said, turning to leave. "The commander will assign each of you an assistant if you choose to remain as guests aboard the *Colossus*. However, do not test my hospitality," he finished, leaving Mr. Eleazar and her dejected on the deck of the airship. Bastiana simply smiled and followed him off the deck with the wisp playing in her hair.

Chapter 10

HYPERION AIRFIELD, CAHIR

Alyssa kicked the loose piece of cement off the landing platform. It sailed and bounced away eager to be away from her anger. She had removed her cloak and left it on the *Colossus*. With the wisp keeping Bastiana distracted, there wasn't a reason for her to wear it anymore. The twin war blades strapped across her lower back and the sixteen shot pistol on her hip brought a lot of un-trusting looks from the soldiers stationed nearby. More than once she heard mumblings that she must be some sort of warrior from the eastern cities. Her pale skin and almond shaped eyes no doubt were the reason behind the guesses.

"Sometimes these things don't quite go as planned," Mr. Eleazar said from a safe distance behind her.

"That's an understatement," she retorted. "Fifteen years, Mr. Eleazar, fifteen years," she said, turning on the time traveler. "Training, learning magic, studying theoretical paradox history. All of it since I was four years old and right now, I am convinced that it has all been a giant waste."

Mr. Eleazar stopped and picked up a piece of the broken cement. Clearly at some point in the past either the *Colossus* or another airship had a rough landing and had damaged the platform. "Time is a strange beast. Go back to kill an abandoned puppy causes a future leader to never learn the meaning of compassion thus leading to some of the most atrocious crimes against humanity the world has ever seen. At the same time you could eliminate an assassin, saving a badly needed hero only to have that hero die in an accident a day later. Save him from that too, and he is struck down by a heart attack or cancer. Try as you might, you can't save him," he said, examining the cement from different angles.

"The river of time flows to the ocean. I know this. But as the Sentinel, I'm starting to wish my life had been with loving parents instead of mapping eddies in time."

"Your grandfather loves you as do your parents," he said. "They all know the importance of what you do and the sacrifices everyone has made."

"You mean someday they will. Right now they are barely holding on by a thread. Their children are gone, their friends lost, and they have the responsibility of saving the world without a clue as how to do it."

"That is why we are here." Mr. Eleazar pushed a tiny amount of Chronomancy into the broken piece of cement. Alyssa watched as it crumbled to dust in his hand. Tiny threads of time flowed in front of them.

"Time flows around Vincent. Magic can't touch him either. He has proven his word is worthless. It was risking a lot to rely on him," Alyssa said, plucking one of the threads of time to see how it vibrated.

"A risk we had to take, one we will have to live with." Mr. Eleazar watched as the thread lead to a homeless man living under an elevated commuter train. Next to him was his wife and a small child. The three of them dirty and twice as hungry.

The ground trembled from another distant pulse of energy from The Eternal Gateway. Alyssa shook her head with a mix of disappointment and frustration. Therion was playing with eternity. "The one thing that is endless is time, and we are running out of it," she said, sending another vibration along the thread of magic.

A vision of what had happened in the past played itself out for them. The homeless man had been a foreman, charged with the task of building the landing platform. As the project neared completion it was discovered that one batch of the steel rods used to reinforce the cement was flawed. The homeless man had a deadline to meet, but replacing the flawed section would have added an additional three days to the project. His superiors refused to set the project back. The man later talked to his wife about it. "You must do what you think is right," the wife said.

Alyssa shook her head. "I've heard that more than once."

"A universal constant," Mr. Eleazar agreed.

The foreman started to replace the faulty section when word reached his superiors. They removed him from the project and demoted him. Six months later when the section had failed, the blame was passed onto him as he was the one in charge of the construction. Then out of work and shamed he and his family now struggled to survive.

Alyssa let the vision pass and sighed. "This war is so crazy. It's even worse than the War of Antiquities. The real fighting is with a handful of people, yet thousands will fight and die never knowing the truth."

She wrapped the thread of time that lead from the broken cement to the homeless man around her hand. Focusing her own magic into the thread, she yanked it free. The homeless man and his family faded away as did the broken section of the landing platform beneath their feet. Closing her eyes she slipped into the meditative state and wove Divination magic through the city. The family was once again living in their home. The wife was now pregnant with their second child. The foreman had stood up to his superiors and fixed the flawed construction.

"You can't save them all," Mr. Eleazar said softly looking at Alyssa.

"I don't have to save them all, just the ones I can," Alyssa turned and made her way back to the *Colossus*.

Chapter 11

WILDERNESS ROAD
NORTH OF THE CANYAMAR JUNGLE

A voice whispered in the back of Camden's mind. Nagging thoughts that refused to rise to the surface. At times it was Suki's voice. Her crying and yelling at him in the dark while the *Snow Break* burned in the city around them. Other times it was Xavier. Mocking him at every turn. The times that scared him the most where when it was Angela or Kail's voice. Phantoms demanding payment and justice for his actions that cost them their family.

He was honestly surprised that Kail had not used his magic to find him. It was impossible by now for them not to know. Perhaps the dirt farmer had his hands full with Angela or was too busy to drop in on him. Those seemed likely reasons. Maybe Kail was keeping her from sticking one of her swords into him if she ever found him.

He looked over his horse again as the jungle loomed nearby. He had no idea how long it would take to make it through to The Eternal Gateway, so he packed everything he thought he would need; extra clothes, especially socks and a second pair of boots. There was plenty of foliage for the horse to eat, and he was an adept hunter so he opted for survival gear over food stocks.

If the information was solid, and he suspected that it was, Xavier had a good month's head start. However Xavier traveled with a group, and Camden was on his own. He should be able to move through the jungle at a quicker pace and catch up to him before reaching the gateway outpost and Therion's forces. But it also meant dealing with whoever was with him as well. One thing he knew for certain was this fight would be nothing like the last one.

Try as he could, the memory of Therion killing Amaya while Xavier goaded him on reared up on him when he least expected it. In the last few months he couldn't fathom ever having children of his own now. If the loss of his friends' children affected him so, what would the loss of his own be like? He hoped that Xavier's head on a plate might be a place to start to ease the pain. It might not be a healthy place to start, but one he was pretty sure would make him feel better.

He pulled out a map to look over it again. There were very few roads that lead into the jungle, the ones listed on the map didn't go in very far. The road he was on simply followed the northern edge. If he were leading a group, he would use one of the established roads as long as possible before trying to carve out a new one. The only flaw with that was if Xavier's intent was not to go to The Eternal Gateway. The man at the mining town had said Xavier seemed to know about things as if he had prior knowledge. If Xavier was going to establish another mining camp, he could be anywhere and until word of the camp got out, Camden would never find him. One radical idea did cross his mind that if he were unable to find Xavier, kill Therion then use the gateway to travel where he knew Xavier would be.

Camden returned the map and started to lead the horse down the road. Each moment he wasted, was a moment of life Xavier didn't deserve.

The farmhouse slowly came into view as he made his way down the road. A two story of early Courduffian design, and by the looks of it obviously abandoned for several years if not decades. Camden stopped his horse to scan the area. It wouldn't do well to run into some highway men who might be using the place to operate from while they preyed on unsuspecting travelers.

He found no evidence of anyone moving around the house. Still he double checked his pistol just in case. There was something about the house however that caught his interest. He was on a mission and stopping to explore derelict buildings wasn't part of his plan. Unable to simply ride past, he stopped at the end of the lane and got off of his horse. Slowly he made his way towards the farmhouse when his memories ambushed him.

"This isn't something I can just forget about Cam" Suki's voice whispered through his mind.

"Cam? Where did that come from?" he said aloud, remembering the smile that her words had brought. "Does this mean I can call you Sue?"

His rubbed his shoulder. She had hit him and even knocked him from his horse.

"I wouldn't want my children anywhere near war," Royce Kelly's words rose from the past to stab at him.

"War is ugly. It makes people do ugly things," Suki's words filled with sorrow brushed past him.

"I don't want to be an ugly person," Camden said, standing at the front door of the farmhouse. He opened the door. The house was full of dust and cobwebs. Empty and abandoned.

"There was a fire," Bailon said as Camden stepped inside. "They did not survive."

"I told you," Suki's words sliced through him as he remembered receiving word about the twins. "We got them killed. It is your fault."

"We bring them home," he whispered, unable to stop the raging flood of memories. "I had given up."

"What do you mean?" He could almost feel Suki's hand on his shoulder as her words spoke to him.

"Like you said. 'He loves her'."

"Is that all?" her voice asked.

"No." He remembered. Before the *Snow Break* touched down in Courduff, there was a moment when all of the small looks, the verbal jabs and even the real ones came together. The moment their lips met. "I love you."

"Suki is waiting for you." Mr. Eleazar said.

Camden snapped out of his self punishing memories. He was in the middle of the room on his hands and knees. Wet drops had turned to mud spots on the floor in front of him. Quickly he wiped away the tears from his face with the back of his hand. A small jolt of fear froze him in mid action. A single pair of footprints were left in the dust in front of him.

Chapter 12

HYPERION AIRFIELD, CAHIR

"The age is changing," Mr. Eleazar said, standing on the outer deck of the *Colossus*.

"Everything changes," Alyssa added. "Steam gives way to direct fuel sources which gives way to steam." She pointed to a line of single man airships. The clockwork factories were producing one about every four hours. Nobody knew it yet, but the new smaller airships were about to change the face of war forever.

"History does seem to repeat itself, even if it's not obvious. Those ships are like your mother, wars fought between people who could fly, and people who could use magic. Now it's people with airships against people with guns."

"How can you be so calm?" Alyssa asked frustrated. "We are locked here, and there will be no second chance if we screw up."

"Actually I find these periods of time to be quite relaxing."

"You're unbelievable. How can you be relaxed?"

"Well, it's actually quite easy. Compared to time hopping and giving people a push here or a nudge there, this is a vacation. It's quite rare to experience this many days that run consecutively."

"Then why can't we relax our way into convincing Vincent to help us?" Alyssa asked.

"By just being here we are." Mr. Eleazar assured her. "He will come around."

"I don't think we have that luxury," Alyssa said as the deck beneath their feet gave a slight tremble. "That was a little one."

"Changes indeed."

Alyssa sighed. She was starting to see why dealing with Mr. Eleazar with anything other than short bursts drove people crazy. "You still haven't explained the prophecy. Why did Vincent say it was self fulfilling?"

"It doesn't mean anything," he said, looking at her. "Everything can be influenced by what one believes. For example, 'The Guardian will fall, and the door will open for revenge yet taken.' It is quite easy I assure you to prophesize death events. The King will die. Not too hard as you can see. Everyone dies eventually. Now add some flair, and you have something like this. 'Forth night of the covered moon the lion is lost, and the country will mourn'," he said with dramatic enthusiasm. "The obvious is obscured, but it means the same thing."

"So you die, and that doesn't bother you?"

"Not in the slightest. It could very well have said the Sentinel will fall."

"I'm not buying it. I've seen too much to ignore it."

"True, but my point is, do not let the prophecy constrain you. Society will destroy itself if Therion is allowed to control the gateway. We have a mission to complete, stop Therion. It's as simple as that."

"And the childless one who will decide the fate of all?" Alyssa asked.

"A metaphor. Nothing more."

"And if it's not?"

"Again, you are letting the words of a prophecy blind you. If you had the chance to stop Therion right here and now, would you? Or would you hesitate because you are not the childless one?"

Alyssa thought about Mr. Eleazar's point. "Actually I am childless, but we don't even know if that part refers to stopping Therion."

"Indeed, but I do know this much. For Therion to be defeated, he needs to be in control of the gateway, and he is. I already sent your mother and father to Vincent to retrieve the magical bindings created by your grandfather. The Duke has already bound Therion once before after the War of Antiquities. However he had to cut a deal in the end to save himself and Catherine. During that same time with the help of Vincent, he was finally able to create the bindings that blocked every form of magic. Not just Necromancy or Enchantment to steal someone's magic. That was part of the deal. However the Duke made Vincent promise that when the time came he would do his part to help against Therion."

Alyssa nodded. "And he has done that, more than once. That's why Vincent feels he has fulfilled his end of the promise."

"It appears so. Though I do believe there is more. The girl Bastiana."

"You think she is influencing him somehow?"

"In a way. I think he is influencing himself on her behalf."

Alyssa turned to face Mr. Eleazar. "What do you mean on her behalf?"

"I think in his own way, he is fulfilling the promise through her instead of to the Duke."

"What?" Alyssa asked surprised.

"It fits. He is very protective of her."

"You think Vincent and Bastiana are the childless one from the prophecy?"

Mr. Eleazar answered with a shrug.

The ground beneath the *Colossus* shook violently, and both Alyssa and Mr. Eleazar had to grab the safety railing on the outer deck to keep from falling. Cracks formed along the landing platform and on other nearby buildings.

"We can't wait any longer," Alyssa said, surveying the city around her. Fires had broken out in a few parts of the city as small plumes of smoke began to rise.

"I believe we should have a meaningful conversation with our host," Mr. Eleazar agreed.

Chapter 13

ARMY HEADQUARTERS, SILVERTON

Kail and Angela met with Duncan and Randal outside the main bunker of the Army Headquarters. Luckily for Silverton, there were few buildings that sustained any damage from the first earthquake, and the ones that had followed these past few days.

"How are the reports so far?" Kail asked Randal.

Angela and he had a close call in the gym when the first earthquake had struck. Kail managed to teleport her and himself out of danger. The same could not be said for everyone else in the city.

"Not good. The headquarters took quite a bit of damage, and we have people on it right now to make it structurally sound as fast as possible. Outside, we have approximately two thousand people in need of shelter."

Kail nodded grimly. "And our defense capabilities?"

Randal looked at Duncan to supply the answer.

"Also not good. We have had to suspend all repairs on the *Seraph*. A support beam inside the repair hanger came down and half of the roof along with it. I don't know how long it will take to clear away the debris before we can get a clear assessment of her condition. Patrols have resumed, but any soldier who has family or homes that were hurt or damaged have been given leave to deal with their own affairs."

Kail understood the need the men would have to make sure their families were safe. "There is more to this report," he said.

"Yes sir," Duncan continued. "There are many who have wished to leave and take their families with them. Several have expressed that they will return once they know their families are out of harm's way."

"Some might come back, but most won't," Kail said.

Both Randal and Duncan nodded.

"Silverton only exists in the eyes of Courduff to provide them with an easy battle they can win in case they feel bored," Kail cursed. "Tell the men that they need to do what they feel is right, but also let them know that I will defend Silverton to its last blade of grass. If Courduff wants to make an example of us, I will make sure the price is paid in blood."

Angela spoke next. "As will I. But we cannot ignore the bigger war. Explain it to them Kail."

Randal and Duncan looked to him for an explanation.

It had taken about six hours after Kail had teleported from the gym to recover enough magic to get the two of them back to Silverton. "The earthquakes are not natural. They are caused by magic." Kail explained to the two officers about their escape from the gym and ending up over a hundred miles away instead of simply outside the building as he had intended. "Not just any magic either, but Chronomancy, or time magic."

"The Eternal Gateway," Randal guessed.

"I believe so," Kail said.

"So this is all an attack from Therion? Shake the earth until we are wiped out?" Duncan asked.

Kail shook his head. "It's not localized to just us. Cahir, Courduff, everywhere has reported the earthquakes. This is bigger than just us."

"It is the beginning of the darkness the Time Walker warned of," Angela stated.

"I believe so," Kail agreed.

Randal shook his head, taking in all of the information. "This is crazy. How do you expect to protect Silverton from this?"

Kail looked into Angela's eyes. "I don't know. I can't be everywhere at once, but I have some ideas. This isn't just about us anymore."

ABANDONED FARMHOUSE
EDGE OF CANYAMAR JUNGLE

The side of Camden's hip hurt as he jerked awake. He had fallen asleep on top of his pistol which had no remorse for his feelings as it dug into him for several hours through the night. Rubbing away the sleep from his eyes, he took a look around the old farmhouse. He must have been more exhausted than he realized if he had passed out on the floor just inside the front door.

He groaned as he got to his feet and limped outside while rubbing out the kinks. His first thoughts were to his horse. He couldn't recall if he had tied the horse up or not. If he hadn't it was probably half way back to the mining town by now.

A quick glance told him that he hadn't tied the horse. "Damn it," he cursed. Why had he bothered to stop to search this old house anyway? Begrudgingly he made his way down the front porch to the dirt lane that led back to the road. This was going to be a serious setback in his ability to try and catch up with Xavier. *One more failure in a long list of failures.*

Turning back towards the farmhouse he looked at the open doorway, and Xavier's voice echoed through his mind, "I see a door with a sign on it that says, 'Arland is an Ass.'"

A wave of nausea passed up his stomach at the same time the ground beneath his feet gave a sudden jolt. Struggling to keep on his feet he watched the old farmhouse give a defeated groan then a sharp crack as the front porch caved in taking part of the outer wall of the second floor down with it. Backing away from the ruined house he couldn't help but think of the obvious coincidence that only moments ago he had been asleep on the floor.

The magic that had passed before the earthquake hadn't gone unnoticed by him either. The thought that he might be running out of time crossed his mind. Those thoughts came to a quick end when he spotted his horse bolting for the edge of a clearing from the side of the collapsed farmhouse.

Not wanting to scare the animal further, he slowly started to make his way towards it. Once the horse disappeared into some trees, he started to run for fear he might lose the horse altogether.

THE ETERNAL GATEWAY

"Fascinating."

Therion looked much different than he had just a few months earlier. Once he had prided himself on his look and dress. Proper grooming and well tailored clothes went a long way in convincing and controlling people to do as he wished. It was far easier to manipulate people if they felt they were doing the right thing and if the person doing the manipulating was charming, good looking, as well as an unconscious image of success that the other people wished to be.

His hair had grown out almost to his shoulders, and his face was covered by a thick beard. Even though he was old, far older than anyone suspected, there wasn't a grey hair to be found. He had The Duke to thank for that. The time they spent together during the War of Antiquities had been insightful.

It really was too bad about Duke. He had discovered so much, yet threw it all away. Nostalgia had him almost wishing The Duke was here with him now. The Eternal Gateway stood open in front of him. The vast expanse of time a mere step away. What wonders he and his old friend could have unlocked. But it wasn't meant to be. Maybe one day it could, but not today.

The first time he had tried to step through the gateway, he had met resistance. The ground had shaken so violently that he had quickly retreated for fear that it might be damaged or worse destroyed again. The Eternal Gateway was far more complex than a simple portal through time. He had returned to studying any lore or history he could get his hands on, but he was still unable to find the answers he desired. His best guess was that there had to be some sort of control device. It fit best with what had happened when the Duke's brat, Kail, and the Guardian were here those many months ago. If they had placed a magical barrier, he would have found it by now and destroyed it. There was a key missing he concluded. However his experimenting also proved that one wasn't needed. He had on several occasions now been able to manipulate the gateway as he wished. Sometimes a strong earthquake resulted, others times a mere whisper of wind as changes rippled through time. Soon, he would be able to walk through unhindered, and he knew exactly when and where he was going to go.

NORTH OF CANYAMAR JUNGLE

Camden had spent the last hour and a half chasing down the spooked horse. He figured that if Xavier was headed into the jungle, The Eternal Gateway was his destination now. The magic that preceded the earthquake convinced him of that. If Therion was about to tear the world apart with the gateway, then it only stood to reason that Xavier would be at his side.

He was surer of it now than ever before, and he was more willing to trust this feeling than some of the crazier things that had crossed his mind lately. Xavier was headed to the gateway, not searching for more riches.

"Time to do some catching up girl," he said, patting the horse on the neck setting the pace at a quick gallop that would chew through the miles but not run the horse to death.

Chapter 14

HYPERION AIRFIELD, CAHIR

Alyssa shook her head for the third time before rubbing her fingers on her temples in frustration. Mr. Eleazar and Vincent had once again become sidetracked discussing their dealings with each other in a time before anyone else in the room had been born. She wondered why the two men couldn't simply stay on topic. What happened after the War of Antiquities between them had absolutely no bearing on today's problem. Bastiana's presence hadn't helped either. Alyssa didn't care how trained or powerful one's magic was. Her fiery arm, bound by runes of protection was unsettling. The blue hue it cast over everything was distracting and downright creepy.

"You were on our side," Mr. Eleazar pointed out.

"Were. Things change over the course of twenty five years. Especially for those who were left behind," Vincent retorted. "My priorities are my own, not yours."

She tuned out their arguing, but wasn't sure how much more of this she could sit through. The original plan was quickly falling apart, and her mind started to formulate alternate plans. Her grandfather, Duke Falconcrest, had been a general during the War of Antiquities. So had Therion. The two of them fought side by side for more than thirty years before the war had ended. The problem was The Duke wanted another life, one that wasn't filled with dark secrets. Therion had other ideas, and in the end it cost them not only their friendship, but it destroyed the very foundations of the Mage Council and its thousands of years of rule.

Duke Falconcrest in his exile had taught her not only the art of using magic, but also military organization and strategy. Her grandfather told her as much as he could about the days after the war, but there were secrets, dark secrets that could never be known again. Her understanding was that Vincent knew the risks and had chosen to be a part of the plan. A plan that clearly after all these years later, he now resented.

"Don't you dare mention her name," Vincent growled, rising to his feet from behind the metal table bolted to the floor of the *Colossus*.

Mr. Eleazar honestly looked stunned at the outburst.

Alyssa started to pay attention again, and the flighty blue wisp also settled down on Bastiana's shoulder and looked at Vincent with weary eyes. Bastiana didn't show it on her face, but Alyssa could tell by the slight dimming of her magical arm that she also was caught off guard by Vincent's uncharacteristic outburst.

She could tell Mr. Eleazar was quickly going through a lifetime of memories. As the Guardian, he hopped in and out of history, and she was convinced that he might even be a bit insane. How else could someone keep everything straight in their head if their mind wasn't already out of order?

"She played a minor role," Mr. Eleazar said to himself as he still tried to put the pieces together. "Why would Cora have anything to do with this moment in time? She is dead."

Mr. Eleazar could be dense sometimes. She let her mind slip into a calm state and began to breathe in through her nose and out of her mouth. This was a method used to prepare for combat and given the people present, three mages and a Moksha, a fight now could destroy not only the *Colossus*, but maybe all of Cahir.

Mr. Eleazar jumped to his feet as he backed away from Bastiana as if seeing her for the first time, pointing accusingly at Vincent. "Her?" he demanded.

Vincent regained his composure. "You are not the only person I have made promises to."

"Impossible, you, you. It's not possible," Mr. Eleazar stuttered.

"You're right. It's not possible, but yes, she is Cora's daughter. I knew it the moment I found her on the streets of Courduff," Vincent said, looking at Bastiana who still hadn't said anything.

Mr. Eleazar slumped into his chair and put his hands over his face. "Oh, this explains so much. How could I have missed it?"

"Missed what?" Alyssa asked.

"The Prophecy. The destruction of The Eternal Gateway. My fall."

"I told you, you were already dead," Bastiana said smugly.

"How does this change anything?" Alyssa asked.

"Everything, everything is so broken," Mr. Eleazar said defeated.

Alyssa cursed at him as she got to her feet. "I won't allow it to be all for nothing." She turned to face Vincent then pointed at herself. "I am blood of Falconcrest." Then with a sweep of her arm, yelled. "Deals off."

"No!" Mr. Eleazar yelled, coming out of his chair to stop her as she stormed out of the room.

"You should know better Guardian," she yelled over her shoulder as she made her way through the *Colossus*. "Always have a plan B and a plan C. Grandfather taught me that."

Mr. Eleazar pleaded with her to not go. Vincent and Bastiana also followed behind as she stormed onto the outer deck of the *Colossus*.

She spun to face Bastiana with the wisp barely hanging on through the rush. "Time to go," she called to the wisp which quickly abandoned Bastiana to fly to her.

Shock quickly turned to anger on Bastiana's face having been tricked by Alyssa and the wisp.

Mr. Eleazar was still shouting at her as she looked into the sky then shot into the air. Her ability to fly came from her mother. Her ability to command magic came from her father. She was the Sentinel, and there was one job for her to do. Secure The Eternal Gateway for a better future. If she got revenge for her sister or she managed to kill Therion, then so much the better.

Chapter 15

PATROL DUTY, SILVERTON

The earthquakes had everyone unsettled. When news came in that they were occurring everywhere in the world, everything started to break down. Most of the men with Duncan Deline were unaware that they were magical in nature. True to his word, Kail had let go anyone who wanted to leave. Duncan had expected a number of the soldiers to high-tail it out of here. Silverton was one sneeze away from being wiped off the map to begin with, and now with the earth shaking everything apart, he was honestly amazed at how few decided to leave.

Silverton was his home, he grew up here, and he was one of the first volunteers to help set up a militia after the *Colossus* had bombed the town all those years ago while trying to flush out the *Snow Break*. Kail and Angela were still here as well. He knew their presence was one of the major factors that held Silverton together. He had to admit, even as bad as things were, when good people like that fought on your side, defeat did not seem a possibility.

Twenty soldiers were with him as well as two armored tractors. Once they had found out that Hyperion Industries equipment had been built with the dual purpose of civilian or military use, they had fabricated their own weapons to mount onto the kerosene powered equipment.

Most of the area around Silverton could be watched from sentry towers and posts. The land was stripped bare of any hiding places or cover that an enemy could use against them. It pained him to see the land that way. Gone were the copse of trees, green grass, and summer wild flowers. Now, everything was a muddy brown mixed with the black char of ash. The air even tasted dirty, and the muck got everywhere, even the roads in town that once were covered with rusty colored paver stones were now grey with mud. One day, if luck would have it, those streets might be cleaned again.

Not today.

"Look sharp men," Duncan called out as the patrol reached the edge of the cleared area. Today they were to check in on six farms and rural houses that lay a few miles outside of Silverton.

Following Duncan's lead, the men formed up to each side of the road and let one of the armored tractors take the lead. The giant behemoth rumbled past them, ready to defend the group.

"Private!" Duncan pointed. "Get up there, and man the repeater gun."

"Yes sir," Private Mance answered, slinging his rifle over his shoulder and quickly caught up to the tractor. He hopped onto the back to ready the gun.

He wasn't expecting to encounter any trouble. They had no reports recently of any enemy movement. However, he wasn't going to let his tombstone read, 'Dead because he was stupid.' He waved his hand down then made a fist and pointed to the second armored tractor. Eight men that were on the same side of the road as himself, followed the first tractor. The rest of the men fell into step behind the second one as it passed.

"Who's first," he asked the sergeant next to him.

"Looks like the Wellington estate," the sergeant answered, looking at a list of names written on the orders.

"Alright, we haven't heard from anyone on this list since the earthquakes started so be ready for anything. We might run into collapsed buildings with trapped people, but everyone stay sharp. Last thing we need is a spooked civilian taking a shot at us."

"Yes sir," came several confirmations.

The Wellington estate was abandoned. The owners hadn't even bothered to lock the doors. After a half hour of investigating, Duncan was ready to move the unit on to the next home that needed to be checked.

"Get that mark off the door, private," he chastised one of the men who had marked the front door of the house as abandoned.

"Sir?"

"We're not out here to case the joint, and we're not going to hang a sign out for every vagabond and looter to see that the place is empty. Now get that mark off the door."

"Sir, you need to see this," one of the men interrupted, waving him back inside the house. The soldier led Duncan to an upstairs room and pointed through the window. "There, just give it a second."

Duncan waited. Then he saw it. A puff of black smoke about two miles out that quickly dissipated just above the trees. "That what I think it is?"

The soldier nodded. "At least four of them I'm guessing."

"Advance party? Too visible for scouts but not enough for an invasion," he reasoned.

The soldier shrugged. It was as good a guess as any.

Duncan quickly rounded up the men to debrief them. "We will set up ambush points here and here with the tractors. Create a cross fire here, here, here and here." The men quickly dispersed and set to work hiding themselves.

"What about me?" Private Mance asked.

"You run your ass as hard as you can back to Silverton."

"Sir," the private complained, clearly upset that he was being sent away and would miss out on the fight.

"If this goes south private, you're going to be the only one that has any chance of saving our sorry hides." Duncan put his hand out, and Private Mance shook it. "Now get!"

"Yes sir!" Private Mance turned and took off down the road to Silverton.

The wait was agonizing. Duncan guessed he checked between the road and the scout on the second floor of the Wellington house over a thousand times. The scout suddenly signaled and about two minutes later he could hear the noise of the armored tractors.

He first saw two men out in front on either side of the road. They were hunched over with rifles ready, keeping an eye out as they came down the road. The armored tractor that followed was a monster. It wasn't some farm plow with a gun mount. It was a weapon of war with two forward mounted cannons and a swivel mounted repeater gun on top. If they had more, their only chance was to knock out the first one and hope it blocked the road, keeping any other armored vehicle out of the fight.

Duncan silently cursed. He was going to have some harsh words with the intelligence group and Kail. How could they have missed this as it rolled across the land?

He signaled to the first armored tractor and made a cross with his hand. The soldier nodded in understanding and waited for the enemy to march into the kill zone. A nod from the second soldier in the other tractor let him know that he had seen the order as well. Now, all they could to do was wait.

He could finally see the emblem on the approaching vehicle. Courduff's colors stood proud as the enemy advanced. There must have been a full unit of infantry as well coming up behind.

Duncan let his mind clear. One thing he had learned early in this new war was if you wanted to survive, you had to keep a cool head and make sure no bullet was wasted. Too many times he had seen a soldier who could shoot straighter at five hundred yards than anyone else or empty a whole pistol into several targets in the a blink of an eye, but when it came to real combat the same soldier missed or ran out of ammunition without hitting a thing.

Keeping your eyes open was critical too. More than once he had seen someone shoot their own ally when battle fear took hold.

Their armored tractor's cannon fired, causing dirt to jump off the ground around him with a noise that rattled his teeth. Their second armored tractor held off its shot when the enemy vehicle was clearly reduced to a fiery ruin.

Bullets poured in from all sides as Duncan and his group opened fire on the exposed infantry. A few of the enemy managed to fire back, but the initial ambush was quickly over. Everyone held their ground knowing there was more than one armored vehicle out there.

The forces of Courduff were quick to react. The smoking hulk that they had hoped would keep the road blocked was smashed into from behind and shoved off the side of the road. The new armored vehicle roared down the road, and its repeater cannon strafed through their cover.

The enemy force was larger than he had guessed. A third armored vehicle joined the second, and together they had his troops pinned down. Enemy soldiers started to pour onto the estate grounds around them. The crossfire they had set up was quickly falling apart, and his men had to defend themselves rather than focus on the larger group.

Duncan fired his rifle, one shot after another with disconnected efficiency as soldier after soldier fell to his gun. Their two armored tractors had managed to disable a second of the enemy vehicles. However the remaining one quickly turned its twin cannons on their lead tractor and tore it to shreds with a quick barrage. He saw the enemy gunner on the repeater gun quickly swing it around to cut down three of his men.

Duncan sighted down his rifle and felt the kick of the shot more than he heard it as he watched the gunner flip off the back of the vehicle like a discarded toy. He was dead before he hit the ground.

Rocks and bits of the ground were suddenly tossed up at him as the enemy returned fire. He whirled out of the way as best he could to keep the dirt from his eyes and retreated from his hiding spot. He found one of his men methodically laying down cover fire, and he added his own fire.

They needed to take out that last armored vehicle. The one converted tractor they had left was out of position. Through the smoke he could see more soldiers from Courduff join the fight, and behind them were two more of the twin cannoned machines of war. Just how big was this attack, and how were they even going to stop it?

Chapter 16

SILVER DOLLAR SALOON, MINING CAMP
300 MILES SOUTH OF COURDUFF

It wasn't very peaceful out here, surrounded by nowhere and people of questionable character and criminal backgrounds. Desperation was the common theme. The world was at war, and with the earthquakes, Armageddon and prophecy seemed to be a popular topic. Perhaps going off on her own wasn't the smartest of ideas.

Suki was already well aware of the eyes that were on her. She knew that she was being watched by a group of local thugs. She needed to keep on her toes to not find herself in a position where they could corner her. If anything went badly, help was not likely going to come.

She paused and looked up the street before entering the saloon. The man following her was no longer being sneaky about it and even winked as she stepped inside. She was going to have to come up with some sort of plan if she was going to have any chance of finding Camden here, or where ever he might be.

The bartender gave her a skeptical look when he saw her and went back to chatting with another customer who was missing a tooth. A loud bang echoed through the saloon as something from the outside slammed into the building.

"What was that?" the bartender asked, coming out from behind the counter to walk past her to check on the noise.

"Hey pretty lady. Why don't you come keep me company?" the man with the missing tooth called out to her now that his conversation partner had left.

She paused, debating whether to stay inside the saloon or head back out the door. The creep at the bar flashed his revolting grin at her. She decided that staying inside was the best solution for now. She was tired being followed ever since she arrived, and she needed to try to find any information she could about Camden. Also there wasn't anyone else in the establishment for her to approach.

Forcing a smile of her own, she pulled her backpack off her shoulder to place it on the counter as she brushed off a stool before sitting down. Inside were her belongings. The most important being the magical bindings given to her by Kail. "What's good here?" she asked.

"Nothing," the man answered quickly. "I mean, nothing's as good as the Yunuan import," he quickly corrected.

"Really?" Suki said, not believing that a cobbled together mining town would have imported alcohol from the eastern cities.

"Yeah. But it's too bad, they ran out of it last week."

"Really?" she repeated with more skepticism.

The man nodded. "But everything is good now that you're here," he said with a nod as if he had impressed her with his witty banter.

"You're not smart enough to be using your mouth, so quit bothering her," the bartender said as he came back into the saloon.

She looked back to the bartender and asked, "What was all the noise?"

"Someone apparently hit their head on the side of the place."

"That was someone's head?" she asked, remembering the loud banging noise.

"A lot of hard headed people around here," the bartender said, eyeing the other man.

The man mockingly parroted the bartender before returning to his drink.

"I'm missing something here," Suki said, looking back and forth between the two men.

"He's missing a tooth for not minding his own business," the bartender said. "What can I get you little lady?"

"Har, har, har," the man replied.

Suki let it drop. "I'll have water please."

"It's not free," the bartender said, disappointingly.

"That's fine."

The bartender shrugged, leaving to get her drink.

She watched the bartender walk away before turning back to the man next to her. "Do you know a lot of people here?" she asked.

"Why, yes I do," the man said, his voice thick with innuendo. "You looking for someone or something special?" he added with a wink.

Suki tried to smile but her stomach almost lost her lunch, while her face looked more of horror or someone with a head injury. She was slow to recover as the man continued to look at her, probably wondering if she was going to have a fit of some kind. She tried to say *yes*, but it came out more like, "Tethss."

The man just looked at her then blinked a few times before slowly turning to face the front of the bar. The bartender came back, placing her water down he could sense something odd was going on. "He do something stupid?" the bartender asked, eyeing the man.

She quickly took a swallow of her drink to help settle her stomach. "No, no. I was going to ask if he knew someone. A big man, blond, might have come through here not too long ago looking for a scarred up man," she said, waving her fingers in front of her face to describe where the scars would be.

"That explains it," the bartender said. "That sounds like the guy who knocked out his tooth."

"Camden was here?" she said. When the man next to her flinched at Camden's name, she knew she was right. "When?"

The conversation was interrupted by the saloon door opening as two men entered and moved to a table behind her, followed by a third person whose face was hidden under a hood that stepped up to the bar on the other side of the man with the missing tooth.

"Yeah, why don't you tell her all about it," the bartender jeered, leaving to serve the new customers.

Suki waited for the man to tell her about Camden as the bartender had suggested. "Well?"

"Well what?" the man said, and his tone told Suki that the encounter that he had with Camden was not something that he wanted to talk about, or relive. Least of all involving going into details about it with some girl he'd just met.

"I'm sorry, I just."

"What? You're the mess between the two of them. Was that why he was all jacked up on something? He almost killed two people after assaulting me."

"No, it's not like that."

"Look lady, I don't know what you're game is, but the last thing I need is more crazy in my life. You seem like a nice enough girl so I'll give you some advice. Go home, find yourself another man. Someone not so big, someone way nicer and stay away from places like this before you get into trouble that you can't walk away from."

"Please, I have to find him," Suki said, reaching out and grabbing the man as he got up to leave.

"Let go lady," he said, giving her hand a hard glare.

Suki slowly let go but continued to plea with her eyes as the man turned away.

A fist smashed into the man's nose, staggering him backwards. The stranger with the hood that had sat down next to him now stood between him and the door.

"What the hell," he said, holding his hands to his nose that was quickly bleeding down his chin. "I think you broke my nose."

"I think you need to sit back down," the stranger said, shoving the now bleeding man back onto his stool.

Suki stared wide eyed at the stranger. "What are you doing?"

"No kidding, what are you doing? You crazy?" the man demanded, trying to keep from getting blood all over the place. "Seems everyone around here just wants to use me as a punching bag."

The stranger pulled back her hood, her dark hair with red streaks stood out as did the array of weapons she wore. "Now, it's not nice to walk away from a girl when she asks you a question. Isn't that right Aunt Suki?"

It was the eyes she first recognized, and the confident attitude she had come to know from the little girl she used to watch over. "Impossible." She shook her head. "Alyssa?"

COLOSSUS, HYPERION AIRPORT, CAHIR

Bastiana paced back and forth like a caged Imaera. Her arm constructed from pure magic would flare as bits of energy floated away like steam above a boiling pot. Mr. Eleazar kept an eye on her as he continued to debate with Vincent. "This won't work without you Vincent."

"Well, I guess you should have followed The Duke's advice like his granddaughter did and have a plan B," Vincent said, growing tired of having to repeat himself.

Mr. Eleazar was at a loss for words, and his voice was starting to betray his uncomfortable feelings. Being in control of everything was what he did best. Now with The Eternal Gateway under Therion's command, he wasn't able to rely on traveling through time to arrange and set everything up to his advantage. His overall plan had already started to show problems when he visited Kail earlier. The sparring match they had on the deck of the *Snow Break* told him that the Duke's son was more powerful than he should be. There was a very fine line to be walked and if either side overwhelmed the other, the world would plunge into an extended era of darkness.

If Therion wins, a world dominated by a power hungry dictator would come to pass. If Kail and his group wiped out Therion without any real resistance or effort, the world would see a rise of mages and eventually the War of Antiquities would start again. No, he had to make sure that his group, the one he had brought together through time with Angela, Kail and Camden were the victors. But they needed to learn about compassion and the value of loss. That way when it was all over, they would understand the dangers of ruling with power and be content to live the rest of their lives without ambitions to rule over other peoples' lives.

"You of all people know that my plans have plans of their own." Mr. Eleazar turned to stare at Bastiana. "Are you sure that your own are under control?"

Bastiana stopped her pacing to stare at him. "You brought her here to mock me," she growled.

Mr. Eleazar frowned.

Vincent shifted his attention to her.

"One of them in this world is enough, and you bring another, no you *made* her with your meddling," Bastiana spat at Mr. Eleazar before rounding on Vincent. "And you have been helping them since the beginning. What else have you lied about?" she demanded.

Vincent stood up. "We all risked our lives. I do what I must, and I will not be brought to question!"

Bastiana took a step back smiling her evil smile. "Fine, let's see you plan your way out of this." With unnatural speed she brought her fiery arm up and blasted Mr. Eleazar with a ball of magical energy. The Guardian managed to block the majority of the surprise attack, but was still tossed to the far side of the room. "I will kill them both, starting with Angela." Bastiana gathered her magic around her to transform into a blue ball of energy, teleporting away.

Vincent stood over him. "Get off my ship."

Chapter 17

MASTERSON GEARWORKS, SCABLANDS

The *Odyssey* was silently waiting in the gearworks. Crews worked along the outer hull and infested the inside corridors in a rush to get the airship ready for flight and combat. Showers of sparks rained down onto the gearworks' floor as welding and cutting crews completed their work. Rayne knew not to look at the welding directly, but at this distance from the other side of the complex the light wouldn't hurt her eyes.

"We are running out of time," Rhonin said, offering her a cup of coffee.

She smelled the dark liquid then let the scent and heat soak into her body before taking a sip. Her internal reserves were already running low from weeks of long days and short nights so anything that helped get her through the morning was welcomed. "I know. I try not to think about it if I can."

"I wish I could stop worrying too. What do we have so far today?"

"Almost finished with the *Odyssey*," she said. Taking a glance at the progress report from the overnight shift, she was pleased with the amount of work that had gotten done. That feeling quickly faded when she considered how much of a strain it was putting on the workers. The last thing they wanted was hasty work that led to shortcuts or defects when lives would be at risk.

"Good. I think I will feel a lot better once she's done."

She nodded in agreement. "Once the *Odyssey* is ready, we won't have any vacation time. It will be straight off to Silverton again." She put the report down to focus on sipping the hot coffee.

Rhonin turned back to look at the ship. "It's amazing you know. Everything we have been through, and here we are. Not a scratch on us."

"I don't agree. We might not have battle scars to show, but I feel bruised and broken every time we get pulled into something by Mr. Eleazar. We might come out ok, but not everyone else does and that hurts," Rayne said, looking deeply into the coffee mug. It was hard to understand the pain and difficulties that Kail and Angela must be going through without their children. It hurt her when she saw their family torn apart like that. It also reminded her that she had no children of her own. Not for a lack of trying on her and Rhonin's part, but they were unable to conceive. Then time flew by, and now they were simply getting too old have children.

Rhonin must have developed the ability to read her mind and rubbed her shoulder. "Once this is over maybe we should look at adopting. I'm sure there will be more than one child orphaned from this war."

"Yes well," she forced back with a sniff. "Let's get through this first."

"Okay," Rhonin said, settling back into work mode. "Looks like the radio and comm systems will be finished and working today. That leaves the weapons platforms and finally the cosmetics."

Rayne finished her coffee. She turned her thoughts back to the situation at hand. "That should be it then. End of the week at the latest, unless I don't like the color you picked out," she teased.

"Right, well we can always take a can of paint with us so you can decorate on the way there."

"Oh, really?" she asked. "I have this shade of lavender in mind. It would go lovely on the outer hull, especially in the spring time when the early blooming flowers start."

"You might have to do it on your own. Conrad wants to get as many people going on the new airship as possible. Purple painting parties are going to have to wait."

"I'll hold you to it," she said with a lopsided grin. "Where are we with the delivery of ammunition and supplies?"

"The ammo storage is already here, as are the long term supplies. Anything else, we will have to wait until we are ready to-" Rhonin's answer was interrupted as Conrad Black approached from overseeing the refit of the *Odyssey*.

"Rhonin. Rayne," Conrad greeted. "Looks like she will be ready, but I have been going over some of the current progress reports for the new airship, and it doesn't look good."

"What is it this time?" Rhonin asked.

"Unless we get a miracle of some kind, it's got at least a month. Maybe two unless everything goes perfectly, and nothing has to be redesigned."

Rayne turned away from the conversation. She had come to the same conclusion as well. It would be a mighty airship when it was finished. Whether or not it got the chance to play a part in this war, she didn't know. Frowning, she moved away from her husband and Conrad to get a closer look at someone standing at the hanger doors observing the two airships and the work being done.

She made a mental note to make sure everyone was conscious of security and the general secret nature of the gearworks. Having people wandering in whenever they felt like it was unacceptable. She didn't care who they might be related to or friends with. "Excuse me. You can't be here," she called out.

The man's piercing blue eyes stopped her cold.

"Just checking in on my ship," Mr. Eleazar said with his heavy accent. "Looks a little unfinished if I do say so myself."

PATROL DUTY, SILVERTON

The sound of his own heart beating, and the rushing of air from heavy breathing overwhelmed every other sense. Private Mance vaguely remembered hearing the explosions as the fighting broke out behind him as he ran as fast and hard as he could back to Silverton. Each time his foot hit the ground his ears registered the impact with a thump through his entire body. His orders were simple: report and get reinforcements. He prayed that he got there in time.

The repeated snap of bullets forced Duncan to pull back behind cover. "You're going to have to run fast," he yelled. "You two grab the repeater gun off of the tractor, and you get the ammunition," he ordered. "I'll provide as much cover fire as I can, but you need to get that gun set up, or we're going to be overrun."

The three soldiers nodded and got ready.

"Pakmon, where's Pakmon?" He looked around as another cannon round from the remaining armored tractor fired off, forcing everyone to brace themselves.

"Right here sir." The private waved.

"Get back into the house and find Stanz. Don't fire more than a few times before moving, they will center on your location, you got that?"

Pakmon nodded and readied his rifle. The tractor fired another shot as it rolled back to find a better angle to use against the incoming enemy forces.

"Now!" Duncan yelled, swinging around to fire his rifle up the road. They were severely outnumbered, and he wasn't sure how many of his men were still alive, but he did know that several were dead or dying. He fired round after round. He knew some hit enemy soldiers when they jerked and fell to the ground. Again he had to retreat from return fire. His position was compromised as more and more enemy rounds pelted around him. He spared a quick glance and saw his men retreating with the repeater gun.

Taking a few deep breaths, he sprinted away from his position. Tiny amounts of dirt jumped up all around him as the enemy fired on him. He reached the edge of an outbuilding on the Wellington estate and skidded to a halt to catch his breath. This wasn't going to be safe enough as half of the enemy had seen him run here.

Enemy fire stopped hitting the side of the building when he heard the repeater gun start up. Now was his chance while the enemy focused on the new and significantly more deadly threat. Sprinting away from the building, he kept low and circled around along the outer edge of the estate. No one fired at him this time, and he felt pretty sure he had gone unnoticed but wasn't about to bet his life on it. He hadn't directly ordered it, but he hoped his men with the repeater gun were smart enough to pack it up and keep moving once the enemy turned on them.

A cannon fired from the enemy resulting in an explosion that billowed black smoke into the air. Their second armored tractor had surely been destroyed. It was the only thing that would go up like that. Duncan checked his ammunition before moving. He had a couple dozen rounds left for the rifle, and his pistol was ready to go with four shots and enough bullets to reload it twice. This was as dirty and real as war got. He hoped that they lived long enough to tell people about it. People only got to hear about the major battles and assumed wars were won or lost right then. There were going to be countless more like the one right now that few would ever hear about. Gripping the rifle tightly, he moved through the brush hoping to find a couple of his men to help flank the enemy.

Pakmon followed his orders to the letter. He fired once from the doorway, twice from the upstairs window, and once from around the servants' entrance. He found Stanz in an upstairs bedroom. He was unconscious and bleeding, but still alive.

He sighted down the rifle and fired, killing a man who had climbed on top of the armored vehicle to man the repeater gun again. It was an easy shot for him when they stood up in the open and he figured he could shoot them all day long like that. He sprinted through the house again and was flung across the kitchen when something outside exploded, blasting the wall in around him. As quickly as he could, with his ears ringing and his head spinning, he checked to make sure all of his limbs were still attached. Wetness crept down the side of his face, and his hand came away covered in blood. Nothing hurt so he ignored it and grabbed his rifle.

Thick black smoke billowed in front of the house. He wasn't going to be able to see anything through the heavy haze. *So much for easy kills*, he thought. He was going to need a new place to snipe from, but first, he needed to move Stanz. He couldn't just leave him there when the house might burn down. Pushing through his disorientation, he sprinted back upstairs.

Duncan had found Erickson and Daly. Both had minor wounds but nothing that would slow them down. "I'll stay on the left, Daly take the middle, and Erikson you go to the right. Find your second target as well. We fire once, shift and fire again. Snap, snap, like that," he emphasized with his hands. "We should easily get two kills each before they can react, then we retreat. If they follow us, we cover each other as we go. Got it?"

Both men nodded before spreading out to flank the enemy infantry that was still coming up the road behind their armored twin cannon vehicles. He sighted down the barrel of his rifle to choose his target. To the front of the man walked his comrade, hunched over in anticipation of the fight ahead of them.

Duncan nodded, and they counted down from three. He fired and could hear both Erikson and Daly do the same.

He fired again, dropping his second target. Both men were dead on the ground before the enemy reacted. He didn't spare a second's worth of time to see if his men also killed two soldiers or not before he tore through the brush and trees as fast as he could.

The enemy returned fire in their direction. Bullets whistled past him and tore parts of the ground and trees apart. Duncan skidded to a halt behind a large birch tree, checking to make sure Erikson and Daly were with still with him. Both men were sprinting through the brush. He didn't see anyone in pursuit as the number of shots fired at them became less and less. He whistled and waved them down.

Daly dove to the ground bringing his gun up, ready to fire on anyone after them. "I think I hit three. Two of them fell on my first shot. I think the bullet passed straight through him."

Erikson joined them and just nodded, catching his breath then letting them know that the plan went well.

Duncan kept his voice down. "Let's not celebrate yet. That's not going to work a second time." He pointed towards the main house. "Let's move."

Pakmon had run out of ammunition a while ago. Luckily he had Stanz's to use. He managed to carry Stanz back downstairs and indeed, parts of the house had started to catch fire from the explosion. There wasn't much more he could do for Stanz, so he dragged him outside and hid his body next to a horse watering trough before abandoning the house all together.

He found a dried irrigation ditch that ran through the middle of the estate. It wasn't as good as the elevated angles the house had provided, but he could move up and down it quickly allowing him to continue the hit and run style of attack his commander had ordered of him.

Pakmon found a spot from the ditch to look up from and surveyed the enemy's advance. There was one hell of a firefight going on in the back. He hoped his fellow soldiers were giving as much as they were getting in that exchange. He even saw the three men with the repeater gun setting up to try to take down the enemy's armored vehicle that was slowly pushing forward. Without even thinking he drew down and fired a round into an enemy soldier who had managed to sneak around the group on the repeater gun. The men continued to set up, oblivious to the danger he had eliminated. It made him feel good, even god-like, to be able to kill and defend so easily. He quickly quelled the feeling though. If there was one thing he had learned from his commanding officer; stupid thoughts led to stupid deaths.

He fired again, dropping the man who had foolishly been chosen to man the repeater gun on the enemy vehicle. Two shots, time to move.

Duncan heard the repeater gun open up, and whatever it was hitting protested loudly with tearing metal and ricochets. "Stay on me," he called to the men behind him.

An explosion, followed by a ball of flame rose high into the air as the repeater gun fell silent. It had to be one of the enemy vehicles. The repeater gun must have punched through the fuel tank. There was at least one more vehicle and an unknown number of infantry. The next sound brought him up short. At first it sounded like some sort of giant cat hissing followed by the sound of a boulder being dropped into a lake or pond. Bright flashes of colored light came from the direction of the main house. *Magic*, he realized. "Kail must be here, way to go private Mance."

"Magic?" Daly asked.

Duncan nodded. "Double time it!" he ordered as he broke into a full run in the direction of the battle.

Angela quietly observed the battle from the top of a tall tree. Guns made her angry. They were a powerful weapon, too powerful, too easily used by untrained hands. She respected it though, just not the people who relied on it. The smoke from the battle had been spotted from Silverton. Kail had teleported her and himself close by, and the *Sky Hawk* would be here in a few minutes as well after hearing from a soldier who had arrived describing the enemy force.

In her haste to arrive quickly, she realized that she had not brought enough arrows. She pulled back on her bow and released. The arrow struck through the back of a soldier's neck, and he fell to the ground. With so much chaos going on from Kail's attack, no one even noticed their felled comrade. Again she held her breath for a brief moment before dropping a second man. Her arrows rained a silent death, one after another until there were none left.

She pulled her ancient unbreakable war blade from her back. It was time to get up close and messy.

"How many of you are there?" Kail yelled to the three men who had just used the last of the repeater gun's ammunition.

"Twenty sir. No, nineteen and two tractors," came the answer.

Kail nodded. "Find everyone and fall back until the *Sky Hawk* arrives. I'll take care of this."

The men nodded needing no further encouragement as Kail waded into the fight. His magic was wrapped around him in a soft white glow, and the enemy gun fire seemed to just evaporate before hitting him.

The first thing to get rid of was the remaining armored vehicle. The twin cannons swiveled to face him but never got the chance to fire. With a wave of his hand a pulse of magic cut through the center of the machine slicing it in two. He instantly regretted it as the vehicle fell in on itself. It would have been valuable to save for their own use. Next time, he wouldn't be so rough.

He strode down the road, past the burning armored tractors and the vehicle he had disabled. He lashed out with his magic as the enemy took ineffective shots at him. It wasn't a fair fight so he set off fist sized blue balls of magic that exploded with electrical and a concussive force. It used very little of his magic reserves but was extremely effective in knocking out the enemy.

Several of the enemy soldiers sounded a general retreat. That too didn't last as the dozen or so remaining soldiers ran into the dead bodies that littered the roadway following Angela's assault. He could hear her call out for their surrender. It was an absurd sight. A dozen armed soldiers against one woman, but not just any lone woman. It was the one with red hair wearing black skin tight leather armor, standing in the middle of the road with more than fifteen dead soldiers lying at her feet with a sword pointed at them.

The soldiers didn't hesitate in complying. They all dropped their weapons and held their hands in the air. Duncan and two soldiers burst onto the scene. "Daly, Erikson, find everyone and report back here." Duncan ordered before turning to Kail. "You're a sight for sore eyes."

"Duncan." Kail nodded. "We saw the smoke and came. The *Sky Hawk* should be here soon. How are your men?"

"Better than the enemy, but we have several dead and wounded," Duncan answered as private Pakmon ran to join them. "Pakmon, gather their weapons and get the prisoners squared away and ready to move back to Silverton."

Private Pakmon nodded then looked at Kail. "Never seen anything like that before sir," Pakmon said, turning to relieve Angela who still threatened the prisoners.

"How did they get this many troops this close without us knowing about it?" Kail asked.

"I was going ask you the same thing. Somebody missed something, and good men died for it," Duncan lamented as Angela joined them. "Angela, thanks for the save."

"You are welcome, Duncan Deline," she said, nodding her head, accepting the thank you. The three of them looked up as the *Sky Hawk* flew by with a deafening roar.

"Let's help with the wounded Angela," Kail said as the airship circled once before landing in the open field behind the Wellington house. Together they helped Duncan's men move the wounded to the *Sky Hawk* and dress the dead for transport. Eight men were dead and three more had serious wounds. Kail looked back over the recent battlefield. This was just the start, and he couldn't help but feel that it was going to get much worse.

Chapter 18

CANYAMAR JUNGLE

Camden pulled back on the reins, slowing his horse. The road south into the jungle ended more quickly than what the map had shown. Traces of the road were there, and it was clear that lack of use had allowed the jungle to reclaim the road. What also was clear was that someone or a group of people had been here in the not too distant past. Branches showed clean cuts, and dead leaves littered the ground where they made their way through the jungle.

This was even better than he could have asked. The path that Xavier had cut made it simple and easy for him to follow, not having to clear the path himself. He briefly considered going on foot, but the path was clear enough that he would catch up more quickly riding on the horse. He clicked his tongue to urge the horse onward at a brisk walk that would chew through the miles that lay between him and Xavier.

MINING CAMP 300 MILES SOUTH OF COURDUFF

Alyssa motioned for her to follow. Tied behind the saloon was a pair of horses. Suki's eyes widened when she saw the unconscious man lying in the mud. She recognized him as the one that had been following her when she arrived at the mining camp. Then she recalled the loud banging noise after she had entered the saloon. *Someone hit their head,* she remembered the bartender saying. Stepping passed the man she asked, "You did this?"

Alyssa stopped to look down at the man. "Yeah, does that bother you?"

"No no. I don't think so. I don't know what to think right now."

Alyssa undid the reins and handed one to Suki while she hopped onto her own horse. "We have a long way to go Aunt Suki. I think there will be plenty of time to explain."

She could only nod. Alyssa was here now in front of her. Not the four year old girl she remembered taking care of, but a young adult woman perhaps only a few years younger than herself. It wasn't possible. "How do I know it's really you?" she asked, getting onto her own horse and following the dark haired girl.

"You could ask me something only you and I would know. But I think you already know inside that I am who I say I am."

She had to admit, it was hard not to see the resemblance to Angela, and the attitude was definitely there, just more mature. "The last time I saw you, who was that man you went with? You called him grandpa."

"Yes, he is my grandpa. Duke Falconcrest. Kail's father," Alyssa said. "I'm surprised you remembered that."

"It wasn't that long ago," she said, recalling that fateful night in Courduff.

"I'm sorry. It's easy to forget that it has only been a few months for you and my parents. But that night was years and years ago for me." Alyssa eyed some people watching them from the mining town. "Let's pick up the pace some." She spurred her horse into a gallop.

Suki didn't need to be told twice, and together they rode out of town.

A half hour later was not a lot of time to think about what was going on, Alyssa pulled her horse back and settled into an easy walk. Suki fell in beside her.

"I don't even know where to start," Suki said.

"Maybe the beginning is a good place," Alyssa offered.

"Alright, six months ago, you said that it was Kail's father. He was there in Courduff all this time, and he took you?"

"Not exactly. You have to remember, I was four at the time. Men came."

"When you were in Aldervale, with the Kellys." Suki wanted clarified.

Alyssa nodded. "Yes Amaya and I were taken. It seemed like forever then, but it was only a few days before you and Uncle Camden showed up." The wisp that had been hiding under Alyssa's cloak finally peeked out at Suki.

Suki stared back as Alyssa continued. She vaguely remembered the wisp being there in Courduff that night.

"Before they came to take her, she told me not to worry. Amaya said that you would come, but it was time for her to go."

"You said she had to rescue Camden," Suki recalled.

Alyssa's voice turned somber, "I guess. But Therion killed her."

"Wait, Therion killed Amaya? I thought Xavier killed her."

"I don't know who Xavier is," Alyssa said.

"That's who Camden said killed her. That's who he is going after."

"Humm. I will have to look into that name. Then Grandpa came for me, and we went."

"Went where?" Suki asked, trying to absorb everything she was being told. The blue wisp had started to warm up to her as well and now road on Alyssa's shoulder.

Alyssa gave her a distant look before answering. "The future, the past, time itself."

"What does that mean?"

Alyssa chuckled. "Complicated doesn't even begin to describe it. Let's just call it 'the other side of The Eternal Gateway'."

"The other side?" She had to admit Alyssa was right, complicated didn't do the situation any justice. It made her head hurt to even try to start untangling the impossibility of it.

Alyssa nodded. "Grandpa, took care of me from there. Don't worry," she assured her after seeing her skeptical look, "I had a perfectly fine childhood growing up with him. I did miss my mother and father, and especially Amaya." The wisp looked sullen as Alyssa talked about her family. "He is smart, unbelievably smart and can do more with magic than anyone else I know."

Suki was thoroughly confused. "I thought he gave up his magic powers. The prophecy about giving up power." She turned to pull open her pack.

"What are you doing?" Alyssa asked.

Suki found what she was looking for. Three sets of runes set in a circle. "These are them, these are the binding runes that were pulled out of Kail," she finished, holding the runes towards Alyssa.

Alyssa pulled her horse to a stop and stared. "Why do you have those?"

"Kail gave them to me before I left."

"Why did he do that?"

"I don't know," Suki almost yelled. "I don't know what's going on. Nothing makes sense to me anymore." It was hard to breath. "I don't. I don't," she said as the words she wanted to say failed to find voice.

"Aunt Suki, take it easy," she heard Alyssa say.

"I." Suki felt hot all over as her vision started to go black. She heard Alyssa call her name again and then she was falling. Falling into darkness.

Chapter 19

ABANDONED BUILDING, SILVERTON

A cloaked figure had circled the abandoned building more than once. Each time there had been someone nearby so he was unable to sneak inside unnoticed. Inside was the makeshift hideout of Treylane Armstrong and his group of trained spies. Originally they had worked for a man from Hyperion Industries, and to some extent, they still did, but for now, they reported their findings to Courduff's military intelligence group.

Treylane didn't turn around when the door opened to the cramped room. He had seen his man on the street earlier trying to enter the building. "Well, how did the battle go?" Treylane asked, keeping an eye on the crossroad of streets where the Silverton Army Headquarters was located.

The man took off his cloak and sat behind the small table that was crammed up next to the wall. "Quite the fight actually, Silverton was outnumbered and outgunned. They held their own and forced some impressive losses on Courduff. They would have fallen in the end except for Falconcrest and the Keratin showed up."

Treylane nodded. "As expected."

"Yup, they are all talking about it. Magic doesn't make for a fair fight apparently."

"It never will," he agreed. "Get the report encoded and ready to go."

"Yes sir. Also they took a bunch of prisoners. Is that going to cause problems?"

Treylane looked away from the window for the first time. "Prisoners are exactly what we want. The Courduff force was specifically misled for this outcome. They won't have any useable information for Silverton, but keep your ears open just in case. Courduff will be forced to attack now."

The man nodded. "I have a shift coming up at the bunker so I'll keep an eye out."

"We only have a few days left now so keep tabs on your targets as well," Treylane said, returning to look out the window. Angela Atagi stepped outside of the headquarters. Treylane pointed his finger at her like it was a gun. "We don't want anyone slipping through our fingers," he finished, pulling the imaginary trigger on Angela.

MAGE COUNCIL TOWER, COURDUFF

Cid entered the map room on the top floor of the Mage Council Tower. He found Admiral Bailon studying the map, and a quick glance showed him that it was centered over the eastern cities.

"What brings you here Cid?" Bailon asked wearily.

"There has been an incident sir."

Bailon turned his focus away from the map. "Incident means it's not good news."

Cid nodded. "A mobile infantry group was attacked by Silverton forces. There are reports of heavy losses on both sides, but our forces were defeated by Falconcrest, and a number of our soldiers were taken prisoner."

Bailon frowned. "This is unlike Silverton. For them to take the offensive like this is very uncharacteristic. Kail and his group have always acted like war could be resolved with a few individual private battles. We can't allow this to go unanswered. This will force us to answer with force."

"I agree sir, we will have to act, but it does seem odd. All of the engagements that we have information on suggest the same thing. The profilers label them as having 'hero complexes'. Even in battles where there were high casualties or property damage, it all stemmed from individual confrontations. In the rare cases of full pitched battles, they were resoundingly defeated."

"I remember the air battle above The Eternal Gateway. Of course they ran into the unexpected brick wall that is Therion."

"Indeed, the loss at the gateway seemed to reinforce their behavior as well. They launched a small guerilla attack against the gateway outpost that seemed to achieve some unknown goal. The incident with Cahir also started out with relatively benign intentions, and we know now that most of the destruction caused was not by Kail and his group but by Vincent's female mage, Bastiana."

"So why the change now?" Bailon asked, refocusing the map over the top of Silverton.

Cid walked over to examine the city. "I have a couple of theories." The city below his feet looked worse for wear. The surrounding area was dead and burned; the city was dark and gloomy as well. "One, they might simply be tired and broken down. It's no secret that we have left them with the threat of annihilation looming over them. Supplies and information to and from Silverton have been blockaded for a while. Travelers are also searched, and eventually desperation will lead any sane person to do insane acts."

Bailon shook his head. "That might explain it for normal people, but I don't see a man with Kail's power and ability, nor do I see his wife who can fly, as people who succumb to desperation."

"Normally I would agree with you sir. They themselves might not, but what about the tens of thousands of civilians still in Silverton. Desperation breeds desperation," Cid countered. "There were heavy losses on both sides according to the report. If Kail had wanted to attack us, he would have done it himself, not with heavy losses. I am more inclined to believe the populous is losing control to desperation and are acting out on their own, and he had to rescue them."

Bailon frowned. "Maybe. You said you had another theory?"

"We're being setup."

"What?" Bailon responded, disbelief clearly in his voice.

"Only a theory sir," he reassured. "The report comes from a reliable source so I do not doubt its accuracy. However I did some fact checking. The infantry group that was attacked, doesn't exist."

"Explain."

"They don't exist, at least not officially. I found no record of a unit consisting of the equipment or man power listed. Least of all there should not have been a unit that close to Silverton. However, there are reports of missing equipment from other groups, as well as a number of personnel reassignments that could create this unit."

"Are you implying that someone or some group put this unit together to attack Silverton on their own?"

"No sir, just relaying a theory."

"Well, if this group doesn't exist, then we won't have to commit to a retaliatory attack. Last thing we need is to commit resources against Silverton when the eastern cities are a bigger threat. Also, with these damned earthquakes, having the military around provides a calming sense of order for the public."

"I'm afraid that won't be possible," Cid added much to Bailon's displeasure. "Silverton has taken several of our troops prisoner. The newspapers right now are printing up a special edition that will be distributed. In a few hours people will start finding out, and by tomorrow morning everyone will know. They will want to know what our response will be."

"I don't like conspiracy theories, but this is sounding more and more like one. A unit that doesn't exist attacks Silverton and gets wiped out. Prisoners are being held, and the news knows about it before I do."

"Just a theory that fits with what we know."

"Any ideas on who is behind it?"

"No sir, I haven't dedicated any resources to pursuing a conspiracy."

Bailon frowned deep in thought. "Alright, start a normal investigation regarding the lost unit. Start with what we know for sure like names of prisoners, back track orders, and see where it leads. Looks like it's going to be a long night while I prepare for a speech. I'll leave it to you to notify the captains and have the fleet prepared. I have ignored Silverton for as long as I can, hoping for another way, but that time has passed. I'll wire the situation to the gateway outpost, but I don't expect a response from Therion. The man hasn't responded to anything else, and I don't expect him to now."

"Yes sir," Cid said with a salute, turning to exit the map room.

Chapter 20

ABANDONED FARMHOUSE
EDGE OF THE CANYAMAR JUNGLE

Suki groaned. The last time she remembered feeling like this was after a large party at which Camden had managed to get everyone involved in a drinking game. Unfortunately, this time there wasn't a fun time to look back on to help ease the suffering headache that she had.

"How are you feeling?" Alyssa asked, ready with a skin of water.

"I feel like the whole world flipped upside down," she said, taking a small sip. The house that she found herself in seemed to confirm how she felt. "This place looks like how I feel."

Alyssa nodded. "It's not in great shape, I will admit that, but it was the first place I found after you fainted. The broken walls made for some easy firewood, and it's pretty stable in the back here."

Suki chuckled at Alyssa's use of words. "I don't even remember the last time I could say my life was stable." Once she had been able to use magic, but not anymore. Nearly stabbed to death, now a wanted criminal on the run with the people she called her friends. No, stable was not part of the vocabulary that described her life.

Alyssa smiled. "A sense of humor is a good sign."

"Did you learn to be a doctor as well?"

"No, but first aid and general psychology were part of my schooling."

"How old are you again?" she asked. Psychology wasn't something she ever remembered being taught when she was a kid.

Alyssa smiled. "Old enough to know what I am doing, but young enough to know that I can't do everything on my own."

Suki paused for a moment before saying anything. "If I didn't know better, that sounded like you're asking for help."

Alyssa shrugged. "Mr. Eleazar is here. He is in Cahir trying to collect on an old debt. It was never going to be as easy or simple as just showing up and taking out Therion."

Suki's heart took a drop. "Is that why you are here with me? We failed to rescue you so now you're collecting on a debt?"

"Oh no, no, no, no Aunt Suki. That's not it at all. No, you should never think that," Alyssa said putting her hand on her shoulder. "I would never do that. I'm here for you. I know how awful it has been for you, for Camden and my parents since that day. You need to see that it wasn't your fault and to not go on punishing yourself."

"I guess," she said, still unsure of herself. "Have you seen your parents?"

Now it was Alyssa's turn to look guilty. "No. I haven't seen them. I mean I have seen them, but they don't know about me yet."

"How can you keep them in the dark about this? They are your parents. They should have been the first to know."

"I have my reasons," Alyssa said, moving across the room to look through the rubble. "There will be plenty of time for family reunions once this is all over."

"When this is all over?" Suki asked. "What does that mean? Do you already know what is going to happen?"

Alyssa looked back at her before answering. "No. The river is uncharted when we don't have control of The Eternal Gateway."

Suki was even more confused than ever. "The river. What are you talking about?"

Alyssa suppressed a sigh. "You have heard Mr. Eleazar talk about time, how it's fluid. It doesn't work linearly. It can wind around, split into forks, even dam up or drop off cliffs."

"I sort of remember. I recall Kail arguing about it once, but it seemed that in the end it all ran to the ocean. Like it didn't matter what you did."

"Trust me it matters. Just like building your house on a flood plain. When the river rises, it can destroy everything."

Suki thought for a moment. "So you're saying that Therion has control of the gateway and because of that, you and Mr. Eleazar don't know what is going on or what will happen?"

Alyssa simply nodded.

"Then why did he do it on purpose?"

"What?"

"He said that Therion had to control the gateway for us to defeat him."

Alyssa turned away, and Suki was sure that whatever Alyssa was going to say next was either a lie or something worse. The truth.

"We already lost," she admitted. "Even when we were fully in control, or at least as much control as anyone could be when dealing with time travel. There are some things about magic that should have been left undiscovered during the War of Antiquities." Alyssa shook her head before continuing. "Monsters were created, abominations."

Suki was truly lost, but she tried to understand. "What do you mean we already lost?"

"This," Alyssa said, holding her arms out around her. "All of this didn't exist. We forced a paradox. We came back and released control of the gateway. We forced the river to break and flow down another path."

Suki had heard enough, and no matter how it was explained, she knew she would never understand. "What does that mean to someone like me?"

"It means we're on our own. This is it, no more hopping through time. If we don't destroy Therion here in this time, there isn't going to be a second chance."

"So you're stranded here?" Suki asked, trying to understand. "Like you can't go back to where or when you were earlier?"

"I don't know," Alyssa said softly. "What we did... It had never been tried before."

There was something in Alyssa's voice that troubled her before she realized what it was. "Your grandfather!"

Alyssa looked at Suki and tried to smile, but the best she could do was shrug. "I don't know. Everything forward from the last six months when Therion took over the gateway no longer exists. He was already gone from this time."

"Why didn't The Duke come with you?"

"Someone had to stay while Mr. Eleazar and I came back. I went through first, but after I arrived, I was alone. Something happened, and Mr. Eleazar only recently showed up. I asked him about it, and all he said was that we were lucky to be alive."

Suki thought about what it must have been like. Somewhere in the future, everything had gone wrong. The bad guys had won. So they did the only thing they could think to do, cheat time. But at what cost? Kail's father, Duke Falconcrest, stayed behind. Sacrificing what? His existence? His life? In some sort of desperate bid to change things. "I don't understand any of it."

"The important thing is we are here now. We have another chance to make things right," Alyssa announced. "How are you feeling?"

"I don't know what to feel," Suki said as the blue wisp darted inside the room and landed on Suki's shoulder.

Alyssa frowned at the wisp who chattered at her. "If you insist," she said to the tiny being. "We should get going. Camden was here. We need to hurry if we want to catch up to him."

Suki looked at the wisp and felt better when its tiny face smiled at her. She had wondered what had happened to the tiny companion of the *Snow Break*. It had disappeared just before Alyssa and Amaya were born but had shown up again when Alyssa was taken away, the same night Amaya had died.

Camden. He was something on which she could focus. Time travel was out of her league, but the big strong blond was someone she knew she wanted to have in her life. "Ok. I think I am good to ride."

Alyssa smiled. "Let's go find Uncle Camden."

Chapter 21

SILVERTON AIRFIELD

Randal Wood looked out of the window that overlooked the Silverton airfield. The *Sky Hawk* and *Renegade* were crewed and ready to launch at a moment's notice. The *Seraph* sat with her wings clipped. It was a hard decision to make, but a necessary one, one that pained him to see the fine ship stripped of her armaments and useable equipment. The deck guns were placed onto converted Hyperion tractors, and her main cannons were being loaded onto trailers to be sent throughout the city for use as ground based artillery.

"What do you propose Duncan?" Angela asked.

Randal turned back to the meeting. Kail and Angela were sitting next to each other listening to Duncan review recent events. The closeness of the attack by Courduff had caught everyone off guard, and finding a solution wasn't coming easily.

Duncan hammered his fist onto the table. "We need to increase the number of patrols," he insisted. "The *Sky Hawk* and *Renegade* need to be in the air full time. We can't have this happen again."

"Is that even possible?" Kail asked as everyone turned to look at him.

"We have enough fuel to last a month if we run two airships full time," Randal said. "Double that if we run only one of the ships."

"What about taking it from the tractors?" Angela asked.

Randal shook his head. "No, unless you want to leave them where they sit. We are already using resources from the airfield to keep the tractors fueled. Fuel, spare parts and ammunition are all in short supply."

Again Duncan slammed his fist on the table in frustration. "How do you expect me to defend Silverton? Should I just politely ask the enemy to leave?"

"Diplomacy may be an option," Angela said, earning her a shocked, disbelieving look from Duncan.

"Did you just wake up today and decide to lose your mind?" Duncan asked. "You want to surrender Silverton?"

Randal also wondered at what was going on inside Angela's head. He never pegged her as someone who even had the word surrender in her vocabulary, and he knew for a fact that she was the most brutal efficient killing machine there was. He didn't know of anyone other than her who had killed so many in battle, and she always lived by a warrior's code.

Angela's eyes took on a deadly glint. "Therion rules Courduff, and their army does his command. Therion is not in Courduff," she said, looking from Duncan then to Kail. "He is at The Eternal Gateway. We send a messenger to

Courduff. Therion will not leave, but Wilhelm Bailon will hear our words and not attack."

"That might buy us some time to open some new supply lines," Kail said. "But remember, Bailon did betray us."

Randal knew Kail wanted to say more, but had held back. He did not want to revive that night Admiral Bailon destroyed the *Snow Break* as well as destroyed Kail and Angela's family.

Angela drew her war blade. "You mistake my plan. The army is busy, we cut off Therion's head." She finished her words with a swipe of her blade.

Kail frowned. "I don't know. I don't think attacking Therion head on, even if it's just a few of us is the answer. Remember what Mr. Eleazar said? We were done. And what about what I saw through the gateway? It was Mr. Eleazar and that other Keratin."

Randal could see the conflicting emotions warring inside Angela. If he were in her place, he would stop at nothing to get back at Therion. With Kail's powers and Angela's abilities, he was surprised they didn't just magic off that first night and kill Therion.

"I, I no longer believe the Time Walker has our fates in mind," she said with obvious difficulty. "Attacking is our best option."

"What if we ask for help?" Kail suggested.

"Ask for help from whom?" Randal asked. "Who would come to our aid?"

"The eastern cities," Kail proposed. "We know they are in Courduff's sights. Why not offer them the chance to fight with us?"

Duncan shook his head as he pushed his chair away from the table. "The only thing easterners care about is themselves. Hell, you can't even trade with them unless you're willing to take a two for one loss."

"I agree," Randal said. "I don't believe they will be of any help."

"Face it Kail, you're the only one with the power to do anything, no offense Angela." Duncan scoffed. "Seriously, why don't you just kill them all? End this war right here and right now."

Kail's voice was filled with anger. "Is that what you want? One sided slaughter against people who can't defend themselves."

"If it saves our lives, yes!" Duncan countered. "Destroy their airships, their weapons and their army. Better them than us!"

Randal took a step back from the two arguing men. A soldier had peeked his head into the room, wanting to say something but feared interrupting. He caught the soldier's eye and nodded him over. "What is it private?" Randal asked quietly.

"This just came in sir." The soldier handed him a report before quickly leaving the room.

Randal could still hear Kail and Duncan arguing over the use magic to go on the offensive. Angela remained neutral as he read the report. Courduff's air force was being mobilized. Word of the attack that Duncan had stumbled upon had spread through the newspapers, and Courduff's response was the immediate use of force.

"What have you learned Randal Wood?" Angela asked him, halting the argument.

He tossed the report onto the table. "Looks like we have a few days at best before the entire might of Courduff is on our doorsteps. They are spinning it as an unprovoked attack resulting in the taking of prisoners to subject them to all sorts of horrors," he said looking at Kail and Angela. "Magical torture."

"That is not true," Angela protested. "They were released after they were questioned."

"We know that. They don't," Kail reminded her. "And it's not exactly like I sent them home. They do have a long walk back to the nearest city after I teleported them away."

"Something I highly objected to," Duncan added.

Kail sighed. "We don't have the resources, facilities, or manpower to hold prisoners of war."

"And they will know that once their soldiers get back to Courduff," Duncan said.

"Releasing an enemy so he can attack you again is unwise," Angela said, siding with Duncan.

"It's done," Kail said putting an end to it. "We have a few days. Randal, get the *Sky Hawk* and *Renegade* into the sky. Duncan, the army is yours."

"What are you going to do?" Randal asked.

Kail stood up from the conference table looking at Angela. "I'm going to the eastern cities. The worst they can do is say no, and I can be back in time to defend the city."

Angela stood. "Do what you think is right Kail." Her eyes shifted to Duncan. "I will fight where I am needed."

KAIL AND ANGELA'S PRIVATE QUARTERS
SILVERTON

"You don't agree do you?" Kail asked while packing a small backpack. He wasn't sure how or even who to talk to in the east that might be willing to help Silverton against Courduff's attack.

"Honor demands that blood be spilled Kail. For our daughters, for the Kellys," Angela insisted. "What was seen in the gateway should not be what decides for you."

Kail stopped packing and turned his eyes towards his wife. Her almond shaped eyes had always been fierce and fearless, but now they were laced with pain. "I want to, so badly. But it scares me. My breath gets caught in my throat sometimes. You know," he said, waving his hand in front of his chest. "At any moment, I can be one second away from tearing a hole through space with my magic, killing them all in the next second." When Angela didn't say anything he returned to packing. "I want to do it. I almost did it when Duncan wanted me to earlier. I wanted to, every fiber of my being wants revenge, and that scares me."

Angela stepped up behind him, placed her arms around his chest and rested her head on his back. "I do not know how you can deny yourself like this. But you do. Any Keratin with your power would have done so that very night. I wanted to, and you stayed with me." She hugged him tighter. "I hated you for not doing it."

Kail jerked.

"It betrayed everything I honor and believe in. It betrayed us, our family," she continued. "But I see better now. If you had given in to a berserker rage, revenge would consume you, us, everyone. There would be no Kail. Only a monster, a new Therion or Xavier."

Kail loosened himself from Angela and turned around to face her.

"I promise you-," Kail managed to get out before she stopped him by placing her finger on his lips.

"No, when the time comes, we will do it together." Angela fiercely pressed her lips to his, stopping any argument. He could feel her need and desire in her kiss.

"Together," he repeated, holding her as close as possible.

ABANDONED BUILDING, SILVERTON

Treylane watched Kail teleport away before lowering the binoculars and turning from the window towards one of his men eating at the small table. "The mage is gone."

Without finishing his meal the man nodded, stood and left the room.

Chapter 22

MASTERSON GEARWORKS, SCABLANDS

Mr. Eleazar looked at his pocket watch. The time read six twenty, and he adjusted the watch back one minute before closing the face. He ran his thumb over the symbol for infinity. The symbol was divided into ten parts, each representing one of the ten forms of magic. The power of ten was not simply symbolic. It was the underlying foundation of most of the universe. Unfortunately only a very few individuals would ever walk the world with knowledge of the ten.

The new airship that he had tasked the Mastersons with constructing would not be completed in time. It still bothered him that everything could be so far off. He had planned, calculated and even tested to make sure everything was in place and would work. Yet everything was off. A minute here or a day there. Worse even was when it was a week late, or a year early. He knew it was the result of going too far. It might even take centuries before things settled down. One more event to add to the endless list of anomalies to check and correct once he regained control of the gateway.

"How is your fine ship, the *Odyssey*?" Mr. Eleazar asked casually, masking any of the frustration or anxiety he felt.

"We should be ready to launch in less than an hour," Rhonin said while keeping an eye on the last preparations. "Conrad and the rest will continue to work on the other ship, but it won't be battle ready for this fight."

Mr. Eleazar sagely nodded. "Its destiny is still bright. It will simply start later is all."

Rhonin looked sideways at him. "Whatever you say. You're sure we will make it to Silverton in time?"

"Oh yes. Plenty of time to swoop in and play the hero," he assured the captain of the *Odyssey*.

"That's not a habit I like starting," Rhonin said. "This is it. Our debt is paid."

"Yes, yes, of course."

Rhonin didn't seem convinced, but he did mean it. If the plan fell apart and Therion won again, then there would be no more heroes to save the day. No more Guardians, Sentinels or Watchers. A whole community of time travelers would cease to exist. Even if he did regain control of the gateway, there was no guarantee that anyone other than Alyssa or himself would be left of the old guard.

Rhonin turned away from the *Odyssey* to face him. "What's wrong? You're acting strangely, and that says a lot considering who you are."

"I am afraid I will not be joining you."

"What? Why not? You haven't even seen or communicated with Kail and Angela," Rhonin said, clearly upset. "You can't keep doing this to them. Not after what happened that night in Courduff."

"I assure you Mr. Masterson, Kail and Angela will be perfectly fine. They have played their roles. They are now in control of their own destiny."

"You are a monster, you know that," Rhonin said, leaving before he had a chance to say anything.

It was alright if they thought he was a monster. Someone had to make the hard choices, choices that made him look like a monster were simply part of the job. There was another monster that still needed to be tamed. He didn't like the prospect of having to return to Cahir to convince Vincent to change his mind. One more hiccup in a series of . hiccups.

SKIES ABOVE ALDERVALE

"Just who exactly is in charge?" Bailon asked with a forced smile through gritted teeth.

Cid understood his Admiral's frustration. The armada of airships had been prepared as ordered, ready to fly on a moment's notice. However the military strategists, generals and other admirals that sat on various committees had somehow managed to schedule the launch of the fleet for the attack with pomp and circumstance. "You are sir, until Therion sees fit otherwise."

The *Lotus* flew point as Bailon's command and flagship. Four Juggernaut class airships followed behind: the

Scopic, *Enforcer*, *Sanctuary* and the *Gauntlet*. The bulk of their massive engines were used to keep them in the air which made for an agonizingly slow pace. They were necessary for a successful campaign against Silverton as each housed over a thousand ground troops and once the fighting was over, they would need to maintain a presence in Silverton to keep any rebellion from reforming.

Also included was a fifth Juggernaut class airship the *Creator Patron* or the *CP* for short. The outer deck had been stripped and replaced with a miniature airstrip made from hardened wood. A crane had also been installed where the bridge normally sat so it could retrieve the smaller one or two person airships that had recently arrived from Cahir.

Cid had gone over the design and had no doubt that the smaller airships could launch from the *CP,* but he doubted their ability to land. It was one thing to get them airborne when they were already in the sky, but another altogether to land them on such a small area. No, he figured the smaller ships would have to land on the ground to be retrieved later by the crane. However, even if the *CP* only provided a temporary benefit to the battlefield it would be worth it in certain strategic situations. Part of the parade that had Admiral Bailon so worked up was giving the *CP* some shakedown time.

Bailon waved to the crowd of people in the streets of Aldervale as the fleet slowly roared by in the sky. There were not as many people as compared to Courduff, but there were still several thousand waving and cheering.

"Does any of this seem inappropriate to you?" Admiral Bailon asked. "Remind me to make sure this never happens again."

"Yes sir," he replied, making a mental note. "We knew that when this day came, it was going to be more for show than tactical advantage."

"What have you found so far in your investigation? Any suspects or suspicions to why we are forced into this action?"

"Not yet sir. Whoever is responsible for sending the unit to Silverton has covered their tracks very well. I would say it was orchestrated by a master of manipulation and deceit," Cid answered.

"I don't think I have ever heard you give such praise before," Bailon said.

"I respect the skill of the opponent is all sir. I will find out who is behind it."

Bailon nodded as they walked to the other side of the *Lotus* to wave to the crowd below, earning them a new round of cheers that could be heard even over the roar of the airships. "It may not matter. The latest report on Silverton puts the amount of resistance just slightly above a training exercise. Their air force is almost nonexistent and Kail, the only real threat, was reported as leaving to petition help from the east."

Cid nodded in confirmation. "It would be unwise to count Kail out of the battle, but I see no reason for the eastern cities to provide aid. Their isolationist culture would be impossible for him to overcome. However, only a novice would dismiss him. No one knows what a mage of his ability is capable of achieving."

"No one knows," Bailon repeated. "I pray we don't have to discover that."

Cid recalled the battle at The Eternal Gateway when Therion with almost casual ease destroyed one of the airships from Silverton. It was only after the ship had distracted him from the gateway that he had bothered to get involved. The power of magic could not be denied. "We will have to offer them the option of surrender. Desperate men will do desperate things. I don't want to see what a desperate mage might do."

"I wish I had your optimism Cid," Bailon said, looking at him. "I would have killed every last one of us if that had been my daughter. How do we even hold a man like Kail if he did surrender? No, Cid, I'm afraid if it comes to it. Kail Falconcrest will have to die."

"Yes sir," Cid agreed with a nod.

Chapter 23

HYPERION AIRFIELD, CAHIR

Mr. Eleazar, The Guardian of The Eternal Gateway, paced back and forth outside on the Hyperion Airfield where the *Colossus* was currently stationed. The one thing he needed the most of right now was the one thing he no longer had control of, time. The universe it seemed delighted in his predicament. He needed time to think, time to make sure the results produced the desired outcomes.

Four of the new single manned airships flew overhead. Their engines roaring as they buzzed the airfield and changed pitch as they passed. *Far too early for this time.* It should have been at least another decade before airplanes, as they would come to be known, were invented and then another after that before they were ready as war machines. This wasn't the first time he had come across disturbing changes.

Years and years ago for him, right after he had made a deal with Angela Atagi to bring her to the future, he had jumped ahead to try to see the results of his plan. He was a young man then, still a bit naïve, but he noticed. The *Snow Break* had turbine engines, *turbine engines*. An inner ship communications system, as crude as it was, was all electronic, and radio systems. Even the weapons systems were decades ahead of where they should have been. The hole in time created by the destruction of The Eternal Gateway had to be the culprit.

Then there was Kail Falconcrest. The Duke was a magical enigma, but as for his son it was as if he had taken all of Duke's ability and history and crammed it into a normal lifetime. Having seen Kail break through his own timestop was all the proof he needed. Mr. Eleazar had intentionally put off traveling back to those early days of Kail's life until the current situation was resolved. There had been no one other than himself to train the boy in magic, so he had no one to blame but himself. Perhaps he should have gone easier during that sparing match, so as to not weaken Kail and allowed him to destroy Therion. *No*, he reminded himself. That would have made things even worse.

He rubbed the back of his neck and sighed, "Oh Bastiana. Why didn't you tell me Cora? Couldn't you have told me?" The rivalry between Angela and Bastiana could only end in one way, and now he had to consider an even bigger issue. The policy of not getting directly involved was already broken beyond repair. The academic answer was easy, never directly change anything. The mess he was in had been debated and argued at length. There was now only one thing he could do, finding himself in the exact situation that made him question everything. If something needed changing, manipulate those who already exist in that time to do it, and never ever get involved in your own history.

"How does it feel to find out you have a heart when you're a heartless man?" Vincent's voice asked.

"Asks the monster to his creator," Mr. Eleazar replied.

Vincent scoffed. "You are not the first guardian I have dealt with, and you won't be the last." Vincent came to stand next to Mr. Eleazar. "I know your pathetic rules prohibiting you from helping yourselves. That is why I live one day after another."

"That is your prison," he corrected.

Vincent shrugged. "That may be so, but what are you going to do Guardian? I know you already know how this is going to end, and I know how you end."

Mr. Eleazar couldn't help but smile. "I am fully aware of how I die. I've known that for a long time. It wasn't hard to read peoples' reaction to me when I show up after they already knew I was a dead person. But I wasn't sure how, or more correctly who, until my killer spat it in my face."

"It must make you proud," Vincent said, knowing the words would twist like a knife, "to sire your executioner. I always wondered what kind of family man a guardian would be."

"I gave that up when I found the gateway. Besides, I can't be proud or disappointed in something I had no involvement. If anything Vincent, you are responsible."

"Typical time traveler dribble," Vincent said, not rising to the bait. "No. You will not absolve yourself so easily. You owe it to her."

"I don't have time to owe anyone anything. Least of all you Vincent," Mr. Eleazar said as his accent showed through more than usual in his anger.

"You're lack of time is not my problem. But if you want your little plan to work, then you're going to have to do what I want."

"What exactly do you want from me Vincent?"

"A guarantee."

It wasn't often that he was ever confused about anything. "A guarantee?"

"Yes, and I have everything you need too," Vincent said, looking back at the *Colossus*. "Shall we?" Vincent held out his hand, inviting him to return to the ship.

Mr. Eleazar reluctantly followed Vincent back onto the *Colossus*. He didn't know what Vincent wanted or what this guarantee was he insisted on. He did know that Vincent was crucial to righting the timeline, and Vincent delighted in that knowledge as well. He would go along with Vincent's game as long as he could, but time was short. The armies he had thrown at each other would soon be colliding. Everything would come to a head to pave the way for the final confrontation with Therion at The Eternal Gateway.

Vincent stopped in front of the heavy steel door that lead to the *Colossus's* engine room. "Here we are," Vincent said, pulling the locking leaver with a clang and opening the door.

Mr. Eleazar immediately recognized the green glow. The ancient rune forge from a time long past. Here at the heart of an airship, its power being used as an engine instead of for the creation of magical items. "What is this? Why do you have a rune forge?"

Vincent rolled his eyes ignoring the question. "You, Mr. Eleazar, are going to create one of those." Vincent pointed to the pocket watch that hung from his vest.

"I will do no such thing!"

Vincent was fast and before he could react, he felt all his magical power draining away as Vincent grabbed him by the arm with one hand, and the other closed around his throat.

"You will," Vincent spat. His unnatural strength lifted Mr. Eleazar into the air, and his back was slammed onto the outer casing of the rune forge. He could feel the intense heat through his cloths and smell the fabric starting to singe. "I am not giving you a choice Guardian. You owe it to Cora, you owe it to me, and you owe it to your *daughter*."

"No," he whispered. "Not for anyone." His vision began darkening around the edges as Vincent squeezed harder.

"Yes, you will. Or you die here instead while everything you have yet to do unravels." Vincent reached inside his vest and removed the pocket watch. "Make me one, and you can have your own back."

Unable to speak, he simply nodded. Vincent released his throat and pulled him away from the rune forge. "This will take some time," he rasped, noting that Vincent still held onto his arm, suppressing his magical abilities.

Vincent smiled. "I have all the time in the world."

EASTERN CITY OF YUNUAN

Kail was starting to think it was a mistake coming to Yunuan. The looks from the people on the busy street were well earned. He stood out of place more in the eastern city than a princess at a farmers market. He wore his black Imaera hide leather armor and a backpack. Everyone else in the city wore loose fitting outfits of bright contrasting colors. More often than not, people would point in his direction and whisper. He wondered if he was doing something so faux-pas that it might even be illegal. Each time he tried approaching someone to ask where their city or military leaders were located, they all scurried away. He even considered using magic in front of them, but decided better of it. Last thing he wanted to do was start some sort of riot. He remembered that day in Aldervale when Bastiana and Vincent had shown up with the *Colossus*. Bastiana had used magic that resulted in a panic.

By all appearances this did not remind him of a city that was preparing for war. Nor a city that seemed to be touched by it. He found it hard to believe that all of the intelligence reports he had received were this inaccurate or had been fabricated. Courduff had been warring with the east for years now.

About an hour later he was shooed away from a food vendor, and he was ready to call it quits. The crowd that hovered around him quickly dispersed as people suddenly found themselves in a hurry to be somewhere else. The reason for their haste became obvious. A man was slowly approaching him, but unlike everyone else he had seen today, this man was clearly an authority figure. His dull colored uniform made him stand out in the crowd as much as he had. Also the man had the same 'take no attitude from anyone' air about him that a lot of police or authority types seemed to have.

"Austrider," the man said.

Kail assumed he meant him but shook his head, hoping the man could tell that he didn't understand what he said.

"Austrider, sum heer," the man said more forcefully and pointed to the ground in front of him.

Kail pointed to his ear and shrugged, hoping the man would finally understand. Even if he didn't understand the man's words, he knew the man wanted him to approach. "I do not understand your words," Kail said slowly as he approached the man.

"Ves to do," the man said, speaking in the same slow manner Kail had used as if he were talking to someone slow in the head or a small child.

Kail frowned and then understood. The man's accent was so thick, it was harder to understand than Angela when she was drunk. Kail nodded and smiled. It was going to take a while to tune his ear, but at least he was making headway. *Austrider must mean outsider*, he thought, *it made sense.*

"Sum," the man said, motioning for him to follow.

Come, Kail nodded and let the man lead him down the street.

The man stopped by a light pole on a nearby intersection of streets. Pulling a key from his pocket, he unlocked a small box that was attached and pulled out what reminded Kail of a set of headphones that wire men used to send messages back home. The man plugged a wire into a hole and a few moments later was talking to someone on the other side. Kail was unable to make out what was being said because the man was talking so quickly.

"Eight," the man said, locking the headphones back inside the pole.

He had to think about the word and the situation before he understood. The man had said *wait*, not eight. Kail nodded and took a look around while the two of them waited. Unlike earlier, there was nobody else in sight. The man remained silent and only stared at him. "Welcome to the east Kail," he mumbled to himself.

Chapter 24

SILVERTON AIRFIELD

From the observation tower of the Silverton airfield, the valley to the north looked as it had on any other normal day. The clear skies were only marred by a few faint high clouds. The wind during the night had slowed to a breeze by mid-morning, and now the air hung still as the sun slowly rose higher into the sky.

Angela tightened the strap that held her ancient Keratin war blade. She harbored no doubts that it would soon see its fair share of battle, and she had no plans of returning with any arrows left in her quiver. Beside her, Randal Wood kept his binoculars to his eyes and did not look away from the valley even when the shadows of the *Renegade* and *Sky Hawk* passed over them. Duncan on the other hand seemed to be one part caged Imaera and one part child on his naming day as he paced around the room.

Everyone knew that Courduff was coming. They had made no secret of it. There were reports that some reporters from other cities like Cahir were setting up observation areas. Some of the reports even said that civilians were with them. She was unsure if it was some sort of a joke, a diabolical tactic to put people in harm's way or if war had somehow become a form of entertainment, and they expected Courduff to smite them quickly.

The radio chirped and the voice of the *Renegade's* captain played into the room. "Enemy sighted approximately one zero miles up the valley, repeat enemy sighted ten miles out."

"About time," Duncan said as he bolted for the door leading out of the tower.

Angela remained poised, but on the inside she understood what Duncan was feeling.

Randal lowered his binoculars and picked up the radio to call back. "Roger that. Keep us informed and good luck."

"Do not stay here longer than necessary Randal. The tower will be a tempting target," she said.

Again he had the binoculars to his eyes and only responded to her advice with a nod.

She turned to leave. Battle was not new to her, but there was a feeling of strangeness none the less. Perhaps it was that she felt alone. There would be plenty of people fighting side by side with her today, but Kail was not here, nor was Camden or Suki. She even missed the Mastersons with their airship the *Odyssey* and of course her old home, the *Snow Break*. The guard had changed so it seemed.

She heard the radio crackle again behind her as one of the airships reported that a ground army had been spotted. That was her preferred target. The trees and low lying buildings outside of the city would play to her strengths and her ability to fly. Out in the open she simply would be as useful as any other soldier, and trying to take on one of the enemy airships alone was foolish and suicidal. Not that she had not ever done that before.

ABANDONED BUILDING, SILVERTON

"This is it men," Treylane addressed the group of five men in the tiny room. "You have your assignments and your exit options. When this is all over, I'll see you back at the office in Cahir." He watched as his men filed out of the room one after another. Some of them might not survive this day, but they had better odds than anyone else on the battlefield.

Returning his attention to the view of the Silverton Army Headquarters he saw Duncan Deline exit with a hurried step fully armed for battle. Moments later Angela Atagi came into view. He shook his head at the woman. Bow and arrows and a sword against armored vehicles, airships and enough firepower to level the city. She truly was someone from the past, however he had read the reports and even caught glimpses of her ability to fly, and he would not be one to underestimate her combat prowess or tenacious ability to survive against all odds.

THE ETERNAL GATEWAY

Therion rubbed his hand across his face and chin. It had almost been a month since he had last shaved, and it felt nice to be rid of the irritable growth of hair on his face. The hair on his head had grown out, and he had it held back with a cord. He felt more alive than he had in decades. It was all due to being in control of the gateway, and retrieving an item that had once belonged to him that had been taken away a very long time ago by his old friend, Duke Falconcrest.

He held his arm out in front of him to admire the runic wristband he now wore. Set in the band were runic glyphs made from carved focusing stones. The stones alone were priceless because of their ability to amplify a mage's magical powers, but that was only a minor reason, a bonus compared to the wristbands primary use. Long ago, during the War of Antiquities, one mage, the most powerful mage ever to walk the world had uncovered a terrible secret. Yet a wonderful secret that he had shared with his best friend, Therion. Duke Falconcrest had found a way to steal another mage's power and add it to his own. And it didn't stop there. Magical items, created by elderly mages wishing to leave a legacy could also be consumed.

There was a catch though, as there always is. Stealing was bad, especially when it was another person's magical power. When it mixed with your own, it became tainted, sour and if there was too much, lethal. One could only hold so much magic in them, like a container. Once it was full if more was added, it starts to spill out. The first symptoms were mild like muscle pain, headaches or uncontrollable shakes. Later symptoms were a bit worse with your insides liquefying and the general breaking down of bones and skin until popping like a balloon.

The Duke made the wristbands to act as a filter for other people's magic, and the focusing stones acted like another container for the extra magic. An elegant and simple solution. Unfortunately, magic users and magical items were incredibly rare these days. He knew of a few people out there he could suck dry like the Duke's brat, Kail, and that simple minded brute friend of his. Bastiana was a tempting and delicious choice, but Vincent posed a problem that just didn't make it worthwhile. There was no reason to get in any hurry. With the gateway his to command, he had all the time in the world.

There were plenty of puzzles The Eternal Gateway still presented. Using it was not as simple as he had expected. Retrieving the wristband had nearly cost him his life. When he traveled to the past, it was like trying to walk through a solid object. Every move, every breath, every ounce of magic he used took extraordinary effort. He barely managed to get back and when he did magic had erupted from the gateway. It was a few weeks later when he had enough strength to resume studying the gateway that he learned that the magic had rocked the entire planet.

It was easier now with the wristband to reach through time, but each time it resulted in a shockwave. The simple answer to his problem had to be a control device of some sort. Clearly the Guardian was capable of using the gateway without such side effects. The man had pulled people through time. Something he had tried on a whim with less than successful results. He did not envy the men who had to clean up that mess.

Another puzzle he had yet to unravel was where had Duke Falconcrest gone. He had observed his friend in the past, right up to when he exiled himself, but after that, nothing. He considered confronting The Duke there, but he knew better than to meddle directly with the past like that, and if he were, he wanted to know how the gateway fully worked before he tried.

"Sir," someone said.

Turning to face the source of the interruption he said. "It better be important, and by important I mean *really* important."

"Yes sir. Courduff is still awaiting your response."

Therion groaned inward. He thought he had left a few capable people in charge, but apparently not. "What response?" he asked.

Nervously the man pointed to a stack of papers that had built up over time. "The fleet left Courduff a few days ago. They should be reaching Silverton any time now. They want to know if you have anything to say about it."

Therion rolled his eyes. "I don't care what Admiral Wilhuff or whatever his name is does. My orders still stand."

"Yes sir," the man bowed and left quickly.

Therion sat back and debated. Continue to study and observe the gateway, or battle. Both choices were equally tempting.

ABOARD THE *LOTUS* NEAR SILVERTON

Admiral Bailon stood on the bridge of the *Lotus* and could see the city of Silverton in the distance in front of them. The two Silverton airships circling around the city reminded him of a pair of vultures waiting for a wounded animal to die. "Have the mobile infantry begin their advance. Helm increase our altitude by one thousand feet. I want a better view of the battle," he ordered.

The map room located at the top of the Mage Council Tower in Courduff had spoiled him. He wished that its creator had produced a smaller version that could be taken into the field. At least the weather was good, and the *Lotus* could hang back to observe, not that there was ever any intention of participating directly in the battle. Perhaps one day when communications technology improved the whole administering of a war would be done from within the map room. Calling out orders with a complete god's eye view of the battle.

The *Scopic* and *Sanctuary* descended to the ground and began to unload additional troops and equipment to augment the infantry that had already assembled. The ships would remain on the ground and act as hospital ships for any casualties they might receive. Having a dedicated hospital ship was something he had been pushing for but could never get approval pushed through all of the committees. It had been his wife Ari's idea to use an existing ship. 'What good was the troop carrier after the troops were gone?' was her simple solution. Her idea to replace a hundred soldiers with medics, nurses and a doctor staff was something that was in his immediate control. It would function as a mobile field hospital.

"Plus one thousand feet confirmed," the officer at the helm called out.

Bailon glanced at Cid then nodded. "Deploy the *CP*, and begin the aerial bombardment."

The airships began to fan out in front of the *Lotus* as the *CP* slowly powered forward. Bailon and Cid watched as the crane system went to work deploying and launching the small one man airships. Each one had two shells to fire from its cannons and a forward mounted repeater gun that could be fired straight ahead, or unlocked and lowered to a forty five degree angle towards the ground. What they lacked in raw destructive power, they more than made up for in speed, agility and the ability to quickly deliver ordinance and return to the carrier ship for reloading.

SILVERTON

Duncan ignored the obvious threat that his men faced as he walked up and down their ranks. There were new faces he did not recognize, but there were several that he did; Private Mance, Pakmon, Daly, Erickson and even Stanz was there recovered and ready to go another round.

"I'm not going to lie to you men. Look at each other because a lot of people are going to die today. Take a good look so you can remember who the fallen are, so you can tell the wife and children of your fellow soldier about what happened today," Duncan said as most of the men nodded and looked at each other. "Keep your heads clear."

"Yes sir!" everyone shouted bringing a smile to his face.

Motion in the back of the ranks caught his attention as men parted to let someone pass. Angela stepped through the men. Her black, tight fitting combat outfit made from the hide of jungle cats made her stand out amongst the rest of the soldiers in their dull green battledress. Her red hair was pulled back into a tight braid, and her weapons couldn't have been more out of place either. *What could you expect with time travelers and magic users*, he thought. But he had no complaints to her being here. The men felt more confident, and he knew just how deadly the woman was. He hated to admit it, but she was worth a whole unit of men.

"A good day for battle," Angela said, stopping in front of Duncan and his men but keeping her eyes forward on the incoming Courduff army. "Songs will be made of this day."

Duncan wasn't so sure about singing songs unless he was at a bar when this war was over. He squinted as tiny specks began to fill the air around the enemy airships. The distant rumble of the Juggernaut's engines could be heard. A low haze of dust was starting to appear on the horizon. He assumed the ground army was advancing. His men waited in calm silence, ready for his order to advance to engage the enemy. Duncan could feel more than hear some of the men shifting around. Undoubtedly double and triple checking their equipment in an attempt to calm their nerves. He would have bet anyone that they were all fearful of what lay ahead. Everyone except Angela, and he wasn't about to bet against her.

Angela must have felt the same unease radiating from the men. "This is our home, our land. We fight for our families," she said. "Find that blade of honor inside of you and embrace it. Let it harden you, temper you, and we will never be defeated."

Duncan looked over at Angela and nodded. She did not return his look. He saw that her attention was on something in her hand. A photo he had seen before. Two little girls with big smiles on their faces without a worry in the world.

"For my sweet little birds," he heard her whisper, "we will soar together."

A rush of dread and worry passed through him, but not for him or any of his men, but for the enemy. He suddenly realized that at this moment, there was nothing in the world more dangerous than the woman standing next to him. "Kail will be here," he said quietly. "It was a good plan."

Angela returned the photo to the inside of her armor. "I know," she said. "I only hope there is some left for him."

Duncan hoped Kail would arrive today. Visions of a battlefield wasteland filled his head, and the only person left standing was a blood covered Angela on top a mountain of broken bodies and equipment. He shook the disturbing thoughts from his mind and returned to face his men. "All right," he yelled. "Move out!"

A few minutes later as they approached the edge of the city's clear cut area, tiny flashes of light blinked followed by a distant thunder from the Juggernaut airships on the horizon. Seconds later the whistle of artillery shells could be heard overhead followed by explosions around and inside Silverton as the enemy gunners found their range. The battle for Silverton had begun.

Chapter 25

TWO DAYS AGO

EASTERN CITY OF YUNUAN

Kail frowned as he concentrated on what the man was saying. He was starting to get used to the thick accents of the people in Yunuan, but every so often all he heard was gibberish. "I am sorry, can you say that again?" he asked, earning him another frown.

"Tu'demand the peephole of Yunuan to white and die," the man said.

You demand the people of Yunuan to fight and die, Kail understood. "No, I am asking the people of Yunuan to help fight against Therion and Courduff." He looked around the room at the gathering of people around him. Some were listening to what he was trying to say, but others were clearly looking at him with curious interest that one might give an exotic animal at a zoo. "Are your cities not at war with Courduff?"

"No our problem," the man said.

Kail didn't need to concentrate to understand that answer.

"Core'duff foolish. Core'duff like child wid child toys. We safe."

"Magic, are you safe from magic as well? The earthquakes, are you safe from them? That is Therion. That is The Eternal Gateway."

Several people put their heads together and whispered. The central figurehead he had been pleading to frowned at them. Perhaps he was starting to get through to a few of them.

"Magic is dead. No magic in fifty years. Infinite gateway a child story," the man dismissed with a wave of his hand.

"Magic is very much alive. I guarantee it. Therion commands magic. Magic that could destroy this world, and The Eternal Gateway is no child's story." Kail stopped short of mentioning that he too was a mage. He wasn't quite sure how the people here would respond if they found that out.

"Lies," the man said with contempt.

Frustrated Kail was ready to leave. He hadn't had too many expectations when he came up with the idea of asking for help, but being insulted was about all he could take. It was a long shot, but he knew that he could at least give them a warning they couldn't ignore. "It won't matter. As long as Therion controls the gateway the entire world is at risk. An enemy who has control of the gateway can't be left to do as they please."

"Why haven't you done something about it then Kail Falconcrest?" a new voice said without the thick accent. A tall man stepped forward flanked by two stoic female guards.

"Yes, we know who you are," the man said when Kail frowned.

Kail looked back at the man with whom he had been dealing and didn't like the smug look he had. Not only were they insulting him, they were misleading him as well. "Then you know what I say is true," he said to the new speaker, putting as much discontent as he could in his voice.

"Perhaps it is true, perhaps it is not." The man shrugged. "Why should we help one such as you? Mages have caused the worst of wars."

"And swords have killed the most people, yet you don't blame the blacksmith," Kail responded.

"Hardly the same," came the man's rebuttal. "The sword can't help who it cuts. You are the same way; it is only a matter of time."

Kail looked around the room. There wasn't a person present that he felt would lift a finger to help him or Silverton. The eastern cities were apparently strong enough to hold their own against Courduff. Therion would probably not personally get involved with any attack on them, but he might. Kail figured that eventually Therion would figure out how to use the gateway, and all kinds of hell would break loose.

Kail looked down at the floor. "I am going to use magic that will show you that there are men like you in Silverton. Every day I know they wish that I would simply use my magic to destroy the armies of Courduff. Destroy their ability to build airships and weapons." He had seen Bastiana use this same magic before when he had first met her, that night at the top of the mage tower when she had made images of the old Mage Council members appear. It was a mixture of Divination and Illusion.

A ghostly doppelganger of Duncan appeared in the room. Angry and upset the ghost said, "Face it Kail, you're the only one with the power to do anything, no offense Angela." The apparition spun to look angrily at Kail. "Seriously, why don't you just kill them all? End this war right here and right now."

Kail's voice was but a whisper as he projected the memory of the argument. "Is that what you want? One sided slaughter against people who can't defend themselves."

"If it saves our lives yes. Destroy their airships, their weapons and their army. Better them than us!" the ghost Duncan cursed at Kail but dissipated before him.

Next, the ghost of Angela appeared. Younger and full of fire, she spun around the room with her twin war blades as she danced through the air. He caught a few faint whispers from those gathered that they recognized her as a Keratin. The ghost settled down and slowly walked around him, keeping her eyes on him. Her voice filled the room. "It may not seem like it now, but what you choose to do may save countless lives."

"It's starting to feel like I don't have a choice anymore," Kail said, remembering that moment so many years ago when he first learned who he was.

Duncan's voice and apparition made another appearance and repeated. "Just kill them all! Better them than us," the ghost said again before disappearing.

"You always have a choice," the ghost Angela said softly.

The next memory he had not intended to manifest, but it reared its ugly head. The illusion changed, and they were aboard the *Snow Break* making an attack run against Therion. Kail had his hand out and was protecting the ship against the artillery shells. A small ghost of a ship, the *Wind Runner*, was fleeing the gateway when lightning tore from the ground and in a flash of light, incinerated the ship along with everyone aboard.

The scene washed away with the explosion, and the ghost of Angela also lost a layer of detail as she was replaced by an older version of herself, still a warrior, but now also a mother who had lived to see her children taken from her. "He said it would be hell," the ghost said.

"Who?" Kail asked.

"The Time Walker. I could choose death a thousand years ago, or go to a future that would be a living hell," Angela's ghost, circling him again, said with loss and pain in her voice. "Honor demands that blood be spilled Kail. For our daughters."

Kail knew what he said next was going to be important. "I want to, so badly. But it scares me. My breath gets caught in my throat sometimes. At any moment, I can be one second away from tearing a hole through space with my magic, killing them all."

"Revenge would consume you, us, everyone. There would be no Kail. Only a monster, a new Therion," Angela's ghost said. "You always have a choice, never forget that." The ghost finished by flicking him on the forehead with its finger.

Kail jerked backwards abruptly ending the spell. Angela hadn't thumped him on the head like that in a long time, but he was sure he hadn't make the ghost do it. He blinked several times to regain his composure. He had revealed some intimate memories to a room full of strangers, and he wasn't sure if his actions had helped or hurt his cause.

Chapter 26

CANYAMAR JUNGLE

The path through the jungle was easy for Suki and Alyssa to follow, and they made excellent time. Suki took it on faith that Alyssa knew where she was going and that Camden had come this way as well. There was also a sense of urgency as if time was running out. There had been another time quake as Alyssa put it. She had said that it was caused by Therion changing things without the proper protections in place. She also said that eventually he would figure out how to completely use the gateway and once that happened, their chances of defeating him would be near impossible.

The wisp seemed to be enjoying itself. It would zip ahead of them and weave through the trees then circle back. It had even spent a few minutes riding on the top of Suki's horse and had braided several strands of its hair together, much to the horse's annoyance. Her horse even tried to nip at the wisp when it flew too close.

"How long do you think it will take for us to catch up to Camden?" Suki asked.

"I don't know. He is moving quickly," Alyssa answered. "He is making better time than I would have expected all things considered."

"What does that mean?"

"There are enchantments that protect the gateway. The jungle will steer you away from it, people will get lost and forget what they are looking for."

Suki understood. "I remember hearing about that. Mr. Eleazar had to show them the way, but Therion has a military base there. The jungle has been cleared away and burned. Its location isn't exactly a secret anymore, and he knows exactly where it is."

"It's more complicated than that, but it might help explain it. He has been there before so he could find it again, but he would need to have a guide to be moving this fast."

"A guide?" Suki asked. "There is someone else with him? Mr. Eleazar?"

Alyssa frowned as she got a vacant look in her eyes for a moment. "No, Mr. Eleazar is still in Cahir. But it is like he has someone who is tied to the gateway with him."

"Tied? Someone like you or Mr. Eleazar?"

Alyssa nodded. "Mr. Eleazar is a Guardian. I am a Sentinel. Others like the Watchers or people who have traveled through the gateway all share a special bond with the gateway. For example my mother could find it because she has walked through it. The enchantments are in place to protect it from outsiders, but not from those who have used it before."

"Maybe it's Therion." Suki suggested. "If he is messing with the gateway, it might be messing other things up as well."

"That is possible," Alyssa said while considering the idea. "We are in uncharted waters."

Suki was just grateful at this point to have Alyssa with her. Given the last several days she seriously doubted she would have made it this far without her. Even the familiarity of the wisp helped lift her spirits. It made her feel like the days before all the responsibility of fighting a war or trying to save the world was forced upon them. Just a group of friends trying to do the right thing.

"Have you given thought to what you're going to say when we catch up to him?" Alyssa asked.

"Umm. That's a good question. If I said I hoped that all he needed was to see me and that would be enough, would you think I was being foolishly hopeful?"

Alyssa smiled and said. "No, I don't think it's foolish. It actually sounds quite romantic."

Suki used that to turn the tables on Alyssa. "Any boys in your life that are worth running through the jungle for?"

Alyssa laughed. "No. I'm afraid there aren't. Training and schooling didn't leave me with a lot of time to pursue a social life. And with grandpa around, I don't think anyone would have been brave enough to try."

"I thought you said he was great and loving?"

"Oh don't get me wrong. You just have to remember that he is the most powerful and talented magic user in history. Tends to skew people's idea of him a bit. Even people who didn't know he was a mage could tell there was something about him that they didn't want to cross."

"That must have been hard," Suki said, thinking about how her life would have been with such a singular focus. She didn't believe that she would have enjoyed it very much.

"It never bothered me. There was always time for anything when you consider The Eternal Gateway."

"How is it you have both of Angela's swords?" Suki asked next.

"What's with all the questions all of a sudden?"

"I'm sorry. I will stop. Just trying to wrap my head around the idea that you grew up from a little girl to a woman in half a year is all."

"Grandfather gave me one blade and told me about the other. One of the first things I did when I arrived to this time was to retrieve it."

"The one your mother lost in the canyon?"

Alyssa nodded.

"Are you as good as her with them?"

"I don't know. We will have to spar to find out," Alyssa said with an eager look in her eye. "And spar dad too, maybe even both at the same time."

Suki tried to imagine what that would look like. "Just exactly how much were you taught on the other side of the gateway?"

"Well, grandpa taught me about magic, how it works, the different types, and several disciplines and philosophies. Like him, I can use all forms of magic. Mr. Eleazar helped as well. He also taught me about how time and time travel works. As far as the sword and gun goes," Alyssa said, patting her side arm, "History is full of teachers, if you catch my drift."

Perhaps it wasn't a boring childhood after all. Suki tried to imagine what her own power could have been like if she had had someone to mentor her. "So you can heal?"

Alyssa nodded. "I'm not that good at it but yes, Necromancy is part of my abilities. Grandpa showed me what he could, but Evocation, Abjuration and Chronomancy were the primary focus. Fire, lightning and teleporting. That and learning how to defend against it."

"I can't," Suki said solemnly.

"Can't what? Defend against magic?"

"I can't heal anymore. I haven't been able to since that night you were taken."

Alyssa pulled her horse to a stop. The wisp also settled down and landed on Alyssa's shoulder. "Were you hurt or wounded?"

Suki shook her head. "I just can't do it anymore. I don't even feel the magic inside me anymore."

"I have heard of mages losing their powers, but only in specific circumstances like creating a magical item with Enchantment. The power of the object comes from the mage. It doesn't come back once it's made. That is why magic items are so rare. Few people are willing to part with their power like that. And if you weren't attacked, then no one could have stolen your power."

"Like Therion tried to do to your father?"

Alyssa nodded. "The War of Antiquities was fought over magic power." She frowned for a moment in thought. "Therion was there that night. Maybe he did do something."

Suki didn't like the sound of that. The idea that Therion had somehow stolen her power, stolen Amaya's life, brought back Xavier and stole Camden from her as well was making her sick to her stomach. The wisp floated over and landed on Suki's shoulder and started to play with her hair. It made her feel a little better.

"We should get going," Alyssa said, spurring her horse.

"I don't think I have ever been this sore," Suki said, rubbing her back after the pair had stopped for the night. "I never thought I would say it, but I think traveling should be done by trains and airships."

Alyssa smiled and checked on the wisp. The tiny blue being had braided most of Suki's horse's hair, and it now rested quietly in a little nest. The horse seemed to have given up any hope of respite from the wisp and had accepted its fate was to be tormented by it.

"Time quake," Alyssa quickly called out. "Hold onto your horse."

Suki nodded her head and quickly forgot about her sore muscles as she grabbed the reins of the horse. "Got it," she said, bracing herself. Moments passed, but nothing happened. Suki looked expectantly at Alyssa.

"I don't understand," Alyssa said, looking around the jungle. "It should have happened, and it's getting stronger."

The tone in Alyssa's voice told Suki that they were in immediate danger. The stillness of the jungle around them compounded the sense of dread. Alyssa scream was followed by a sound like a cannon going off. Alyssa's horse reared and fled into the jungle as fast as it could run. It was all she could do to keep a hold of her own horse while trying to figure out what had just happened.

The ground where Alyssa had been standing was scorched and burned. Suki's first thought was that they had just been struck by lightning, but what she could see of the sky that shown through the canopy was clear. Hearing a moan coming from the underbrush, she tied the horse down and discovered Alyssa's smoking body. "Alyssa!" It wasn't smoke she realized but magical energy evaporating off.

"Get it off," Alyssa hissed, struggling slowly with her cloak.

Suki helped untangle and strip the cloak away. "What happened?" she asked, assessing how badly Alyssa was hurt. "Are you okay?"

The wisp landed on her shoulder and with a concerned look pointed at the source of the whatever? The attack, an explosion, she wasn't sure.

"What the hell?" Alyssa asked, sitting up. She reached down and from inside the cloak pulled out an ordinary looking pocket watch. "It was Chronomancy for sure, but I have never felt or seen anything like this before." She turned the watch over several times in her hand.

"Was that an attack?" Suki asked, trying to piece it together. *Was it Therion or maybe Bastiana?* she wondered.

Frowning but seemingly unaware that she still had magic drifting off of her, Suki watched as Alyssa got off the jungle floor while completely focused on the pocket watch. Suki looked at the wisp and even its reaction was an unknowing look and a shrug.

"I don't understand," Alyssa said confused.

"What is it?" Suki asked as Alyssa looked at her with fear. Suki wanted to take her question back. Anything that would make Alyssa that scared was something she never wanted to face.

"It's the key to The Eternal Gateway."

Suki had no idea what that meant.

"I have to go," Alyssa suddenly said, marching through the underbrush back to where the event had happened. "I have to go," she repeated.

"Where? What's going on?" Suki followed her.

"I'm sorry," Alyssa said.

The wisp chattered angrily demanding Alyssa's attention.

She waved her hand. "Then stay."

Confused Suki looked at the wisp. A new fear crept into her as the realization that she was moments away from being left alone in the jungle. "Wait, tell me what's going on."

"I don't know. I have to go." Alyssa looked at the wisp who was determined to stay. "Look after her."

"Wait," Suki called out as Alyssa flew into the sky and with a blue flash of magic was gone.

MASTERSON GEARWORKS, SCABLANDS

Conrad Black pulled his glasses down so he could rub the inside corners of his eyes then shook his head in frustration. The blueprints of the unfinished ship were spread over the work desk in front of him. Some of the design he understood, but a lot of it was simply fantasy, and he did not see how he could continue in good faith to the Mastersons. The amount of power required to lift the ship would be impossible with twenty engines, let alone only the four that the design called for. That level of thrust to weight ratio simply did not exist.

A change in the noise of airship construction caused him to look up. "What's going on out there," he yelled, not expecting any real answer before going back to the problem of the airship. He made a mental note to tell the construction crews that even though the original deadline to have the ship built was no longer an issue, it was no reason to goof off.

The cat call whistle was the last straw. Tossing his glasses onto the desk he got up to reprimand the crew. "Back to work!" he yelled, coming down to the production floor. Several of the workers looked at him but did not return to work. "What's going on here?" he asked again as several of the men pointed to the entrance of the gearworks' hanger.

Conrad with a touch of impatience walked to the front of the Masterson's secret facility. Secret was starting to become too loose of a description for the place. A young serious faced woman, far more serious looking than he suspected she had any right to be, was running a critical eye over the work being done. "I would ask what you're doing here, but somehow I don't think you're the type to answer me," he said, noticing that she was armed with a mean looking pistol and a pair of swords.

Alyssa frowned at him. "This is worse than I thought."

"It might get even more worse unless you tell me what you're doing here," he said not shying away from the fact that she was armed.

"I am here for my ship."

Conrad raised his eyebrows and glanced back at some of the men who had found her comment amusing. "Your ship? And whatever gave you that idea?" he asked, folding his arms and waiting for what undoubtedly would be the most absurd answer he would ever hear. "You're not the first to show up making that claim."

Alyssa turned her full attention to Conrad. "I designed it. I commissioned its construction six months ago, and it's not even close to being finished," she said, unable to hide the rising anger in her voice.

He didn't understand the hole he was digging himself into when he smiled even more. "Well, that explains it. Leave it to a little girl to want the impossible." Turning back to his crew he continued. "Do you want a white pony too? Maybe one with a little horn on its head? I'll see if I can get one that flies too," he finished, flopping his hands up and down, earning him laughs.

"Conrad Black, father to Eleanor Black who was the pilot of the *Snow Break*. Deceased. Sons imprisoned and forced to work in the clockwork factories of Courduff. You are one of the most capable ship builders ever to live. I expected more from you," her words had some bite, as did the look on her face.

"Who do you think you are missy, insulting my family like that?" he demanded as all humor drained away from him.

"I am Alyssa Atagi. Perhaps you have heard of me?"

Conrad frowned. The name was familiar, but the girl in front of him could not be her. "Last I heard the Atagi girls were four years old and not exactly in the best of shape. One dead, one kidnapped."

"We're even then," she said firmly, responding to the family jibe. "How long is it going to take to finish my ship?"

"Look lady, even if you somehow are who you say you are, and there is nothing that's going to convince me you are, this ship will never fly. We need a month at least and a miracle. She's never going to fly no matter how much wishful thinking you have, it isn't going to make it true."

Alyssa pulled out a pocket watched and thumbed open the face. "We have all the time in the world," she said, winding the watch. "As for a miracle." Alyssa opened her hand and focused her magic. Threads of multi colored magic started to wind around her and through the air. She pushed off with her foot and used her flying ability to float into the air. "I'll worry about that."

Conrad watched as the floating girl started to work her magic on the unfinished airship. A grin slowly crept onto his face. She was definitely Kail and Angela's kid. "You heard the boss!" he shouted. "Let's make this ship fly."

Chapter 27

BATTLE OF SILVERTON

Duncan could hear the crashing of trees and the sounds of tractor engines in the distance. The underbrush was thick enough that he wasn't able to see the enemy yet. His men were fanned out around the area, waiting in ambush. Angela hid in the cover of the tree tops ready to rain death from above with her bow. He checked his rifle again making sure it was ready to fire then patted his hands to feel if the rest of the ammunition that he had brought was still where it should be. He whistled to get some of his men's attention and took out his bayonet to attach it to the end of his rifle. His men nodded at the order, and passed it along, and also attached the blades to their rifles.

A flicker of movement caught his eye as the first lead scout of the Courduff army made his way towards them. Duncan sighted down on the man as he held his breath. He wanted to wait as long as possible before firing and revealing their position. He frowned when the man tripped on a piece of uneven ground and didn't get up. At first he wondered if they had been spotted then he saw the real reason. One of Angela's arrows had found a new home in the man's neck.

They didn't have to wait long before the front lines of the enemy rank started to come into view. Right behind them were Hyperion heavy tractors fully converted for war. The tractors were going to be a problem. His men didn't have any heavy weapons that could disable one. Just how much they were out matched became apparently clear. They really were not much of a threat anymore to Courduff, and he understood now why they had waited to use Silverton as a morale boosting victory.

Gunfire opened on the far side of the glade, and every enemy soldier responded quickly by dropping to their knees. Duncan cursed as more gunfire erupted. Wasting no more time he sighted down his rifle and pulled the trigger.

Angela calmly watched the battle erupt below her. She had picked off a lead scout that would have stumbled right into Duncan's position. There were so many easy targets below her, she reasoned that she if she wanted to she could go through her entire compliment of arrows right now. She could also see that the largest threat they were up against were the four armored tractors. A smile crept up on her lips as a plan began to form. One of the tractors had lagged behind the others. It had to detour around a thick group of trees that it couldn't simply smash down.

The group of soldiers that had been surrounding the tractor had wandered ahead, eager to help with the fighting or eager to start dying, she wasn't sure which, but it left the vehicle exposed to the type of attack that only she would be able to pull off. There was a gunner on the outside of the tractor in control of a repeater gun. She could easily kill him with an arrow, but she was not positive he would go down silently. If he called out, her plan would be over before it really got started.

Securing her bow, she retrieved the war blade from her back. The silvery runes of indestructibility glowed with a faint eagerness that she also felt from battle. Angela stepped forward off of the branch. The air rushed by as she fell towards the ground. At the last moment, she slowed her fall just enough to keep from hurting herself and brought her blade down through the gunner's right shoulder and out through his left side. It took a lot of force to cut a man in half like that, but the eternally sharp blade was up to the task. Severing the lungs made it physically impossible for the soldier to cry out as he fell off the back of the tractor in two pieces.

Keeping herself afloat she came to the side of the tractor that had the thick steel access door. Yanking open the door, she caught the two men inside by surprise. As they turned to look at her, she stabbed her blade through the closest man's neck then angled the blade downward and continued to push it into the next man. A couple more hard pushes and jerks left both men skewered on the blade.

She pulled the driver out of the cabin to take his place behind the controls. Everything looked the same as other tractors she had been inside, and she quickly got the vehicle moving forward again. Glancing out the viewport her attack and commandeering of the tractor appeared to have gone unnoticed. The only extra equipment she saw that was not present in normal tractors were the controls near the second dead man. She assumed that they were used to fire the twin cannons because there were two sets of the same levers and buttons.

In front of her and to the right she saw one of the enemy tractors getting ready to open fire against the men from Silverton. There were half a dozen enemy soldiers escorting the tractor. Lining up her tractor as best she could she leaned across the dead man so she could press one of the buttons. Nothing happened. Looking at the controls again, she jerked one of the levers. Again nothing happened. "Fire you beast," she cursed, slapping a third button. One of the cannons fired. The noise was so deafening inside the tractor cabin that it knocked her cross-eyed.

Outside the enemy tractor had exploded in ball of flame that billowed above the tall trees. The soldiers were gone as well, either annihilated in the blast or blown back. Her ears were not ringing from the explosion, but everything was completely muffled. A quick wipe of her hand to her ears showed blood. It was something to worry about later. She rolled the tractor forward and to the left. The enemy was in total chaos trying to figure out what had just occurred. She had no intention of being inside the tractor when they found out. Lining up for the second shot, she hit the correct button this time, and the second cannon fired destroying another enemy tractor.

Angela found the third tractor and pushed the control leavers all the way forward. She didn't know how to reload the cannon, and the enemy had figured out where the sneak attack had come from. All she could hope was that her tractor ran over a few of the enemy. If luck was on her side it would push into the remaining enemy tractor as well. She pushed open the steel door abandoning the tractor. She did not look back as she ran through the trees.

Duncan rubbed the back of his hand across his eye, trying to remove the bits of dirt and debris that blurred his vision. He had no idea how they lucked out when the enemy tractors had decided to attack each other. He did have one suspect in mind however, and he intended to use the sudden advantage to its fullest.

"Pakmon. Mance. On me," Duncan ordered. "Enemy ahead and to the east."

Trained and experienced in combat, his men readied their rifles and followed his lead. A moment later they were confronting the soldiers from Courduff. Duncan dropped down next to a tree. His aim was steady as he fired off several rounds as Private Pakmon and Mance advanced their position and opened fire on the enemy.

The enemy surged forward, and the three of them made the Courduff army pay for their mistake. Without the support of the armored tractors, the enemy soldiers were at the disadvantage of fighting on unfamiliar ground against an opponent that had everything to lose: family, homes, friends and their way of life. One by one the advancing soldiers fell to the determined defenders. Duncan glanced around not finding any more soldiers from Courduff coming at them. All of the gunfire had also ceased.

"Call out!" Duncan yelled, slowly getting to his feet but keeping an eye out for any remaining enemy soldiers. Around him he could hear his men calling out, and he was relieved at how many shouts he was hearing. One voice that he had not heard was Angela's. "Pakmon. Take a quick run and see if you can find the flying girl."

"Yes sir." Pakmon reloaded his riffle and sprinted off.

"Mance, with me, and start gathering the troops, look for wounded and check the dead."

Private Mance nodded and jogged ahead into the smoke.

Duncan made his way towards the row of destroyed armored tractors to see if there was anything they could salvage. While their battle might be over, he could hear other units battling it out in the distance. Checking bodies as he went he headed to the first ruined tractor. Nothing would be salvageable here. Erickson and Stanz met up with him.

"Who took out these vehicles?" Stanz asked. "They went down pretty quickly before anything else really started."

Duncan shook his head. "Don't know, my money is on Angela that she had something to do with it. Anyone see our sword swinging friend anywhere?"

Both men shook their heads. "Negative Sir."

"Salvage what you can, but keep an eye out," he ordered, moving to check the next smoking pile of armored tractor.

"Sir," someone called out.

Duncan turned to see Private Daly coming towards him. "What have you got?"

"You're going to like this sir. We have an armored tractor. Intact, loaded and ready to go," Daly said, unable to keep from smiling.

"I am liking this," Duncan agreed. "Get it fired up, we're moving out in ten minutes."

"Yes sir." Daly left, grabbing two other men to help man the Hyperion manufactured weapon.

Private Mance returned. "We have two dead and one wounded," he reported. "Can't get an accurate count on the enemy dead, but it's all of them. We didn't find any survivors."

Duncan nodded. It had been a complete rout with minimal losses. He wanted to find Angela however. If she was hurt or even worse, dead, he wasn't going to be the one who had to tell Kail that they hadn't found or helped her. "We head out in ten minutes. Use that time to find Angela."

"Over here," one of his men called out. "Medic."

Duncan hustled over to where several of his men had huddled around. Pushing through them, he saw Angela walking towards them. She looked ok, then he noticed that the sides of her face and neck were smeared with blood. "You ok Angela?" he called out. She nodded, then pointed to her ears.

"I cannot hear anything," she said, almost shouting.

Duncan felt a wave of relief. Better deaf than dead.

Chapter 28

LOTUS, SKIES ABOVE SILVERTON

Admiral Bailon stood on the bridge of the *Lotus* with both hands clasped behind his back. Silverton appeared to be putting up quite the fight on the ground. However, the armada he commanded in the skies would be the deciding factor. The smaller single manned airships were nearing Silverton now. The two airships defending Silverton would not be enough to save the town. Even any anti-airship cannons the city might have in place, wouldn't be able to stop them entirely.

"Admiral," Cid addressed him. "There is a high chance of Silverton surrendering once they realize the might our airships can unleash."

Bailon nodded. "I intend to offer them that chance. However, we need to see how well the new ships perform. But I see no reason to spend any more resources than needed. Every round saved will be one we have when it comes time to push into the east."

"Understood sir."

Bailon heard a bit frustration in Cid's voice. "You don't agree?"

"The new ships do need to be battle tested, but the ground fighting has been quite fierce." Cid pointed towards the wooded areas that billowed smoke into the sky. "If we start razing the city there is a chance that the defenders will hold out to the last man. It will take more of the same resources we wish to save. Perhaps if we call back some of the ships to have them concentrate on Silverton's ground force we will fare better and still get the test we desire."

"Interesting observation." Bailon turned to look at Cid and raised an eyebrow. "More profiling of the enemy?"

Cid remained stoic. "Partially sir. We have dominance in the skies, and previous battles show that civilian governments will quickly concede once they are defenseless. However, when faced with annihilation even the most docile of animals will attack when backed into a corner."

Bailon watched as the ships approached Silverton. Another large explosion on the ground billowed a fireball up through the trees. He hated being forced into this position by politics, and he agreed with Cid's assessment of the battle. "Comm. Open a channel to the fleet." The smaller airships had radio receivers, but they were not outfitted with transmitters. He leaned in towards Cid to say. "Sometimes you can do both."

"Channel open sir," the comms officer called out.

Bailon stepped over to the microphone and pressed the transmit button. "*CP* air-fighters, this is Admiral Bailon. Concentrate fire on the enemy airships. Reserve ground targets to any anti-aircraft threats while focusing on

Silverton's ground forces and provide support to our ground troops. Good luck and fight well." He released the button and nodded his thanks to the communications officer.

"Military targets only," Cid agreed.

"It should work. Gives us our victory, and whomever is behind our being here won't have the satisfaction of seeing Silverton removed from the map." Bailon watched with satisfaction as one fifth of the airships started to turn back towards them.

DUNCAN'S UNIT, OUTSIDE SILVERTON

Angela watched as small airships flew overhead, casting shadows onto the ground as they passed. She could only make out a faint buzz of their engines. Her ears were still numb, but in one ear she was starting to make out some sounds. She recalled once when Kail had been struck deaf that she had written down what she had wanted to say to him. She hoped that he would not have to do the same for her for the rest of her life. A shadow passed directly over her, and she wondered briefly if Suki had found what she desired. Something bounced off of her shoulder, and she turned to see Duncan waving her over to him.

"We have forces here and here," he said, pointing in each direction. She read his lips more than heard him. "If we bring the tractor with us and can win another battle, we can combine groups and continue to flank them."

She nodded in agreement that they should push their hard fought advantage. Rarely when one side had been so out-armed and outnumbered had they won the fight. And that they had only lost a few men was even more outstanding. "This section here." She pointed on the map. "If the enemy has advanced as far as they have here, we should be able to come in from the back."

Duncan nodded as well.

"What about those airships?" Daly asked, pointing back at Silverton.

She glanced back towards Silverton, and she saw Duncan shake his head.

"That's not something we can worry about right now. The *Renegade* and *Sky Hawk* will have to hold the line. Silverton has flak cannons in place as well." Duncan looked at everyone gathered. "We need to stop the ground army. Let's move out."

"Wait," Angela whispered still watching the ships in the sky. Several of the ships were circling back as others continued on to Silverton. Glancing back at all of the smoke rising into the sky from their battle she understood. "They are coming for us."

"Are you sure?" Duncan asked, watching the skies.

Angela glared at him. "I know the skies."

Duncan met her glare for glare before finally going with her assessment. "Mance. Pakmon. Take B group and get that tractor moving. Leave us the repeater cannon from the wreck and remove the one from your tractor. If those ships are coming here, it will be our only defense. The rest of you, fan out." Duncan looked back at Angela as she nodded, "We're about to have incoming."

Angela frowned from the treetops. The airships were heading right towards their position. What they needed were flak cannons to fill the sky with metal and shrapnel. They also needed more airships of their own. The *Renegade* and *Sky Hawk* were not going to leave the air over Silverton to provide any backup for the army in the field. "Where are you Kail?" she said out loud. It had been three days since he had left for the eastern cities to plead for help. He promised her that he would be here in time to defend the city.

She checked the string on her bow. Aside from the two repeater cannons and what rifles the men carried, her bow was all there was to try to defeat the new enemy. The ships could fly faster than she could, but they took time to turn around. She also had faith that they would not be able to shoot her out of the sky, none the less an arrow started to seem inadequate.

Below her on the ground she could see Duncan's men strapping a rope around one of the repeater guns. The gun was too big for one man to use, and it needed to be able to turn and move quickly while pointed skyward. It looked like it should work, but she guessed they had less than a minute before they found out.

She whistled loudly to grab their attention as she launched herself into the sky. Looking behind her she could see the *Lotus* flying high to observe the battle. The Juggernauts were slowly advancing; sky cities with their troops and support craft. She remembered seeing the first one of that size at Stalbridge, and now there were two of them here. No four she corrected herself after seeing that two of them were already on the ground. That was over four thousand troops they faced. A little less than four thousand now after she and Duncan's men had defeated a four armored tractor squad.

The repeater gun opened fire at the approaching ships, clipping one causing it to bank and weave in her direction. She slowly drew in a full breath of air and held it. She put the minimum amount of energy into her flying ability and started to drift with the breeze as the airship started firing its own gun towards the ground. The pilot was protected by a rounded plate of glass from the front so only an attack from the sides, directly above or behind the pilot would be effective. Angela could see in her mind's eye what the pilot was going to do. She knew exactly where he was going to be. Almost by reflex she drew back on her bow and released an arrow, leading the airship by over a hundred yards.

The ship continued its banking turn as it shot past her to come around to take another run against Duncan's troops on the ground. As she had seen, the airship and her arrow met. She blew out the breath she had been holding as it struck the pilot in the back. The airship pulled out of its turn and slowly rolled onto its side before crashing into the ground below. Fiery black smoke quickly filled the area where the airship had crashed, igniting the fuel. It was a perfect shot and, even she doubted that she could do it again.

Having seen their comrade's airship go down, the rest of the incoming airships switched up their tactics. Angela flew higher into the sky as they approached, and the ground below her erupted as the airships started to use their cannons. Duncan was on his own from here. Her only hope for helping them was to stay above the airships and harass as much as she could. If she could distract some of them, they might get lucky enough to catch one or two not paying attention to the gunfire coming from the ground.

A second airship suddenly exploded in midair having flown into the line of fire from the ground. She did not stop to worry if the fire raining down to the ground from the ignited fuel was landing on Duncan. She fired off another arrow at a passing airship and cursed when it missed the pilot. The arrow had impacted just in front of him and she could see him, looking around for the source of the attack. It did not take him long to spot her basically standing in the air. This time she did not suppress a curse when she saw him wave and point towards her.

"You are not alone in the sky now are you?" she said as three of the small airships banked away and formed up to attack her.

Duncan yelled "Three o'clock!" and started to shoot his rifle at an airship that was making an attack run on them. Two lines of bullet impacts raced through his group from the passing ship, followed by a roar that vibrated the ground around him. Two of his men were cut down by the strafing airship, and he watched as the pilot pulled the ship back up into the sky. "It's coming around," he yelled to Erickson who had been manning one of the repeater guns salvaged from the earlier fight.

He could see Erickson look at him then swing the gun around as the airship slowed in its climb and fell back towards them. It was a fatal error on the pilot's account as Duncan watched Erickson punch more than a dozen rounds through the airship, then enjoyed a job well done as it crashed out of sight into the ground.

A flicker of movement in the sky pulled his attention as he saw Angela shoot by as fast as she could. He instantly saw her dilemma. "Erickson. Cover fire. Now!" he ordered, pointing to the sky as three airships were about to pass overhead.

Erickson nodded and pivoted the repeater cannon around, opening fire.

Duncan fired his rifle as fast as he could, reloaded and fired again. "Damn it," he cursed as only one of the passing ships seemed to have been hit. A trail of smoke started to pour out of the damaged ship, but the pilot seemed unconcerned as he continued to chase Angela.

Angela stole a glance behind her at the three ships giving chase. One of them was venting smoke yet ignored the damage to the ship. She jerked her flight to the north towards the advancing Courduff fleet noticing that the damaged airship was slower to respond as it swung a bit wider than the other ships. An idea quickly came to her from her training years from her youth. Young Keratins were not necessarily the best of fliers, nor were they experienced. Twisting in midair she pushed her ability as hard as she could and flew back towards Duncan's area.

Like a group of eager toddlers, they banked their airships in an attempt to cut her off. The lead airship collided with the damaged ship sending both spinning out of control and crashing into the ground. The remaining airship was forced to pull away and disengage. Angela smiled, but didn't hesitate to dive back below the tree tops. Three airships taken out in just as many minutes was pretty good.

LOTUS, SKIES ABOVE SILVERTON

Admiral Bailon stood at the viewport, arms folded but unable to keep from frowning as he watched the battles unfold. Clearly the pilots that were chosen for the new airships were handpicked by a committee for the equal opportunity of guaranteed disaster. He leaned towards Cid to ask in a low voice. "Are we being betrayed again? I can't believe what I am seeing. Ships running into each other."

He heard Cid take a deep breath then let it out before answering. "I have no evidence that the conspiracy extends beyond the initial attack on Silverton, but knowing what we do and looking at the results of the fighting, I clearly see possible evidence of it."

"Add it to your list," Bailon mumbled. "Get me the fleet on the radio." He turned away from the battle and pressed the transmit button harder than he needed. "*Enforcer* and *Gauntlet*, concentrate your long range cannons on the city. Keep an eye out for the flying Keratin, and use your close range defense guns if you see her." He released the button and said, "Last thing we need is someone from a distant fairy tale storming one of the Juggernauts and single-handedly bring it down with nothing more than three feet of sharpened metal and a bad temper."

Cid remained silent.

"Shelling the city will force them to rethink their position. If we're not careful these small battles that they have won have a way of snowballing into a victory."

As the Juggernauts opened fire they could hear the long range cannons blast one after another. The distance to

Silverton was still a few miles away so it took several seconds before explosions started to dot throughout the city.

Chapter 29

SILVERTON

Randal held the binoculars to his eyes to view the battlefield. Throughout the city the anti-airship batteries were being fired. Shells designed to fill the air with engine clogging debris rather than raw explosive power were detonating high in sky leaving miniature dark clouds of smoke.

He frowned. The flak cannons were proving to be fairly useless against the smaller airships as they started to fire their cannons at the fortifications throughout the city. The *Renegade* and *Sky Hawk* were doing their best to protect the city, but the smaller craft were proving to be too fast for them to track with their main cannons. Their crews had to use their deck mounted repeater guns to defend the city.

The windows rattled from a nearby explosion. "This isn't good," he said, seeing one of the hangars at the airstrip go up in smoke. What remained of the *Seraph* had been stored in there, and it pained him to know that the ship was gone forever.

One of the airships that had been attacking Silverton rolled over onto its side crashing into the city. A row of flame and smoke erupted where it had died.

The radio crackled, "Silverton, come in."

"*Renegade*, this is Randal come in," he answered.

"Better get out of there Randal," the Captain said. "Looks like they are gunning for anything that looks important. We're not going to be able to stop them all."

"Copy that *Renegade*." Randal stopped transmitting. There really wasn't much he could do from the tower. The captains knew their roles better than he did, and he silently wished them luck. He took one last look around the headquarters before heading out to the main bunker.

DUNCAN'S UNIT, OUTSIDE SILVERTON

Duncan cursed. "We have to go. Now!" he yelled as another airship buzzed overhead forcing everyone to find cover. The repeater guns had run out of ammo, and they were methodically getting picked off with each pass. The air was so thick with smoke from nearby fires and artillery craters that it was getting hard to see or breathe.

"We must fall back," Angela said, landing next to him. "The other units have already fallen, and troops are marching on Silverton."

Frustrated, he ran to the nearest soldier and hauled him to his feet. "Private move out." He shoved the man forward then continued on. Angela followed him.

"If we attack the enemy, the airships will not fire upon us for fear of killing their own," he heard her yell. Duncan had to agree with her logic. Leave it to a Keratin to suggest the safest place was with the attacking enemy.

"Let's move, let's move, let's move!" he yelled, waving his men back towards Silverton. "We're all dead if we stay here any longer." His men were finally starting to understand and began to retreat. More artillery fire from the airships and repeater guns ripped apart the ground around them. He broke through the tree line to see several of his men just standing there. "Move you fatherless cows. You going to make your dying easy for them?" He then saw why they had stopped but was too busy getting everyone moving to truly process it. Silverton, was on fire. Dozens maybe even hundreds of fires were burning throughout the city. Airships circled overhead like hungry buzzards over a corpse. The hair raising whistle of cannon shells screamed as they passed before striking into the city.

SILVERTON

"We need volunteers to help with the fires," Randal Wood said. "If we don't get them under control, there won't be a Silverton left to defend."

"It's suicide to go out there right now," someone complained. "We can't go out there while we are under attack."

Randal thought about it for a moment before calling up the airships above the city. "*Sky Hawk*, *Renegade* this is Randal Wood. Come in please."

"*Renegade* here," came the call.

"What's your status?"

"*Sky Hawk* is shot up pretty badly but still flying. We're faring better but running low on ammo. The air attack seemed to be winding down with some of the airships from Courduff returning. We're guessing they are running low on fuel."

Randal nodded and then stopped when he realized the captain of the *Renegade* couldn't see him. "What's it look like outside *Renegade*? How badly are we burning?"

There was a long pause. "Not good. Most of downtown and the industry sector is on fire. Outer edges of the residential areas are going up. There are more spot fires than we can count. Most of the bombardment seems to be focused on downtown though."

"Copy that *Renegade*. Randal out." He set the radio down and turned to the men gathered in the room. "People's homes are burning. Your home, my home, our homes."

Most of the people shook their heads.

"You heard the *Renegade*. They are attacking downtown, not the residential areas."

Again everyone shied away from volunteering.

He found the nearest officer and promoted him to man the radio. "I'm going out there. There are people already out there that need our help." No one moved. Randal took a deep breath and headed out of the bunker. It was bad. As bad as they said it was. Ash was falling from the sky like a grey winter snow storm. Explosions could be heard as cannon fire from Courduff landed throughout the city. He almost went back into the bunker when he heard.

"We're with you sir."

Looking back he saw over a dozen volunteers had left the safety of the bunker to join him.

DUNCAN'S UNIT, OUTSIDE SILVERTON

"Angela?" Duncan asked, keeping his head down as his men traded gunfire with the enemy.

Angela shook her head at him but held her bow at the ready with an arrow already nocked.

She was right he admitted. Out in the open her ability to fly wasn't much of an advantage. She would be an easy target for them.

"Running out of time," there was an edge of urgency in Erickson's voice, "If we don't meet up with more of our own people, this becomes a fight we can't win."

Duncan saw Angela pop up then back down just as fast.

"Two on the edge of the lane behind fence posts." Angela nodded at him.

"Erickson," he called out to signal the plan. Duncan counted down on his fingers, and the three of them opened fire on the two soldiers that had them pinned down. It was over quickly. "Good shot Erickson," he said. Angela had a scowl on her face like none he had seen before. "You too

Angela," he added.   When she didn't ease up he asked.
"What?"

Erickson still had his rifle pointed towards the two
dead soldiers. Duncan's stomach dropped. Erickson's hands
were limp, his body still, his eyes still open but looking at the
ground. Duncan pulled down his own helmet and for the
moment was glad that Angela's hearing wasn't at its best as he
ran through every curse he knew and then invented some on
the spot.

Angela touched his shoulder.   "We sing for him
later."

Singing wasn't his way, but he vowed to have a drink
to toast Erickson. Maybe a whole bottle's worth of drinks.
Forcing himself to get up, he pushed the loss of Erickson
aside. Dwelling on it now wouldn't do anyone any good. As
they passed by the bodies of the dead soldiers he noticed that
each of them had an arrow sticking out of them. "Don't let
anyone tell you that a bow isn't a good enough weapon."

Angela tilted her head to the side at the complement
but said nothing.

"We got a long ways to go," he said, feelings time was
over. The sun was approaching the horizon. Rays mixed
with the battle smoke in the air were starting to cast a rose
colored hue across everything.

SILVERTON

Treylane Armstrong shouldered his rifle and joined in with the group as they passed. He recognized Randal Wood and some of the other men. "Where are we going?" he asked with genuine concern.

"Going to help put out fires and help people," one of the men said clearly unconcerned that Treylane was armed as was most of the group.

Treylane nodded. "I'll join you. Can always use an extra set of hands. I think the shelling is worse over there too."

The man nodded and waved him up to the rest of the group.

He was improvising now. The Courduff army should have been invading the city by now, but apparently Silverton was putting up more resistance than had been expected. His original plan was to simply work as a sniper, but that plan had been abandoned. It wouldn't be to his advantage if he was the only one doing the shooting, too much attention. He also reasoned that if he kept near someone as high up the Silverton ranks as Wood, he would soon be in the company of much more valuable targets.

Chapter 30

CANYAMAR JUNGLE

A day ago Camden had set his horse free. He hoped that it wouldn't become a meal for an Imaera or some other jungle predator, but honestly he didn't have the luxury of worrying about the animal. He had come upon a clearing in the jungle where Xavier's party had camped for the night, not just any night, but the night before. There were warm campfire coals and bits of food that the jungle hadn't found and carried off yet. He decided that it was time to continue on foot, favoring stealth over speed, and he had yet to find a way to make a horse tromping through the jungle stealthy.

The jungle was proving to be quite cooperative with him. It seemed that the group he stalked was not trying to hide their trail. He fell into a rhythm of half run, and half jog by keeping his eyes on the jungle floor. It was an easy pace to keep up as he moved through the jungle with surprising ease and quickness.

Now that he could feel Xavier almost within his grasp he started going over what he was going to do when he caught up. Xavier's men would need to be dealt with first, or distracted in some way. A night attack was also a tempting option; get in, kill Xavier and get out. Of course there was always the possibility of a full on fight. That idea brought a smile to his lips as he imagined turning his body into steel. Camden pictured the looks on their faces when they discovered they couldn't hurt him as he smashed through them in a one sided rampage.

As Camden hurried through the jungle, he noticed some small changes. The ambient noises were less, and he caught a few whiffs of odd smells. He supposed that he must be near to reaching The Eternal Gateway. Large areas of the jungle around the gateway had been cleared as a military outpost was built within the vicinity. He also remembered there being a lot of fire from the last battle they had. When the wind shifted just right, that could explain it. One thing he didn't want was Xavier to reach the outpost. Even if bullets did bounce off of his skin, taking on an entire base was more than even he could handle, especially if Therion got involved.

Suki had seen a lot of things in her life; a woman born a thousand years ago, time traveling mages, and a four year old girl who looked twenty. Even flying in the skies with a guy who could turn his body into other materials didn't strike her as odd compared to what she now saw. Ahead of her came the wisp, and it wasn't alone. Apparently it had found a horse and not just any horse, but one complete with a saddle and tack.

"Where did you get that?" she asked. The wisp had a look of smug satisfaction on its little face. Suki suppressed a laugh. It struggled with the reins it had tucked up under each of its arms as it sat in the saddle.

The wisp chattered.

"It's Uncle Camden's horse?" Suki raised an eyebrow. "No, I don't think he will mind if you ride his horse," she answered another chirp.

Her own horse even seemed a bit jealous, shaking its head a few times and trying to nip at the other horse, earning it some well deserved glares and an angry scolding from the blue wisp.

"If that is Camden's horse, he must be near."

The wisp nodded and spoke again before urging the horse back down the jungle path.

"Ok, I'll follow, you lead the way." Suki understood that they were very near to catching up to Camden. If he was on foot and they hurried, they should be able to catch up by nightfall. Something else that had astounded her was that she had understood what the wisp had said. She filed that away as one more thing to ask Alyssa when she saw her again, but for now, it wasn't as important as finding Camden.

Tracking, Camden concluded was aggravating. Even though he knew he was close to catching the man he hated most, each passing moment seemed to tease him with the chance of finding his prey, only to realize they had already passed through.

He almost missed it. The faint sounds of people talking and moving about brought him to a halt. His heart was already beating quickly from the fast pace he had been running, but now it felt like it was ready to pound its way out of his chest. Even the voices he had heard were drowned out by the pulse of blood hammering through his ears. His breathing sounded like shouts to his own ears, and he hoped they couldn't hear him.

He crouched in silence as he tried to calm down. Looking around he didn't spot anyone or see any movement. Relief drained through him that no one had spotted him sprinting through the jungle. It would be just his dumb luck to blow everything in a careless moment by accidently charging through the middle of their camp.

A few deep breaths later he had calmed down enough to move forward. He estimated that they were forty to fifty yards ahead of him so he made his way through uncut jungle to swing around to the side of them. He needed to find out how many men he was going up against, but most important of all he needed to see Xavier's face. He was positive that he had tracked the traitor down, but until he saw him, there was always the possibility that he might be following the wrong group of men, and Xavier wasn't here.

Moments later he sat crouched in the shadows of the jungle underbrush after he had evicted a large ground rodent from the hiding spot. He could make out parts of the conversations between the people he was watching. It appeared that they were done hiking for the day and were busily setting up camp for the night. He counted six men, but there might be more out in the jungle gathering wood for fires or looking for fresh food. One person wasn't among them. Camden held back silent curses as he settled in to keep watch.

Through the gaps between the plants, he saw the men going about their tasks. None of them seemed concerned that someone might be following them. *Why should they?* he figured. They weren't military or doing anything particularly sneaky or illegal. They looked like a bunch of down on their luck miners from the last town. *Maybe not so down*, he corrected. There were small things he started to notice. Their boots for starters were of quality sufficient for jungle hiking. Most of them were armed as well. Not for protection against an unruly jungle encounter, but armed sufficiently for much more. He quelled his own suspicions quickly when he remembered where they were headed. Showing up out of the jungle like a group of lost adventurers onto a secret military base probably wasn't the best of ideas.

Xavier Ross, as he was now known, inhaled as deeply as he could. The glow on the end of the cigarette crawled towards his fingers before he stopped to flick the butt away with his middle finger. He had a problem. A six foot, two hundred fifty pound, hiding in the bushes like some dim witted child kind of problem. The easy solution was to just shoot him in the back of the head and let the bugs carry him off. However, today didn't feel like an easy kind of day. This called for something more satisfying.

Xavier quietly took off the rifle he had slung behind his shoulder. Earlier in the day, he had broken away from the group in the off chance of finding some big game like an Imaera. Its hide would prove very useful in the next few days. Instead he had found Camden Arland of all people charging through the jungle like some primate in heat. Holding the rifle by the barrel he took all of three steps before swinging the rifle as hard as he could. The funny noise Camden made wasn't nearly as satisfying as the bone shattering crunch was when he caught the man across the back.

Camden frowned. He smelled smoke, but he hadn't seen any of the men start a campfire. Pain like he had never felt before exploded through him as he was falling forward through the underbrush. The pain was so unexpected he couldn't breathe as his surroundings began to spin. Something had gone horribly wrong. Someone used their foot to kick him over onto his back. Xavier Ross stood over him.

"I liked that gun too," Xavier said, eyeing the broken stock before tossing it away. "How have you been Arland? Get anyone killed lately?"

Anger consumed him turning his vision red, but he couldn't get up. His legs refused to move regardless of how hard he tried to put his boot across that burned face.

Xavier lit another cigarette then pulled out a knife. Camden watched as Xavier looked at the blade. "You know, I just can't figure something out," he said, squatting down next to him. "Losing your ship might piss you off. I know. I saw it happen twice."

He watched as Xavier stabbed the knife about an inch into his thigh without him feeling it.

"But there has to be something else," Xavier said, poking him a couple of more times. "What could I have done that created such hate? I really want to know. It's like I slept with your sister or maybe your mother." Xavier looked at him with concern. "Did I sleep with her? I was like you once you know, so full of hate and rage. Obsessed with my own sense of self and power." He pulled the cigarette away to look at it. "Then I took up smoking." Xavier smiled. "Much better after that."

Camden tried to sit up or at least spit on the man, but it was all he could do to keep from passing out.

Xavier stabbed him several more times causing the entire side of his pants to darken with blood then he gave him a pathetic smile. "Looks like you're half a man now." Xavier stood up as several of the men from the camp came to investigate.

"Who's this?" someone asked.

"A special friend," Xavier said, walking away. "He's going to need a little assistance though to make it to camp and be mindful of his legs. He's a bit sensitive about them."

Camden couldn't even focus enough to struggle as they started to drag him to their camp. The pain overwhelmed him.

Suki didn't want to stop for the night, but traveling through the jungle on horseback in the dark was a recipe for disaster. Even if her wisp companion could continue to follow the trail, it would only take one misstep by the horse to cause a fall or something worse. She got off her horse and tied them both down so they wouldn't wander off. The wisp seemed to share her anxiety about stopping.

"It's getting dark," she said. "Besides, not all of us are fearless little wisps."

The wisp grumped at her as it zipped off into the jungle.

"Be careful," she called. Suki hoped the little wisp would return soon. The jungle made her claustrophobic, and the bravery of the horses was limited to how fast they could run away if anything decided to jump out of the dark at her.

Several minutes later the wisp returned and excitedly circled her.

"What?" she asked.

The wisp chattered at her as it pulled on her sleeve.

"Ok, I'm coming. I understand. I need to be quiet." Suki let the wisp lead her into the darkness. It wasn't too long before she could make out the light of camp fires in the distance. The wisp took a very winding path that she assumed kept them from revealing themselves as they got closer.

The wisp finally stopped and softly chattered as it pointed.

Suki eyed the camp. Several men grouped around a couple of fires were eating or settling in for the night. Then she saw him, and it stole her breath. Camden was lying on his back not moving. She knew that he was badly injured. She could see that his leg was covered in blood, but her experience with healing the wounded told her that it was much worse than that, much worse.

"Ouch," she said as the wisp pulled on her hair. She hadn't even realized that she was trying to make her way to him. "He needs me," she whispered.

The angry glare the wisp gave her stopped her short. While it had always been rather playful, she felt a sudden chill run down her spine. According to Camden, the wisp had torn Xavier apart all those years ago. She hadn't quite believed it until now.

The wisp chirped and turned its glare to the camp.

Fear gripped its icy claws around Suki's heart. In the glow of a campfire she saw him. The stringy hair, the melted face and that damned careless demeanor as he sucked on the end of a cigarette. Camden hadn't gone crazy that night. Xavier Ross was alive, and he was right here.

Her hand unconsciously rubbed the scar in the middle of her chest. The scar left when Xavier had stabbed her in the back so hard that the knife had pushed out through her chest. The same chill she remembered from almost dying crawled over her again. It was only by some miracle that she had managed to stay alive long enough to let Camden back onto the *Snow Break*. She remembered that he had done his best to save her.

Now there was no possible way for her to save Camden. If she revealed herself, Xavier would kill her. Maybe even worse, bring her back from the dead somehow to kill her again.

The wisp looked at her with sadness. It patted the back of her hand in understanding.

"I, I can't." she whispered. "I'm too scared." Suki slowly moved back out of sight and sat down. Tears flowed down her cheeks as she cried. "I'm so sorry."

Chapter 31

SILVERTON

"Help me with this door," Randal called out while throwing a bucket of water into a broken window, pushing back the flames for a moment. "Someone's inside."

"Here," someone said, pushing past him slamming a metal fence post like a battering ram into the door.

Randal came around to the other side to help beat the door down. Another volunteer tossed him a wet blanket which he put over his head as he rushed inside. Just past the foyer he found an unconscious man. Hoisting him by the shoulders, he dragged the man out of the burning house. He hoped that there wasn't anyone else inside as a few minutes later the roof caved in, sending a fountain of sparks high into the smoky night air.

The shelling from the Courduff airships had slowed. He guessed that they were now letting the fire do the damage for them. However, every fifteen to twenty minutes one of them would fire a round into the city, keeping everyone from finding a moment's peace or rest.

"Get this man some help," Randal ordered. "How are doing on Sixth Street?" he asked, taking a moment for himself to catch his breath.

"Fires are being contained, but it's going to be a while before we get ahead of this," he was answered. In another part of the city a fireball rose into the sky, and a few seconds later he could hear the explosion.

"Start gathering civilians so we can get them out of the city," Randal said, turning away from the fading fireball. "We need to start evacuating while we still can." He wished it was different, that somehow they would be able to push back the forces from Courduff. He could read the shock on their faces, but he could also see them start to come to the same conclusion; Silverton was falling. "I need to get back to headquarters to oversee things from there," he declared. "Save as many as you can."

The soldiers and volunteers looked at him before they started to nod and some saluted.

Randal saluted back. "Good luck men." He turned back towards the center of Silverton.

Treylane Armstrong lowered his salute, and started to fade back from the group of men who had heard Randal Wood's little run away speech. This development needed to be reported, and he couldn't help but smile as Randal took off alone through the city. Opportunities he couldn't pass up were starting to present themselves.

Duncan tossed his helmet onto the floor as he entered the bunker. "We have status on anybody?" he asked the room. "Where is Randal?"

"He left to oversee fire and rescue efforts in the civilian parts of the city," someone answered.

Duncan frowned at the older man. "Who the hell is in charge here then?"

"I am sir," the same person said, raising his hand.

"Who are you?"

"Jonathon," he said. "Jonathon Chambers."

"Ok Chambers, what's the status with our air ships? How much of a ground force do we have left?"

Angela stepped inside the bunker barely tolerating the medic that hovered over her trying to examine her ears.

"The *Renegade* and *Sky Hawk* are still holding over the city. They have taken a few hits, but nothing they haven't been able to handle while in flight. As for our troops, I don't know. There hasn't been a report from anyone in several hours. They don't have radios like the ships do sir."

"Don't make excuses for them," Duncan said. "However it would be nice if they did."

Jonathon nodded.

"The enemy has pulled back their attack as night has fallen," Angela said. "We need to use this time to gather our forces."

Duncan agreed. "See if you can get to the *Sky Hawk* to help. You up to being messenger boy for a while Angela?"

"What is your plan?" she asked, pushing away the medic.

"Fly up to one of the ships. Spot any of our troops and relay orders."

Angela inclined her head then nodded.

Duncan turned back to Jonathon. "Call them, and let them know she's coming."

Angela turned to leave the bunker.

"Angela," he said, stopping her. "He doesn't show up soon, there isn't going to be a Silverton left."

Angela didn't turn around. "He promised," was all she said as she left.

Treylane lowered his rifle, smoke trailed up from the end of the barrel. Randal Wood, officer in charge of the Silverton Air Field, was dead. Only one of several targets he and his men had been tasked to eliminate once the fighting had started. The glow of the burning city cast its light on the fallen officer as if it knew it should be mourning the loss.

Movement caught his eye as he ducked backwards into the darkness. It wasn't anything with which he needed to be concerned he quickly realized. It was the Keratin woman. She had taken flight and was headed into the dark sky. He brought up his rifle again to peer through the scope and watched as she flew upward with her hands flared out to her sides. The hovering smoke swirled as she passed. He had to admit, she was something else. He even entertained the idea of what it would have been like if she had been a part of his team instead of a target. A talent like flying would have endless uses. "Bang," he said out loud, imagining that he was close enough to be able to shoot her from the sky.

Chapter 32

SILVERTON

Duncan had managed to grab about four hours of sleep. Between relaying orders on the radio to the airships with Jonathon, and Angela flying to the ground troops, he had managed to organize what remained of their military into what he felt was their best options for holding onto the city. He had left orders for the *Sky Hawk* and *Renegade* to meet the smaller enemy airships head on. It was just too hard for the ground forces to effectively combat them.

Courduff hadn't been content either to just sit back through the night. Angela had reported and mapped out their advancements. The enemy ground troops and equipment had marched up to the very edge of the clear cut that surrounded the city. When they decided to push forward, it would be known. Every bit of artillery or heavy weaponry that Silverton still had was moved into position. It wasn't much but if they advanced, Silverton was ready to make them pay for each yard. Adding to the frustration was the missing Randal Wood. Duncan wanted to lead men on the battlefield, and staying in a bunker trying to coordinate various groups wasn't his strong suit.

The first rays of the morning dawn were starting to light up the horizon. He was about to go back into the bunker to wake Angela, but there was no need. The radio crackled when the captain of the *Renegade* called them, snapping her awake.

"This is Duncan. Go ahead," he answered the call.

"Got a problem sir," the captain said. "We're counting several new airships."

Duncan eyed Angela who sprinted outside, probably on her way into the air to see for herself.

"More juggs?" he asked.

"Negative. These are more standard airships, same as we are."

That was going to be it, he thought. They would overwhelm them from the sky so the ground army could walk right in and sweep them all under the rug. "Copy that *Renegade*. Stand by."

Angela returned and shook her head. "I do not see a way to victory Duncan."

"Nothing in your book of prophecies?" He had to laugh at himself. It was plainly clear on her face that she did not find any humor in the question. "Never did buy into any of that myself."

"I have had doubts," she admitted, drawing her war blade, looking it over. "Then I remember where I came from, whom I have met and battled, and the people who have been lost." She turned her gaze to him. "There are people out there I have yet to kill. My revenge has not yet been taken."

Duncan knew then. If anyone was going to walk away from today, it would be Angela. "Alright then," he said, turning back to the radio. "*Renegade, Sky Hawk*. Get in range of the clear cut and start shelling them for us. Keep the air busy as long as you can." Duncan released the transmit button as the ship captains acknowledged. He turned back to Angela. "What kind of songs are they going to make about today?"

Angela shrugged. "I am a spear, not a song maiden."

Duncan laughed this time.

LOTUS, SKIES ABOVE SILVERTON

"Here is the intelligence report Admiral," Cid said, handing Bailon the report.

"Thank you," Bailon said, looking over the highlights of the information. Overall their forces had not fared well. The ground army had sustained some heavy one sided losses early on, but by the end of the day, they had secured the line. The new airships that had been deployed made for some interesting analysis. For a new weapon technology, it wasn't unexpected to see some poor numbers until the data could be used to improve training, tactics, and design improvements. Cid had arranged the information in a way that let him know he had already done his own analysis. The ground army, when they were on their own did not fare well. The same was true for the new individual airships. However, when the ground army was supported by the new ships, their combined effectiveness was spectacular. "Has this been relayed to the rest of the fleet and ground commanders?"

"Yes sir."

"Good. Let's keep the forces combined then. If we continue forth with this level of success, the morale boost will be impressive. Also I want more information when we prepare to move on the eastern cities."

Cid nodded, jotting down notes.

"Interesting," Bailon said, reading further. "Do we now know who is in charge of the Silverton force?" he asked, pointing to the headline that Randal Wood was reported as being killed.

Cid shook his head. "No, but the chain of command should have fallen upon Duncan Deline. There still has been no report or sighting of Kail Falconcrest, however we have seen the Keratin."

Bailon nodded, remembering some of the early losses they had witnessed. "What should we expect if he is in command?"

"He is a fighter. I would not be surprised if he directly joins the battlefield. I do not foresee their tactics changing because of this. The chances of them taking a surrender offer however are pretty much nil at this point."

"Seems like everything is going exactly as planned by whoever setup this confrontation," he said softly.

Cid nodded. "It does appear that everything is lining up to wipe Silverton off the map."

Bailon returned the report to Cid as he made his way to the front viewport. Silverton was still burning in many places, but they still had their two airships. Their own fleet had been reinforced by the *Interceptor*, *Morning Star* and the *Deterrent*; returning airships that had been deployed on earlier missions. "Begin the attack," he ordered.

SILVERTON

"Thank you," Duncan said, dismissing the officer that informed him that Courduff was advancing. He smoothed down the hair on the back of his head as he eyed Angela. "Here they come."

Angela nodded and started to leave the bunker.

"Silverton, come in Silverton. This is the *Odyssey*," the radio call came.

Duncan's jaw dropped. He stared at the radio in disbelief. Angela stopped to turn around.

"Silverton. This is Rhonin on the *Odyssey*, come in please."

Duncan grabbed the radio microphone. "*Odyssey*, this is Silverton."

"Is that you Duncan?"

"Affirmative Rhonin. It's a relief to hear your call, but I'm afraid you might have arrived only to bear witness to our defeat," Duncan said.

There was a pause before Rhonin replied. "I take it then you're on your own? Where's Kail and the others?"

Duncan looked at Angela, and she shook her head. "He's not here, and I don't know if he is coming. It's complicated. Angela however is here."

"Understood. Silverton is just coming into our view. I can see it's not looking too good. Can you put on Angela?"

Duncan stepped back from the radio.

"It is good to hear your voice Rhonin," Angela said.

"I can't explain it to you, but we're not alone. There is another airship with us."

Angela frowned. "This is good news, yes?"

Rhonin didn't answer directly. "The other airship is the *Snow Break*."

Angela quickly faced Duncan. "Suki found him," she said quickly before turning back to the radio. "This is very good news. There is hope for this day after all."

Duncan wasn't so sure. There had been something in Rhonin's voice that told him everything wasn't quite what it seemed to be. He wondered if on the other hand Angela might be getting her hopes up a little prematurely.

"Reunions can wait. We have a city to save first," Rhonin said.

Duncan saw Angela clearly go back into warrior mode.

"Agreed," Angela replied. "I am putting Duncan back on, he can fill you in." She turned away from the radio and rushed to leave the bunker, but Duncan managed to stop her.

"Keep your head clear," he said.   Angela nodded, leaving the bunker as he turned back to the radio. "Two ships double our air force, but it might not be enough. They have four Juggernauts and five other airships against us out there. That's not including these smaller craft," he relayed to the *Odyssey*.

"Understood Silverton."

ODYSSEY

Rhonin released the transmit button and looked back to the center of the bridge. "That work for you?" he asked.

Alyssa nodded. "I know you disagree with me, but it's for the best. When this is over, I will talk with my mother, but for now, she doesn't need to know, and we can't afford anyone being distracted."

Rayne stepped forward. "I hope this doesn't backfire."

"How so?" Alyssa asked.

Rayne looked to Rhonin for help. "It would be wrong for her not to know. If something were to happen."

Alyssa sighed. "I have given this a lot of thought. This is the best way. The only way. You won't be able to change my mind on this. She already believes that her family has joined the battle, and she is right. That is enough. I ask that you keep your promises."

Rhonin disagreed but said, "It's your call."

Alyssa nodded. "The planes are weak. Focus your repeater guns on them, and they won't be a problem. The airships will be harder to defeat, but the *Odyssey* is faster, better armed, and more than a match for any of them. As is the *Snow Break*."

She wasn't wrong there Rhonin agreed. The *Odyssey's* refit made it even better than the original *Snow Break* had been. The new ship that Alyssa had put together from the gearworks in less than a day was downright scary in its capabilities. It was a spectacular blend of magic and technology that he would never want to be on the receiving end in battle. Then there was Alyssa herself. If there ever was an argument for or against eugenics she was it. He suspected that Mr. Eleazar knew exactly what he was doing when he brought Angela and Kail together. Alyssa was a weapon.

Rhonin sat into the captain's chair and pressed a button for the inner-ship intercom. "All hands, prepare for battle." Looking towards Alyssa he nodded. "Good luck Captain," he said.

Alyssa smiled. "Fortune watch over us, Captain." In a blue flash of magic, Alyssa teleported off the bridge, returning her to the *Snow Break*.

"I love you, you know that," Rhonin stated, eyeing the array of forces against them.

Rayne nodded. "I know."

Chapter 33

LOTUS, SKIES ABOVE SILVERTON

Through the front viewport of the *Lotus*, Admiral Bailon watched as the *Gauntlet* and *Enforcer* along with the three reinforcement airships positioned above the ground force. During the night they had deployed the remainder of the ground force to provide fresh troops and equipment for those that saw combat the day before.

The *Lotus* remained at a higher altitude away from the fighting. The wind also played in their favor by keeping the majority of the smoke away from his fleet, giving him a clear view of the battlefield. The *CP's* cranes were swinging back and forth, depositing the single manned airships onto its outer deck.

He was also calm as two additional airships arrived to help defend Silverton. By a stroke of luck, they had intercepted the transmission from the *Odyssey*. Strategically it should make no difference if the *Odyssey* arrived with their experienced crew, the Mastersons. Even the second ship renamed after the *Snow Break* brought their numbers to only four airships against his armada of three airships, four Juggernauts and the *CP*. That wasn't even counting the *Lotus*, or four thousand ground troops and their equipment.

The smaller airships started to form up in three and four ship groups. Their goal was to bait out the Silverton airships so they could be engaged on their own. The main cannons of the Juggernauts and other airships would be able to destroy them from the sky.

"Here they come," Cid said, stepping up to his side.

"I don't believe there will be a third day of fighting," Bailon said. "They are outnumbered two to one in the air without the *CP's* airships, and the ground force has already eliminated half of the remaining defenders."

"I agree sir. And the transmission confirmed that Kail Falconcrest is not here."

Bailon nodded. "Keep your eyes on the *Odyssey* and this new *Snow Break*. I don't want to lose any ships unnecessarily."

"Yes sir."

ODYSSEY

"Brom, keep an eye out for the planes," Rhonin warned the pilot of the *Odyssey*.

"Aye sir," Brom Carter acknowledged.

The *Snow Break* eased ahead of them as they approached over Silverton. Rhonin had mixed feelings about the incoming battle. They were significantly outnumbered, but he was also eager to see how the *Odyssey's* new upgrades performed and how the *Snow Break* handled herself.

He opened up communications to the *Sky Hawk* and *Renegade*. "Soften up the ground forces as much as you can. *Odyssey* and *Snow Break* will provide cover against their airships."

"Copy *Odyssey*. Good to have you with us," the captain of the *Renegade* answered.

"Good to be here," Rhonin added before ending his transmission.

Rayne held a pair of binoculars to her eyes as she called out. "The carrier Juggernaut is launching the planes. Looks like one about every twenty or thirty seconds."

"Got it," Brom said.

"The rest of the fleet is pushing forward. Two of the airships are leading, the other seems to be hanging back to guard the other juggs."

"Covering for their ground army," Rhonin guessed. He pressed and held the transmit button. "Are you seeing this Alyssa?"

"Yes, we're seeing it," came the response. "Keep to the plan, and don't let the planes get a bead on you with their larger cannons," Alyssa's voice trailed off over the radio. Rhonin looked ahead and the first salvos were being fired from the *Sky Hawk* and *Renegade*. Before the shells even landed in the trees Courduff's fleet was already filling the sky with their own barrage against the city.

Explosions started to fill the air as flak cannons from the Juggernauts started firing. The clumps of smaller ships started to break out of the main groups to harass the two original ships from Silverton.

Rhonin hit a switch on the console to turn on red warning lights throughout the ship. "Let's go."

"Aye sir," Brom said as he throttled up the *Odyssey* to try to catch up to the *Snow Break* and join in the fight. The *Snow Break* had just opened up with its repeater cannons. Streaks of light traced through the sky, reaching out to shred a pair of smaller planes that had gotten too close.

"Get those guns firing," he ordered. The ship vibrated as the main cannons started to send shells at the larger fleet. They were long shots, but the Juggernauts were not agile enough to do much about it other than to take the hits.

"Incoming," Rayne called out as a group of four smaller airships came at them from above.

"Defensive fire now," Rhonin called out and sixteen repeater cannons on the starboard side of the *Odyssey* came to life. It sounded like a giant had found a plate of steel to rip in half. One of the smaller ships exploded in mid air, forcing the rest of the group to break away. "Nice shooting."

Two of the larger airships banked and moved towards the *Snow Break* and *Odyssey* and started to fire their cannons. "Hang on," Brom called out as he pulled the *Odyssey* into the air. The new turbine engines whined as he throttled up the power to swing them around, providing a firing solution to the gunners.

"It's a feint," Rhonin tried to explain, but it was too late.

Before Brom could bring them around, both of the airships along with the smaller planes had circled back and had the *Renegade* caught in a two sided flank. Enemy shells started to slam into the side of the *Renegade*.

"Get out of there," Rhonin said in frustration as the *Renegade* started to billow smoke from several places. The *Snow Break* came in fast and hot. The smaller ships fell from the sky like birds with broken wings, but Alyssa's ship wasn't able to destroy anything else. The enemy ships had dealt their damage and retreated.

"*Renegade*, report." Rhonin called.

"We're done *Odyssey*, sorry," her captain called.

"Understood, get out of there." Rhonin turned to Rayne. "We're down one ship, and all we have to show for it is a few swatted bite flies," he said with anger rising in his voice.

SNOW BREAK

Alyssa held back a curse as she gripped the flight controls of the *Snow Break*. With the loss of the *Renegade*, they had lost a quarter of their air defense. "Conrad, get ready to fire the cannons."

"Aye," Conrad Black called out.

The *Sky Hawk* was outmatched although she didn't want to tether the *Snow Break* to the weaker ship to protect it, she didn't see she had much of a choice. She knew there would to be losses for both sides in this battle, but she hadn't thought they would lose one of their own so quickly.

"See if we can push them back a little from the *Sky Hawk* while softening up the ground army too," she said.

Conrad keyed in the controls for the main cannons. "Ready."

She rolled the ship onto its side then cut back along the tree line as Conrad waited for her command. "Fire."

The main cannons and the repeater guns roared to life. The *Snow Break* bucked as the army on the ground responded with fire of its own, but the *Snow Break* was well armored and incredibly fast. The *Snow Break* poured its fire power into the trees where the Courduff ground army was positioned. As the ship passed, explosions and fire erupted in its wake.

"*Sky Hawk*, this is the *Snow Break*, come in," she called.

"*Sky Hawk* here."

"Pull up and focus on the armada. We've done as much as we can for the ground. Now we need to keep the skies clear for them."

"Roger, *Snow Break*."

ODYSSEY

"It's going to get rough from here on out," Rhonin assessed as the *Snow Break* lit up the ground army. As expected the Courduff fleet advanced as a whole group. They had intended just to wash over them and sweep them away since they had the force to do it.

Alyssa had correctly called it. They couldn't devote anymore firepower against the ground army with the entire air fleet now gunning for them. Their repeater guns opened up again as Brom took the *Odyssey* through a series of evasive maneuvers as two groups of the smaller airships tried to herd them into range of the larger more powerful ships.

"Roll to port *Odyssey*," Alyssa's voice called out over the radio.

Rhonin held on as Brom brought the ship over as the *Snow Break* shot over the top of them, destroying most of the smaller airships that were hounding them.

"Nice shooting." Rhonin could see the *Sky Hawk* taking fire in front of them. "Let's do the same."

The *Odyssey's* main cannons fired toward the advancing airships from Courduff, forcing them to break off their attack. The repeater defense guns convinced the pilots of the smaller ships to either retreat or be shot out of the sky.

Courduff was playing it safe. They were poking in, doing damage then quickly retreating before they took any real losses. He had to begrudgingly admit that he would be doing the same thing if the roles were reversed. "Keep each other covered," he called into the radio. "They are just waiting for one of us to get separated and be easily picked off."

Both the *Snow Break* and *Sky Hawk* acknowledged.

"Bring us up and concentrate the long range guns on the juggs," he ordered. "If they want to play it safe, so can we."

LOTUS

"Heavy losses are being reported from some of the ground units," Cid called out, manning the inner fleet communications. "*CP* reports a thirty percent loss of its airships."

Admiral Bailon listened to the rest of Cid's report as he watched the *Snow Break* and *Odyssey* dance around, protecting the *Sky Hawk*. He had to admire their construction and their pilot's skill. He was correct to not underestimate them. Even though Silverton had shot down only a handful of smaller craft, it was clear the two ships were dangerous and deadly.

"Call off the *CP* and fill the sky with cannon fire and flak," he ordered. "Soften them up while we push forward on the ground."

Cid nodded relaying the orders.

"Keep the long range cannons firing on them, and try forcing them into a cross fire. We might get a lucky shot if we don't we will still shell the city." It was now only a matter of time. Even if the ships escaped, Silverton would fall.

SILVERTON GROUND

Angela got a second soldier right through the chest with her bow, but as soon as he fell, two more took his place. It was frustratingly hard to get an arrow off against the enemy armed with guns. Now that they were aware of her and her ability to fly, most of her advantage was gone. Still after the *Snow Break* had razed the tree line, there was enough confusion, smoke and other cover for her to continue her attacks. She was going to have to remember to thank Camden for that when she next saw him.

Angela flipped sideways through the air, forcing the nearest soldier to prematurely fire his rifle, sending both soldiers back a step. It provided the opening she had been hoping to get. Her war blade flashed to their left, down, then across, picking both of them off.

She took only a moment to glance around for anyone else before shooting back into the sky. She had lost track of Duncan and his men during the fighting and wanted to check in with them. One position she did not want to find herself in was ending up behind enemy lines with no chance of support.

She caught sight of four men from Silverton battling it out with half a dozen from Courduff. They were trading cover fire as they reloaded. If she timed it right, she figured that she could at least even the odds. She quickly fired an arrow followed by another before diving down on top of the enemy. One arrow struck home, causing the soldier to fall, the other however missed a fatal blow. The enemy was alerted to her now as they swung their rifles up towards the sky.

She wasn't going to make it to the ground before they opened up on her. Luck granted her a pass this time as the soldiers from Silverton saw her attack and opened fire when the enemy became distracted. They gunned down the five ground troops with brutal efficiency. She nodded her thanks as she took off through the smoke in the direction of more fighting.

ODYSSEY

The *Odyssey's* cannons thundered away. Several shells exploded along the side of the nearest Juggernaut. Unfortunately they seemed to have little effect on the advancing armada as the massive ships seemed to be able to just shrug off the damage.

Next to the ship, the *Snow Break*, with better maneuverability and more advanced cannon control seemed to have an easier time of landing hits, but like them it seemed to have little effect. A bright flash forced Rhonin to turn his head as the back quarter of the *Sky Hawk* exploded.

"What happened?" he called out.

Rayne shook her head as she scrambled to find an answer to his question.

The radio crackled, but he wasn't able to make out much of the words. The only thing that did make it through was the desperation of the *Sky Hawk*. There was little he could do as another shell punched through the crippled ship, exploding out the other side. The static cut out as a third shell made contact. It was all overkill at this point as the *Sky Hawk* broke apart in front of them.

SILVERTON GROUND

Angela dodged back from the swing of a rifle. The soldier was out of bullets and now used his rifle against her as a makeshift club. She spun about bringing her blade in line to block the strike coming from the other direction. She could see that the man fought with fear and desperation against her.

She made the block then countered by stepping inside his range with a spin and stab maneuver that sent her blade sliding into the man's stomach. She jerked the blade free as she spun around slicing it through the man's neck, ending his suffering before his body had a chance to fall to the ground.

The sky above her exploded, and the *Sky Hawk* was dead. She felt the brush of death's hand caress her chest as the valiant ship broke apart. She steeled herself remembering that they were not the only people who had died in this battle. Now was not the time to mourn.

She could barely hear shouts coming from the other side of the smoke in front of her. Glancing once more at the fire filled sky, she bolted for the top of a large oak tree that had survived the razing. More than half of her arrows were gone when she saw another whole unit of soldiers from Courduff making their way beneath her marching towards Silverton.

There was no mistaking it now, she was too far out. She needed to rendezvous with her own forces and start to fall back to the city. Soon Courduff would be directly invading Silverton.

Duncan's face it seemed was set in a permanent frown. The airships had their hands full trying to keep themselves from becoming additional fireballs like the *Sky Hawk*. It also meant that they were pretty much on their own in dealing with the incoming ground army from Courduff.

"Pakmon, Stanz, find Daly and start rounding everyone up and begin falling back," he ordered. Turning he pointed. "Set up a firing line there while we retreat. It should slow them down."

Both men nodded and hurried away to follow his orders. There wasn't much more they could do here. There were still armored tractors and artillery encampments on the edge of the city. They weren't much, but right now, it was all they had. He hoped the *Snow Break* and *Odyssey* would shoot down at least one airship for him.

Angela shadowed the Courduff unit staying out of sight as best she could. One of the soldiers had made the mistake of going around the remains of one of the smaller crashed airships. She easily picked him off with her bow. None of the enemy seemed to notice he was missing.

She wasted no time, jogging aside, bow and arrow at the ready. She angled herself away from the unit while keeping an eye out for other soldiers. It was going to take luck, patience, and most of all skill to get back after being this far behind the advancing enemy. If she managed to pick a few of them off, then so much the better. Each one being one less Silverton would have to worry about.

ODYSSEY

"We need to start falling back Alyssa," Rhonin called through the radio. "The ground army is advancing, and our own troops are falling back."

"Understood *Odyssey*," Alyssa's voice came over the speaker. "We're going to come in low to see if we can't push them back or at least slow them down a bit."

"Copy that. We will keep you covered." Rhonin turned away from the radio microphone. The battle was disintegrating around them. The ground army was surging forward; the air battle had seen the destruction of half their force while the enemy fleet seemed to laugh at their attempts to deal any significant damage.

The *Snow Break* pushed ahead and began to dive towards the ground. The enemy soldiers had apparently learned their lesson from earlier and were well spread out. Most of the cannon fire from Alyssa's ship scattered only small handfuls of troops as the repeater guns produced more missed shots than hits, but it did slow the enemy surge.

The armada had enough of playing it safe. The smaller ships pushed forward like a swarm of angry bees while the main airships continued to advance with the slowly moving Juggernauts. They were the only two ships left in their way. Rhonin didn't know how they were going to make it out of this one. But he did know that they would take as many of them with them as they could.

Chapter 34

SILVERTON

It was raining ash in Silverton, the former small mining and farming town, tucked in a low valley away from the large city states of Cahir and Courduff. It had been transformed years ago by an unprovoked attack from Cahir with the arrival of a group of branded outlaws. Outlaws that were not only wealthy beyond reason, but also powerful and unique. The town quickly grew into a city. Industry, schools, and innovation prospered, but underneath there was a secret. Magic, time travel and prophecy lay the foundations of conflict that would shape the path the world would take for generations.

Treylane Armstrong wrapped a torn strip of cloth across the front of his mouth and nose. He had changed clothes and did his best to *help* with the defense of Silverton. His job was nearing its end as well. There was little intelligence left to gather or report, and it didn't take a military genius to see that Silverton had little time left.

Once the troops from Courduff started to invade the city proper he figured he had two options; retreat to the rendezvous point, or change uniforms and continue to hunt. He wanted to hunt, but the bombardment from Courduff was methodically pounding the city into rubble, and it was starting to become hazardous to his health. His prey was too rare, too exotic to pass up, and he reasoned that once the ground forces pressed forward far enough all he had to do was wait, and like well-trained hunting dogs, Courduff would flush out his targets right to him.

SNOW BREAK

"No matter how hard you try, some things can't be changed," Alyssa said, pushing the throttle forward, sending the *Snow Break* through the end of its turn. She had seen the ruins of Silverton once before when she was younger. Her grandfather, Duke Falconcrest, had once taken her there to show her how important it was for them to succeed in eliminating Therion. Until now, she hadn't thought she would actually see its destruction first hand.

Mr. Eleazar had a favorite mantra when it came to changing the past and guiding the future. For the first time, she really did understand what he meant when he would talk about being unable to change some events, no matter how hard he tried.

"*Odyssey*," she called over the radio. "We're going to have to provide cover for each other. If they manage to divide us up, we won't survive."

"Agreed," Rhonin replied. "What about the ground army?"

"Not a lot we can do for them now. Besides the airships will be too busy keeping up with us to worry about hitting the ground force."

"Wonderful so now I have to worry about where their ships crash if I manage to shoot them down."

Alyssa smiled. Rhonin probably didn't realize how right he was. The Masterson's reputation and the *Odyssey* were legendary in the future. In all of the battles they fought not only did they always survive but as the stories go, they never even took a hit or scratch. "Just make sure they land on their own forces then."

Seriousness returned to his voice. "Line them up, and we will knock them down."

"Copy that, *Odyssey*. Cover my six." Alyssa shifted to Conrad. "Ready to go on the offensive?"

The control board where Conrad Black stood indicated that all of the guns were loaded and ready to go. "As ready as we can be," he replied. "Weeks to build inside, while a day passes outside. What's not to be ready?" he mumbled to himself.

She still had the key to The Eternal Gateway. It was a small pocket watch with countless uses like stopping time or securing control of the gateway. It also had its limits, and she had used it to those limits to complete the construction of the *Snow Break*. It would need time to recharge before it would be useful again, and she honestly didn't know how long that would take.

Alyssa veered the *Snow Break* hard to port, bringing the ship to face the oncoming armada. Two Juggernauts loomed in front of them dwarfing the other airships and scores of smaller planes that were providing escort. A lone ship floated high in the sky observing. The *Lotus*, captained by Aunt Suki's half brother.

She still had a few tricks up her sleeve as the planes started to come into range. "Clear us a path Mr. Black."

The *Snow Break's* repeater guns flared to life, sending countless bullets towards the enemy aircraft. Alyssa heard a sound like gravel being dropped onto a metal roof as the smaller ships pelted the *Snow Break* with return fire of their own. The hull of the *Snow Break* was more than capable of dealing with the hits. She had transferred a portion of her magic into hardening the ship's hull. The downside was the magic she used would not return to her unless she removed the enchantment.

The *Odyssey* followed in her wake taking out any of the smaller ships that managed to slip past the *Snow Break*. Two of the airships started to come around trying a flanking run against them, but she wasn't concerned with that. The third ship was positioning itself to be in perfect firing range once the *Snow Break* completed its attack run.

That was definitely the *Lotus* up there calling the shots. "*Odyssey*, you see that ship positioning to the outside?"

"Copy. We see it."

"Start firing your main cannons at it now, and convince it to keep moving or we're going to be easy pickings," she ordered.

The *Odyssey* started firing on the distant ship. They were long range shots, and as long as the other airship kept moving the odds were low that it would get hit. But if it held position like she knew it wanted to, the *Odyssey* would be able to inflict some serious damage.

Shrapnel and debris joined the bullets bouncing off of the hull as one smaller airship and then another fell to the onslaught of gunfire the *Snow Break* and *Odyssey* were able to unleash. Alyssa focused on the two larger airships coming into range. "Hold fire on the main cannons," she told Conrad as she angled for a path that would take the *Snow Break* streaking between them.

Alyssa tipped the ship on edge ignoring Conrad's cry of surprise and protest to keep the ship upright and steady. The angle of the cannons on the airships from Courduff had a fixed range of motion, and if she piloted the *Snow Break* correctly there was a narrow path between them that would allow her to broadside both ships with their main cannons while they were unable to fire back.

Rhonin's voice came over the radio. "We're not going to fit *Snow Break*."

"Understood *Odyssey*," she replied, focusing her concentration on the path between the other ships. "Do what you can to keep up with us." She could tell that the captains of the airships finally understood her maneuver, and she had to give them credit as they peeled away from each other. Jerking the controls, the *Snow Break* righted itself, and she pushed the throttle as far forward as it would go. "Fire!" she yelled as the *Snow Break* lurched forward to shoot between the enemy airships.

Every cannon on the *Snow Break* fired in succession, shaking the ship almost as hard as if it had collided with another ship. Her teeth rattled as she fought to keep control of the ship. It only took a few seconds for the *Snow Break* to pass through. "Reload, we have nothing for that third ship," she ordered. "Hang on," she cried out as the enemy airship that had been angling for an ambush opened fire at them. She dropped speed and dove. The first shell screamed past them, but the second clipped the front bow, rocking the ship.

"Break back," she heard Rhonin's call. "Break back!"

Visibility was nonexistent as smoke from the hit billowed up across the bridge viewports. Pulling back the smoke began to clear as the *Snow Break* gained altitude. Relief flooded through her as the damage to the ship seemed to be only cosmetic. Protected by her magic and the fact that it had only been a glancing blow, a dark bruise was all that showed on the front of the ship.

"How did we do?" she called, turning the ship.

"Please don't do that again," Conrad begged.

Both ships that they had fired upon were still in the air, both were smoking from direct hits but were falling back to the safety of the Juggernauts. The ship that had delivered the glancing blow however was in worse shape. The *Odyssey*, unable to participate in her attack, had managed to score several hits, and the ship was slowly losing altitude. Probably going to land as best it could and either abandon ship or enact some sort of emergency repairs she reasoned. Disappointed that her attack run resulted in only one enemy ship being forced to land added to her frustration. It was going to take a lot more than they had she realized to defend Silverton. Once again, Mr. Eleazar's words about being unable to effect change haunted her.

SILVERTON GROUND

Angela discarded her bow. The last arrow had been fired, now only her immortal war blade remained. Camden and the Mastersons were slugging it out in the skies above her. Making herself a target by flying was out of the question at this point, and she still had a long ways to go by foot before reuniting with any of Silverton's forces. How she had managed to get herself so far behind enemy lines was a mystery to her.

Ahead which was where she wanted to go was blocked by a group of six soldiers. She debated attacking them but decided against it when she saw that they were moving away. She frowned when they stopped and started to look around. They could clearly hear something she could not. Her ears still did not work very well after the first day of fighting, but soon she could start to make out a faint scream.

A bolt of blue lightning shot through the sky causing the soldiers to look up. The sound intensified, and she flinched backwards when the bolt intercepted one of the enemy airships. It punched through the other side of the vessel before arcing towards the ground. *It could only be Kail,* Angela thought as the airship tore in half before exploding. Making her way to him was going to be difficult. The display of his arrival had attracted everyone's attention.

Shrill laughter froze her where she stood and for the first time since the fighting began, real tendrils of fear crawled across her skin. She dared not believe it until she was sure. Confirmation was quick in coming. Just about two hundred yards away stood a dark-skinned woman. Her black and white hair whipping about as if she was the source of her own wind, but most notable was her arm. Angela remembered the fight she had with Bastiana's ghost, smashing the rune staff and shattering the arm. It was the only thing that could explain the fiery blue appendage she now saw. She now wished that she had the rune staff with her, but she had chosen to leave it behind as she had no realistic way to carry it with her, along with her bow, arrows, and sword.

The air cracked as a blinding flash erupted in front of her, and her wish was granted. The rune covered staff filled one hand and the war blade the other. The staff's arrival to her call had not gone unnoticed.

"That is mine!" Bastiana screamed.

Angela didn't need good hearing to make out the rest of Bastiana's words. Their meaning was quite clear as the disturbed mage advanced on her.

Chapter 35

OUTSIDE SILVERTON

The rune staff gave her hope against Bastiana. It had defeated the mage in their last encounter, and it had saved her from fatal injuries as well. Along with the Imaera leather she wore it would have to be enough.

Bastiana stopped. "No," she shouted, raking her hand through the air. Crimson and white waves of magic shot away from the mage. "Don't you dare, she is mine!"

Angela flinched as the magic sliced through several soldiers that had come near. More than one had their weapons raised at the both of them. Their bodies fell into piles where they stood, and their rifles and weapons clattered to the ground. She was Bastiana's only target. Anyone else who got in her way was expendable.

Angela sprinted to the side while Bastiana was distracted, kicking gravel up beneath her feet as she closed the distance. She pushed off to fly ten steps away from the mage giving herself force and momentum as she whipped her war blade down.

Bastiana's eyes glinted, and Angela could have sworn she saw her own reflection in them as she followed through with her strike. Her whole body jarred as if she had tried to cut into a block of granite instead of a flesh and blood enemy, steel or iron gave less resistance. The fiery blue hand caught her sword by the blade.

Bastiana twisted the blade in her grasp yanking Angela closer. "Hello, my pet," the woman purred. "You're going to have to do better than this," she said, eyeing the indestructible blade. Bastiana's lip curled in a sneer as her magical arm flared with power. The runes that held the blade together were unaffected, and their silvery glow did not diminish.

Angela could feel the unhealthy amount of heat and power radiating around the blade so she did not hesitate to oblige her request. Yanking herself to the right she brought the rune staff, locked under her arm, around to strike at Bastiana's other side. All she managed to get was a mild grunt from the woman.

Bastiana had her natural hand braced to her side, palm out and fingers splayed. Inches away raw magic pushed against the staff, blocking her attack and distorting the air between them as if it was suddenly thick and fluid. Energy billowed away from them, kicking up wind and dirt. A grin, evil and forced, crept up on Bastiana's face. "This is going to be so much fun," the mage said.

"Where is the rest of you," Angela taunted, referring to Bastiana's new arm. She knew from past confrontations that the more unstable Bastiana was the better the chances that she would make a mistake. Of course, it also meant that at any moment she could totally lose control of her powers.

Angela would much rather take her chances with chaos, over whatever represented a level headed Bastiana.

"This is your gift to me," Bastiana said, forcing Angela almost over as she brought her rune wrapped magical arm holding the war blade down to her side. "It's so much better like this." Bastiana kicked forward, her heeled boot caught Angela just above her waist.

Magic from Bastiana's kick exploded, sending Angela flying back while her breath was pushed out of her with a groan. Angela landed hard on her back, her head smacking against the packed ground. Tiny flashes of light filled her vision, but she managed to keep ahold of both her weapons. As fast as the pain had hit her, it was gone. A rune on the staff burned brightly then faded to a dull black. Sounds came rushing in at her from every direction. She could hear the burning of fires and even the bits of debris falling to the ground in the distance from the airship Bastiana had destroyed upon her arrival.

The staff heals, she remembered. Her ears were fixed. It was almost disorienting processing the amount of sound that she had been missing. Angela was instantly on her feet, launching another attack. Bastiana was quick. Her hand shot up pointing in her direction. Angela barely managed to bring the rune staff and sword up in front of her to block the bar of magical energy that struck out at her.

It was as before when they had fought in the bottom of the Hyperion Tower. The blade and Imaera armor resisted the magic, but this time the rune staff stood in for the binding runes. The magic might have been neutralized, but the raw kinetic force of it wasn't. Angela dug her heels into the ground to keep from being forced back. She dropped forward rolling under the magic while bringing the blade up with her.

Bastiana made her pay for the attack in blood, swatting away the war blade with her magical arm while with the same move, landing a backhand across her cheekbone that split flesh and crunched bone. Angela cried out as the blow also burned the side of her face. Again the staff quickly repaired the damage, and Angela felt like the blow had never happened.

A hand wrapped around her neck hauling her to her feet. Bastiana looked at the rune that now marked Angela's face. "There isn't going to be a pretty piece of skin left on you by the time I am finished."

Angela brought her sword up, spinning it in an attempt to sever the hand at her neck from the arm it was attached to. Bastiana simply turned, letting go to deflect the sword with her magical arm. Angela jumped and spun the instant she was released, throwing a kick that landed solidly across Bastiana's chest, staggering her backwards. She didn't let up against the dark-skinned mage, bringing the rune staff down and around. Exploding energy echoed each time she slammed the staff into Bastiana. She had to give the mage some minor respect as she caught the blows with her magical arm.

Angela battered away at Bastiana, driving the mage back, step by step. Laughter confused her, and her next blow swung through empty air. By reflex alone, Angela dropped to one knee and rolled to the side, bringing her war blade up at an angle behind her as a twisting ball of energy barely missed her. She knew she had struck home when she felt the familiar resistance on her blade as it stabbed into someone.

Bastiana teleported away from Angela's assault to reappear behind her with magic blazing, but Angela wasn't there as she felt the stab of pain penetrate her hip. Her stomach clenched and fluttered. She didn't know how she should feel. The pain was sharp, but at the same time it made her entire skin crawl. Grabbing the blade with her magical arm she forced the blade back. She knew that it was bad to be stabbed like that, but she couldn't ignore how much she liked it. Her magical arm was as strong as she wanted it to be by the amount of power she gave it. As the blade slipped free from her body the sensation almost overwhelmed her.

"Oh, you never disappoint do you?" she gasped, stepping back from her angel of death, war and now pleasure. She touched the wound and found that it hardly even bled, but it was exquisitely distracting each time she took a step.

The ground erupted around them as one of the smaller airships passed overhead with its repeater guns firing, seeking revenge for the destroyed airship. She ignored the pest as it made its run. Her breath stopped however, and all of the pleasure she had built up quickly turned to anger. She saw Angela covering up crying out as the rain of bullets cut right across her.

"I said no!" she screamed as every part of her body shook. In the blink of an eye she teleported into the sky as the airship that had dared to interfere was coming straight at her. The look of shock on the man's face when he saw her was all the inspiration she needed for his death. Swinging her hand out in front of her, she snapped her fingers. It was a cruel perversion of something she had seen the Guardian do in the past. She teleported the airship away, where it went, she wasn't concerned with, its pilot on the other hand she watched flail, screaming past her as he started to plunge to the earth. She watched as it took several seconds for him to finally hit the ground. It was disappointing in the end. She expected something more than a single broken bounce from the man.

A second snap of her fingers brought the airship back letting it slam into the ground on top of the man's body exploding with a much more satisfying fireball.

"Flying is my domain," an angry voice called out.

Bastiana got her magical arm up just in time to catch the razor edge of the war blade. Angela kept coming as the both of them were pushed higher into the sky.

SILVERTON

"This changes things," Treylane said to himself after seeing the arrival of the mage from Cahir. The destruction of the airship had created a pause in the fighting as both sides tried to figure out whose side she was on. It seemed Courduff clearly viewed her as an enemy.

He wasn't going to get a much better chance than this to move out of the city. He had tracked down Duncan Deline's location and decided to make his way in that direction. Randal Wood had failed to produce other high value targets, but the display of magic should bring them out like moths to a flame. "Who knows, I might just end up doing the world a favor," he said, as he eyed the mage and the Keratin flying in the sky.

SKY ABOVE SILVERTON

Angela hoped Bastiana was using up a sizeable amount of her power to keep herself in the air, but by the laughter and fun the mage seemed to be having, it was probably not an accurate assessment. Angela felt her head spin as Bastiana struck out. She let her body twist, bringing the rune staff around with her in a clearing arch. Predictably Bastiana tried to duck under the attack as Angela kicked upwards, bringing her boot toe up under the mage's chin with an extremely satisfying crunch of teeth on teeth.

The mage's concentration clearly faltered as she started to fall from the sky. A blink of magic, and she was gone. Angela grunted as Bastiana fell on top of her while both of them tumbled out of the sky. Angela called out in pain as Bastiana began to crush her wrist with that magical arm of hers. Her skin beneath the mage's hand began to bulge and blister, turning from red to a disturbing dark purple color. Light flared from the other side of her as the rune staff's magic tried to counter the attack. "No," Angela pleaded as her hand holding onto the war blade curled open against her will, causing the blade to come free and fall away.

Angela kicked and thrashed around with the only weapon she had left, the glowing rune staff. She caught a lucky hit and broke free from Bastiana. Twisting around the ground was rushing up at her as she poured all of her will into her flying ability to avoid slamming into the ground. She didn't make it but managed to angle the impact so that she tumbled along the ground, kicking up a trail of dust and dirt behind her before sliding to an aching stop.

"Fly!" Bastiana yelled, grabbing her by the back of her leather vest she jerked her off of the ground to send her back through the air again. She landed hard on her back. The world spun, and she had trouble shaking it off this time. She managed to sit up but instantly felt sick to her stomach. Bastiana was stalking towards her.

Angela brought the rune staff up in front of her in a weak defense. Her hand that Bastiana had tried to burn off was dark and completely covered with overlapping bloody tattoos. Seeing her own blood caused her to forget about the mage for a moment as she noticed for the first time all of the cuts and scrapes she had from the fall. The staff had not protected her this time. All of the silvery runes that were etched onto the staff were now dark. She could tell by its feel that it had protected her for the final time.

"You broke it, didn't you?" Bastiana accused her, seeing the depleted staff. "Now I break you."

Angela didn't have time to brace herself against the magically reinforced kick. Only the hide of the resistant Imaera saved her from a killing blow. She didn't know how many times she rolled across the ground, but each bounce, each impact delivered a blow to her like an angry mob armed with clubs.

When she came to rest, it hurt to breathe as sharp pains on her left side told her of other broken parts on the inside. One thing that wasn't broken was Bastiana. She could hear the mage's laughter grow louder with each step she took towards her.

Chapter 36

LOTUS, SKIES ABOVE SILVERTON

"I am going to have words with our *allies* in Cahir." Admiral Bailon clenched his fists in frustration as the wreckage of the *Interceptor* littered the battlefield. "A temper tantrum isn't going to be an acceptable excuse. Vincent is going to answer for each and every victim."

Cid frowned as well. "This does complicate our battle plans."

Trying not to let his anger influence his voice any further, Bailon slowly turned his head towards Cid. "Indeed. However we may be able to use her to our advantage."

"If you have an idea of how to direct Bastiana at the Silverton forces, I am curious," Cid said, returning his focus to the ongoing battle.

Bailon watched as magic started to flash around on the ground near where Bastiana had appeared. "I believe that certain elements; certain people for example are abnormally influential compared to their equal counterparts. For example, Kail Falconcrest and his wife, Angela," he said, eyeing Cid from the corner of his eye. "I would favor either one of them in combat over any of our best troops, even a unit of troops with air support. I would still favor them even if she couldn't fly or his magical powers were removed."

"Perhaps, but I would not favor them that greatly with that handicap," Cid said as a frown appeared on his face.

"As long as Bastiana is here, Angela is effectively removed from the equation all together. Eventually one of them will prevail and either way, we come out ahead."

Cid cocked his head. "That's assuming Bastiana doesn't decide just for the fun of it to destroy more of our ships."

"True and I don't intend to give her that reason. There is another potential benefit for us as well," Bailon said, leaving the sentence hanging for Cid to draw his own conclusion.

A few moments passed before Cid said. "Kail, if he arrives then there is an element," Cid quoted him, "she would counter his influence."

"Just because we might not be able to directly control her, does not mean we cannot use her presence here to our advantage. Sometimes the only way to fight a fire is with more fire."

"I would prefer not to have to fight fire at all, sir. Least of all with kerosene." Cid replied changing the metaphor.

"Order all of our forces to keep their distance, and call for a local retreat if they find themselves in her vicinity." Bailon raised one eyebrow then shook his head as one of the *CP's* airships vanished after retaliating against the mage.

"Aye sir." Cid turned away to relay his order to the rest of the fleet.

An explosion seemed to erupt from the ground for no reason, but the dark fireball suggested that a sizeable amount of fuel was involved.

"Admiral," Cid called to him with a concerned tone.

"What have you got?"

Cid didn't answer, but instead hurried to the starboard side of the bridge to scan the horizon with a pair of binoculars. "There." He pointed, holding out the binoculars. "A new airship."

Bailon looked to where Cid had pointed. An airship was indeed headed in their direction. He didn't need Cid to tell him whom the airship belonged to. He was able to recognize the design.

"It's the east sir. They have joined the battle."

YUNUAN AIRSHIP

"Your city doesn't look so good mage." Commander Bei said, observing the destruction.

Kail couldn't help from frowning, but he held his tongue. The city that he had called home for the last five years was burning. The temporary alliance he had forged with the Commander from Yunuan was exactly that. They had made it abundantly clear that it only existed while it suited his interests. Helping him defend Silverton was low on that list. Commander Bei hadn't come out and said it, but this was more of a heavily armed reconnaissance mission for them, one that if an advantage or opportunity presented itself they might act upon it.

"I don't see any Silverton forces either. I hope you don't expect us to commit lives and resources for a lost city."

Kail surveyed the airships. Commander Bei was correct. There seemed to be little to no defense for Silverton. He recognized the *Odyssey,* and the sight of it brought a slight smile to his lips. A second ship also danced in the sky with the Mastersons. He didn't recognize it so he assumed it was the project they were working on in the Scablands Gearworks. "They fight," he said, pointing to the two ships. "I hope you see what you need to. Therion and his allies won't stop with us."

Bei shrugged. "Perhaps they will."

Kail closed his eyes. "I don't understand. You have come this far. Why are you resisting now?"

"There is no army, no airships here." Bei pointed out. "You have already lost, and we shall not lose with you."

"Leaving was a mistake," Kail said. "If I had stayed, this wouldn't be happening."

"Perhaps," Bei said dryly, "Instead of your city burning it would have been the enemy ships."

"You use the same words a lot, but at the same time you don't say much at all do you?"

"Perhaps. It might be that it is not my words you need to listen to."

"You sound a lot like Mr. Eleazar," Kail said, growing tired of the circle talk of the eastern commander.

"Your people are fighting for their lives and dying. You left to ask for our aid when you could have defeated your enemies on your own. Tell me mage, why *are* you still standing here?"

It was a good question, one he was asking himself over and over. Ice ran through his veins when realization hit. Commander Bei was not here to assess Courduff's forces. He was here to watch him and observe what he was going to do. That didn't matter now. Angela and the Masterson's were out there. He had promised Angela that he would be here, and breaking his promise wasn't something he was ever going to do to her again. "I made a promise," Kail said softly. Turning to face the commander he said, "Now I put my own faith to the test. I did what I felt was the right thing to do, and you're right; I came to you for help. Now I am going to save my home, but I will be watching what you do as well Commander Bei."

Kail pulled his magic to him as he teleported to the *Odyssey*.

ODYSSEY

"Bring us around, I want to get a look at the new ship," Rhonin ordered.

Brom called out acknowledging the order, bringing the *Odyssey* up and around to bring the new arrival to the battle in front of them.

"Who are they?" Rhonin asked Rayne.

Rayne looked back over her shoulder at him. "I don't know for sure, but it's not Courduff or anyone I have seen before." She cried out in surprise as Kail appeared on the bridge. "Kail!"

Rhonin spun out of his captain's chair. "Kail. Where in the hell have you been?"

Kail didn't answer his question right away but instead walked to the front of the bridge next to Rayne. "That is a ship from Yunuan." Kail nodded at the airship that held position away from the battle. He turned back to face the center of the bridge. "How are we holding out?"

"The east? Why would they be here?" Rhonin asked. "And we're not doing well at all. The *Sky Hawk* and *Renegade* are down. We're all that's left, and the *Snow Break*," he added, meeting Rayne's eyes.

Kail looked out the view port at the *Snow Break*. "Camden?"

Rhonin shook his head. "Conrad Black is over there," he said, not exactly lying. "Ellenore's father. She piloted the original years ago. Remember?"

"Another family torn apart," Kail said, turning away from the view of the *Snow Break*.

"You had nothing to do with Conrad being forced to work in the clockwork factories or Ellenore's death," Rayne said. "Stop this Kail. Put an end to it right now, and we can take the fight to where it really belongs."

"And where would that be? Cahir, Courduff?" Kail asked.

Rhonin had enough and stomped towards Kail. "You need to snap out of it boy," he said, landing a right hook that sent Kail to the deck. "This isn't some stupid moral debate." Rhonin reached down and hauled Kail to his feet. "You need to get yourself together." He pressed Kail's face against the viewport overlooking the burning city.

"Stop it Rhonin," Rayne cried out.

"That right there Kail. That is the darkness everyone fears, and you are going to just let it happen." Rhonin released him.

"I won't kill them all," Kail said, rubbing his jaw.

"You don't have to," Rhonin shouted. "But you have to do something. Many have already died. There is an entire prophecy wrapped around you, and you're acting like a child."

"I didn't ask for this!" Kail shouted back shoving Rhonin away from him. "I didn't ask to have my family killed, my children slaughtered and stolen. Everyone I know is scattered or dead. To hell with prophecy!"

Rhonin felt a twinge of guilt. Months of keeping everything bottled up inside it seemed had finally caught up with Kail. They couldn't afford for him to fall apart now. Rayne had a pleading look in her eyes, and he knew she wanted to tell him about Alyssa on the *Snow Break*. But the girl had specifically asked them not to reveal her presence until the battle was finished. "Just stop this fight then. Save what remains of Silverton before it's too late."

"Before it's too late," Kail repeated, "too late."

The change in Kail's voice when he repeated the words a second time set off alarms inside of Rhonin's head. He looked to see if Rayne had caught it. She didn't appear to have and still looked torn about whether or not to tell him about his daughter. "What are you doing?"

Kail rubbed his eyes then covered his mouth. "I'm going to do something about it."

"Wait," Rhonin called, reaching out for Kail, but it was too late. He was already gone.

Chapter 37

OUTSIDE SILVERTON

"Mance, Pakmon. Cover the east," Duncan ordered, pointing his hand towards their exposed flank. He waved Stanz and Daly to the other side as well. Duncan began giving orders and assignments to others under his command. He was trying his best to keep together what little control he had left. Pakmon and Mance opened fire. It flushed out a couple of soldiers from Courduff that should have been easily taken down. However one of them managed to scramble away, and suddenly there was an armored tractor headed their way.

"Cover me," Duncan yelled. He knew that the tractor would rout them. Their only chance was to rush the vehicle before it had a chance to unleash its cannons and repeater gun on them. No one heard. He yelled again putting more force into it. "Damn it, cover me." He gestured towards the incoming tractor as he sprinted towards it.

Enemy fire started to zing past him bouncing off the ground in front of him, but that didn't scare him as much as the cannons on the tractor did. It was a whole new sensation to look down the twin barrels. Problem with cannons, they didn't have to hit him, just hitting near him would kill him.

Someone apparently had heard him. He saw the soldier manning the repeater gun fall off to the side after being shot. The danger lessened by only a hair. Something hard rebounded from his helmet with a dizzying clank forcing the air from his lungs. He didn't remember falling, but Private Mance was there pulling him up to his feet.

"Are you crazy?" Mance yelled.

Duncan shook him off. "Just be ready to fire." The tractor tried to pivot to get a second shot at them, but Duncan made it to the door first, yanking it open.

Mance didn't hesitate to fire his rifle into the cabin of the tractor.

"Turn it." Duncan ordered Mance as he jumped onto the back, pivoting the repeater gun back in the direction of the enemy. The tractor jerked, causing him to lose balance, almost falling back onto the ground as Private Mance got the tractor moving. The gun shook his whole body as he fired round after round through the rank of the Courduff soldiers.

Mance cried out when the tractor took a hit from above. His head appeared out of the door complaining, "What the hell was that?" he asked, pointing.

Punctured through the armored plating of the tractor was a blade; a blade covered in runes.

Duncan scanned the skies, "There." He pointed.

Angela had someone covered in blue fire on her back as she fought a losing battle. As they fell from the skies,

Duncan yanked the blade from the tractor roof, "We have to go," he shouted. "Get this thing moving and follow her."

Treylane figured he might not have to kill Duncan Deline. The man must have his own death wish to be charging a weaponized vehicle. The fight in the sky between the Keratin and mage was coming to an end. He saw Duncan making his way to where the Keratin had fallen. Three targets: the Keratin, Duncan and Bastiana all grouping up together.

This is it, Angela thought. Her sword was out of reach. The rune staff was reduced to a depleted stick. She barely had the energy to scramble away on her back. Pain caused by bones grinding against each other in ways never meant to be, threatened to push her into unconsciousness.

Bastiana threw back her head and reveled. "You've never been better than me," she taunted. "How does it feel to have your wings clipped little duckling?" Bastiana literally glowed with pleasure.

Angela was not going to spend any energy with an answer. The photo of Alyssa and Amaya lay on the ground in front of her just past her reach, and the wind threatened to steal it away. Unable to crawl she rolled onto her side dragging herself towards the tattered photo and to her daughters.

She could hear Bastiana's footsteps coming up behind her. "Crawling away are we? Going to find some rock to crawl under and die?"

Angela cried out when Bastiana kicked her, forcing her over onto her back.

"I want you looking at me when you die. My face will be the last one you see."

Angela fell back against the ground and took a small bit of solace in what would be her final breaths. She could see the wind take the smiling faces of her daughters as blue shards of sky peaked though the smoke filled air. Oddly she wondered if there were tiny tattoos on the inside of her ears. That first blow from Bastiana that the rune staff had protected her from also restored her hearing that had been damaged from the previous day. She could clearly make out the sound of Bastiana's heels crunching on the hard ground. *Hard ground.* If she was going to die, she at least wanted to be comfortable, but something on the ground beneath her dug into her back. Wincing she managed to get her hand underneath her and around the offending object.

"Any last words I should tell Kail? Something meaningful that I can deliver when I present your corpse?" Bastiana asked, basking in her victory.

"No," Angela said, pulling her hand out from under her. She had immediately recognized the object when her hand wrapped around the hilt of a pistol. She pulled the trigger, and the gun went off once then again. Then another shot, and again before clicking empty. Four growing stains appeared on Bastiana's chest.

"You, you shot me," Bastiana said in disbelief, looking down at the wounds in confusion. Her arm made of magic flickered then dimmed. "You cheated," the mage said, dropping to her knees. "I can't believe you cheated," were her last words before slumping over.

Angela fell back to the ground as tears welled up in her eyes. Bastiana was dead. She could not keep the tears from coming. "Help," she cried softly. "Help me. Please Help." Wiping away the tears with the back of her hand made her eyes sting. She could see the dirt, blood and now tears smeared on her shaking hands. She had cheated death once again. Every emotion seemed to crush down on her making it hurt to breathe. "Where are you Kail?"

Chapter 38

CREATOR PATRON, SKIES ABOVE SILVERTON

"Move all ships away from the city," Captain Blake Aaron ordered. "Have wings one, two and three return for refueling and arming. Position the fourth wing between us and the eastern ship."

"Aye sir."

Captain Aaron clasped his hands behind his back and watched the small airships maneuver as they received his orders. The Silverton defenders had proven to be an ineffective test of the new airship's designs. They had simply circled their city while they let it be shelled and burned, their captains content to be shot from the sky like overfed geese. The *Odyssey* and the other remaining ship reminded him of soap bubbles circling a drain. It was only a matter of time before they were gone as well. "Man the defensive batteries too. I don't expect them to be needed, but rate the men according to live fire drills," he ordered a sub commander.

The man saluted. "Yes sir."

Aaron started his own assessment of the bridge crew. If he found any shortcomings in anyone he made a mental note to see it resolved before the next campaign. He was not going to tolerate failure, not during his command, especially when it could cost over a thousand lives. He didn't even try to calculate what the cost and time to replace the *CP* and its ships would be.

Frowning at an anomaly on his bridge Captain Aaron called out. "You there, pilot. Identify yourself and your commanding officer," he demanded, finding a man in dark leathers looking over his bridge. He wasn't against crew seeing the bridge, in fact he encouraged everyone to familiarize themselves with every inch of the *CP*, but doing so now during an active combat mission was completely against protocol.

"How long does it take a ship like this to land?" the man asked, ignoring his question.

"Who are you? Security, restrain that pilot, and get him off my bridge." That got the man's attention.

"I don't have time for this," the man said, eyeing the two security officers moving towards him. He raised his hand and a flash of magic slammed into each man, sending them to the floor.

Captain Aaron took a couple of steps backwards as the man approached. He made a mental note that even with the intruder and an obvious magical attack, his bridge crew hadn't panicked. "Who are you?" he asked again.

"Kail Falconcrest. And that is my city you are destroying. How long to put this ship on the ground?"

Aaron reacted by drawing his sidearm, but with a wave of Kail's hand it was sent clattering across the bridge.

Aaron held his head high preparing for the worst. "You will get no satisfaction from me terrorist."

Kail closed his eyes as several large runic symbols glowed on the deck floor of the bridge. A low groan and shudder came from deep within the ship.

"What are you doing?" Aaron demanded, helpless to stop Kail.

The runes on the floor solidified changing color before Kail opened his eyes to answer. "You have fifteen minutes, maybe more. I weakened the structural integrity of this ship, and it will continue to grow weaker until it falls apart." A loud ping rang through the bridge as a rivet lost its hold. "It's up to you if it falls apart in the sky or on the ground."

Aaron frowned as he began to feel the subtle changes in the ship through the sounds and vibrations. Kail Falconcrest teleported himself away, leaving him to deal with the dying ship.

"Launch everything. Every airship, every support craft. I want the ship evacuated now!" he barked. "Get me the Admiral." He made his way to the radio before turning back to face the bridge, seeing his crew awaiting his next order. "Abandon ship people. That's an order."

SNOW BREAK

"Something has changed," Alyssa said. The movement of the smaller ships made sense now that the

Yunuan ship had arrived, but the Juggernaut carrier ship was in trouble. "Rhonin, ready to take the fight to them?" she called into the radio.

"Lead the way *Snow Break*," came the reply.

"Ready the guns Mr. Black." Alyssa shoved the *Snow Break's* throttle forward bringing the Courduff fleet into view in front of them.

"Do you see that?" Rhonin's asked over the radio.

If she had to guess, it looked like the carrier ship was disintegrating. Parts were shedding off the bottom and falling to the ground. The support and evacuation ships were launching as fast as they could. The crane system used to help the attack ships had been abandoned. Some of the planes were even trying to launch off the side of the ship without getting proper airspeed. One pushed another to the side catching its engines on the wing of an abandoned ship causing all three to explode covering the deck of the *CP* in flames.

"We'll draw the fire *Odyssey*, why don't you help it out of the sky?"

"Copy that," Rhonin said, clicking off the radio.

Conrad looked over his shoulder. "Draw their fire? That's your plan?"

"Do you doubt your construction skills or this ship?" Alyssa asked, keeping an eye on all the airships to find a route through the enemy fleet.

"No, no, I just have an understanding of physics is all, including basic math concepts like survival odds."

"Or is it my piloting skills?" Alyssa continued, banking the *Snow Break* hard to port and pulling back on the controls. "Fire."

Conrad kept one eye on the weapons controls and the other on where Alyssa was taking the ship. The repeater guns across the ship came to life, spraying bullets into the sky keeping the smaller attack planes at bay. The main cannons fired in turn, punching holes into the side of the *CP* as well as the *Morning Star* that was trying to provide cover.

Flames erupted behind them as a secondary explosion billowed up from the hull of the *CP*, washing over the *Odyssey* as it followed Alyssa's attack run.

Conrad called out in surprise when Alyssa pushed the *Snow Break* into a dive, barely missing a collision with another airship that had appeared from behind the massive carrier ship. The *Snow Break* bucked sending Conrad to the floor.

Alyssa bit back a curse as the ship still clipped them. "How did that happen?" she called out, trying to stabilize the ship. "I missed that ship."

"You alright over there?" Rhonin's voice crackled over the speaker.

"What happened?" Alyssa asked, bringing the *Snow Break* back over gaining altitude.

"Our friend decided to join the battle instead of watching," Rhonin explained. "They destroyed that ship just as you dove under it, and it caught you."

Alyssa looked to make sure Conrad was on his feet. "I'm billing them when we decide to paint this ship."

Conrad just nodded, returning to the weapons controls. "Everything looks good here," he said.

"Got it *Odyssey*. Keep your eyes out for them," she said, clicking off the radio. "Just don't die for them," she added under her breath. The east had always had its own agenda. In the future before she and Mr. Eleazar came back, they had played on every side of the war supplying arms and mercenaries one moment, then devoting official military resources in the same battle for the other side, all while providing humanitarian aid to anyone who needed it. The most un-neutral of neutrals as her grandfather Duke had put it.

LOTUS

Cid kept silent as the *CP* fell apart below them, and the *Morning Star* was destroyed by the Yunuan airship. He kept one eye on Admiral Bailon, looking for any signs of what he might be thinking. Being able to anticipate Bailon's line of thinking was a skill he had honed over the years, but now, he was at a loss as to what might be going through the Admiral's mind.

"Sir, I have Captain Blake Aaron on the radio," the comms officer said.

Cid took a step towards the console but stopped when Bailon said to put it on speaker.

"We're going down Admiral. The mage did something to kill us from the inside. We're falling apart faster than those bastards can shell us."

"Bastiana, the girl from Cahir did this?" Bailon asked.

Cid looked out towards Silverton. There had been signs of magic seen on the ground, but nothing had flared recently. If she had taken her rage to the *CP*, that would explain everything.

"Negative sir. Kail Falconcrest came aboard and did this."

Cid clicked on the internal intercom system of the *Lotus* while Captain Aaron and Bailon continued to talk. "All personnel, be advised we may have intruders aboard. Repeat possible intruders aboard."

Cid turned back, missing the last part of Captain Aaron's transmission as the radio cut out. The *CP* started to break apart crashing over the battlefield. Most of the ship collapsed onto itself with only one large section catching fire where the main fuel was housed. It was an oddly anti-climatic end to the carrier ship.

"Bring us within firing range of the *CP*," Bailon ordered the helmsman, drawing a few confused looks from the bridge crew.

Cid understood at once and approached the weapons officer. "High yield incendiary rounds Lieutenant."

Bailon nodded in agreement. "The *Creator Patron* is a wealth of resources and technology that cannot be allowed to fall into enemy hands," he addressed the crew. "Understand that it was lost at the hands of a single person. A single terrorist with unnatural magical powers to use against us without consequence." Bailon stoically gave the order for the *Lotus* to fire on the remains of the *CP*. The incendiary rounds did their job, igniting and melting the metal. Even at their altitude and distance the magnesium and phosphate fire was almost too bright to look at.

OUTSIDE SILVERTON

Duncan jumped off the tractor and hit the ground running. Angela was lying on the ground in front of them. "Mance. Grab the med kit, and get over here now," he called, skidding to a halt by Angela.

"Here," Private Mance said, tossing the med kit to him.

Angela was alive, but unconscious and not responding to his attempts to waken her. Duncan upended the pack until he found the smelling salts. "Check that monster," he ordered Mance, pointing towards Bastiana lying a few yards away. "Stay with us Angela, stay with us," he said, cracking open the packet and holding it up to her face.

"She's dead sir. Four to the chest," Private Mance reported.

Angela jerked her head away and came across with a backhand, catching Duncan by surprise and sending him sprawling. Angela struggled to get away from them.

"Whoa, there," Mance said. "We're on your side."

"Stop," Duncan told Angela, wiping away the blood from his split lip. "It's us. It's okay now."

"Foolish," Angela's voice was hoarse as she quit scrambling away.

"You're hurt." Duncan grabbed the gauze and shook out some of the dirt that had gotten on it and began to wrap her arm. "This looks like a burnt log from an old camp fire. Where else are you hurt?"

"Where am I not hurt," she answered as he continued to dress her arm.

"Women are crazy. There is a reason the men do the fighting," Duncan mumbled as he worked. "Magic and flying around with swords and bows and arrows."

A wet slap covered both Duncan and Angela with fresh blood. Angela scrambled back and rolled away as Private Mance with a red hole in his chest almost fell on her.

One down, two to go. Treylane Armstrong pulled the slide bolt back on his rifle, ejecting the smoking shell casing before sliding a new bullet into the chamber and locking it down. The Keratin wasn't going anywhere so he lined up the sights on the General.

Duncan cursed, scanning for the source of the attack. Tossing Angela her war blade he said, "Stay down."

Angela pointed. "There. In the low spot."

Duncan turned and fired his rifle where Angela pointed. He found the sniper trying to sneak away after being spotted and flushed out from his hiding spot. The sniper, despite losing his advantage, fired back with a side arm forcing Duncan to stay low. He glanced back as gunfire came from behind him. Angela had picked up Private Mance's weapon and was doing her best to fire it at their attacker. He knew she hated guns, but she obviously hated dying more.

The sniper spun back to bring up his rifle. Duncan shouldered his rifle and charged, firing as he went. He could see his bullets hit near the sniper as he closed the distance, then he felt hot pain in his stomach that made him want to vomit. He knew he had been shot, and his legs tried to buckle, but he refused to let them.

Duncan's rifle pinged empty, ejecting the clip. He had hit the sniper and could see the man trying to limp away. His chest started to feel like it was filled with lead as it became hard to breathe, and his mouth tasted like metal. "Damn it," he managed to say when his legs finally gave out. He didn't remember clutching the wound, but when he withdrew his hand, his palm was covered in blood. Dark blood, not the lighter kind from cuts or a nose bleed. What made him angry wasn't the wound, but the sight of the sniper who had killed Private Mance, getting away.

Treylane spared a glance back and saw the General on his knees holding his gut. He would die, but the man had gotten off a lucky shot with that charge, hitting him in the thigh. His fleeing was stopped short by a cracking hiss and flash in front of him. Kail Falconcrest stood in his path. Treylane Armstrong didn't have time to finish the curse before Kail brought up his hand.

Duncan chuckled when he saw the sniper explode. He wondered if perhaps one of the airships had hit him with one of their cannons, but knew that wasn't quite right. There would have been a lot of noise and smoke if a shell had landed this close. He blinked a few times and as the sniper mist cleared he saw Kail standing there looking very pissed off. "That works too," he said as darkness came.

LOTUS, SKIES ABOVE SILVERTON

"Order the fleet back," Admiral Bailon said.

"Are you sure sir?" Cid dared to ask.

"If any give chase, we will destroy them. But we have accomplished what we set out to do. Silverton is in ruins, and I will not see any more of our ships lost today."

"Understood sir," Cid said, relaying the orders to the rest of the fleet.

"This battle is not over. It will take some time for the troops to be recalled," Bailon reminded him. "I think we have satisfied the conspiracy element as well," he added.

Cid nodded in agreement as Bailon pulled him to the side.

"There is more," Bailon said. "Something about what Captain Aaron said doesn't sit right. I haven't been able to pin it down, but it has to do with Kail."

"What are you thinking sir? Remember, he destroyed the *Creator Patron*."

"I don't need to be reminded of that," Bailon said a bit harshly. "I think your profile assessments are spot on. No one would have given Aaron time to evacuate his ship like that in the middle of battle. Not after we destroyed half of their air force and shelled Silverton into ash."

"I don't know sir. Who really understands the mind of a mage?"

Bailon thought for a few moments before continuing. "As soon as the fleet is ready, they will return to Courduff."

"By they, I assume you're not talking about us sir?" Cid asked.

"I want you to ready us a flight plan to Canyamar. We're going to The Eternal Gateway."

Chapter 39

OUTSIDE SILVERTON

Kail walked past Duncan. The General deserved more, but right now there was only one person he cared about in the world, and he needed her. The world needed her for him just as badly. Every cell in Kail's body screamed for him to unleash his magic and destroy the Courduff fleet in the sky. Eliminate every soldier still on the ground even as they retreated and not to stop until every last one of them was dead from here to the end of the world.

Kail's throat tightened as he knelt next to Angela, taking her hand and brushing away a stray lock of hair from her face. Kail ran his eyes over her exposed skin covered in tattoos from the rune staff. "You look like you fought a printing press and lost."

Kail felt Angela squeeze his hand. "Do not make me laugh," she said trying to suppress a smile with a wince.

"I can't help it. That's my job remember." He smiled, kissing her hand and squeezing it back. Kail looked over his shoulder towards the south. "Hang on, here comes another quake."

The earth rumbled, shaking the area around them as Kail wrapped the both of them with his magic as the disturbance from The Eternal Gateway washed past them.

"There never seems to be enough time anymore," Angela said as the ground settled down.

"I've been thinking the exact same thing," Kail said. "But I have an idea about that."

Angela reached around for her sword. "Help me up."

"Are you sure?" Kail hesitated.

"My injuries appear much worse than they actually are," she insisted. "I know what you are thinking. You want to take the gateway back from Therion, hopefully killing him and then use the gateway yourself." Angela pulled herself up onto her feet with his help, heavily favoring one leg.

"I know that tone. You don't believe it can be used that way, do you?"

Angela put some weight on her injured leg to test it but fell.

Kail caught her, scooping her into his arms. Again he was amazed at how deceptively light she was. "I've got you."

He could see her start to complain, but she held back, letting him carry her. "I think it is possible to use the gateway like that, but I do not think we can."

Kail looked at his wife's face and couldn't help but kiss her on the forehead. "Explain," he asked, hoping that her reasoning would be flawed.

"We are not its Guardian."

Kail thought about Mr. Eleazar. "Neither is Therion," he said quickly.

"And the world shakes," she countered. "I have walked through The Eternal Gateway Kail. With him, with the Time Walker, and I do not believe it is that simple. Therion fights the gateway, but eventually he will master it."

"Why can't we master it then?"

"That is not our destiny Kail," Angela answered.

"But we have to save it. You believe that, right?" he asked.

Angela nodded her head. "The fight for the gateway is not over."

The wind picked up forcing them to shield their eyes from blowing dirt as the *Odyssey* circled past them before landing on the ground. Still carrying Angela, Kail started to make his way over to the Masterson's ship when the second airship landed, followed by Commander Bei's airship from Yunuan.

"The *Snow Break*," Angela said. "They built another one."

"I know" Kail said, watching the dust settle around the new ship. "It looks unfinished and a bit strange."

"Set me down," Angela insisted. "You can help me walk."

Kail did as she asked while the boarding ramps were lowered on each ship. Rhonin and Rayne were the first off of their ship.

"Kail, Angela," Rhonin greeted them. Rayne gingerly hugged Angela. "Looks like you two have been busy."

Rhonin pointed Bei's airship as the Commander disembarked from the ship.

Kail shrugged. "Not exactly what I hoped for." No one had exited the *Snow Break* yet. "Been busy yourselves as well. I knew you had left for the gearworks, but I didn't know you were building another *Snow Break*." Kail waited for Bei to join them before introducing the eastern commander.

Rhonin glanced at Rayne and pinched his lips while keeping an eye on the commander. "We refit the *Odyssey*. Turbine engines, electronics, the works just like the original *Snow Break*. We ran out of time on building a new ship so we took what we had to come to Silverton's defense."

"Suki and Camden?" Angela asked.

Rhonin shook his head. "Afraid not. I know that's who you thought was on the ship, but we haven't heard any word from them."

Kail felt like he was missing some important information. "What do you mean it wasn't finished when you left?"

"Not even close. A month out at least," Rhonin said. "Maybe more," he finished, feeling uncomfortable that the eastern commander was hearing their secrets.

Kail focused on the *Snow Break*. "There's magic here. I can feel it." He turned to face Rhonin. "What's going on here?"

Rhonin shifted uncomfortably.   "She made us promise not to tell you."

"She?" Angela questioned.

Both Rhonin and Rayne nodded towards the *Snow Break*.

Standing at the bottom of the *Snow Break's* ramp was a young dark haired woman.

"That's her," Kail gasped, taking a step towards the girl.   Angela hopped when he moved, causing him to stop. "That's the Keratin I saw in the gateway." He pointed. "The one fighting Therion with Mr. Eleazar."

Kail felt Angela stiffen next to him.

"You know who she is?" he asked, remembering that before when he had described the woman in the gateway that neither Angela nor Mr. Eleazar had known who she was.

Angela held her hand over her mouth as the girl walked towards them.   She clearly knew who the girl was. Ignoring her injuries Angela stepped towards the girl to hug her.

"Hello mother," she said, hugging Angela then looked at Kail. "Hello father," Alyssa added with a smile.

Kail felt his stomach drop. He had never considered that the girl he had seen in the gateway might have been his daughter. None of them had. No, Mr. Eleazar had to have known, maybe. It was hard for him to think clearly. He joined them in the hug. "Can it be? My little bird how is this possible?"

Chapter 40

CANYAMAR JUNGLE

Red flashed to black then back to red again. The floor and walls were smeared with blood. Harris McAllister looked at him through hollow eyes, pleading with him to explain how it was that he was dead, but Xavier was alive.

Camden turned to run down the hall of the *Snow Break*. The red turned to black. Ellenore Black stood on the bridge holding a knife. He could see her lips moving, but no words were coming out because of the wound across her neck. He didn't need to hear what she was trying to say. It was the same as McAllister. Where was the justice? Everything flashed red as Ellenore was covered in it, bathed in it from Xavier's killing attack. Camden turned and ran.

The engine room of the *Snow Break* was loud, so loud that it hurt. Camden looked around for the protective ear muffs but instead found Pyron Redstone and Montoy DeSantos. They wouldn't help him. They just looked at him with disgust then went back to communicating with each other through hand signals. Camden tried to scream over the noise, but the two engineers refused to hear. He looked down, and in his hands was an oversized wrench. The same wrench that Xavier had used.

Camden looked up, and now he was in the infirmary. "No," he cried. On the bed was a body, covered by a cloth. Everything turned red again. The cloth was stained with it. He knew she was under the cloth. He knew he had saved her though. She shouldn't be dead. His blood stained hands reached for the cloth to pull it back. He felt his soul die. It wasn't Suki as he had expected, but Amaya instead. Her little blue eyes frozen open and dull. The light that had use to shine in them was gone. Light that he had done nothing to save.

Someone walked past the infirmary door behind him. Camden turned and called out, but the person was already gone. He caught sight of the person again turning the far corner at the end of the hall. He ran, trying to catch up. He just missed the person again as they went up a flight of stairs, ignoring his calls. He heard the door to the outer deck of the ship slam shut.

Through the viewport Camden could see someone standing outside. Now he knew who the person was he had been chasing. The man whom they had trusted. The man who had killed them all. A man whom he had seen torn to pieces in a nightmarish death. Camden threw the door open and charged with a yell.

The man turned towards him as he ran. He expected Xavier Ross to be standing there, the same way he had found him all those years ago. Therion stood there instead, looking at him then raised his hand as a blast of cold magic splashed over him.

"Wake up," Xavier said after tossing a large bowl of water on Camden.

He coughed and shook away the water as best he could.

"We've got a long walk ahead of us." Xavier paused. "Well, you don't. You're going to be dragged along for some conversation, and you can't do that sleeping."

"You're dead," Camden spat.

"I know," Xavier said sarcastically. "You guys tried really hard and almost succeeded too."

"Come closer, and I'll correct that." Camden eyed Xavier as the burned man packed up part of the camp.

"Come closer, and I'll correct that," Xavier repeated, mocking him. Xavier balled his fists and threw a few practice punches. "Come on big boy bring it on. Hop up on those feet, and do something about it." Xavier kicked him in his legs. Camden could only feel the bump through his body. "What's that?" Xavier asked, holding his hand up to his ear. "You're a cripple. Well how rude of me."

Camden seethed. Xavier was more insane than he ever imagined. The old Xavier that he had known had never said half as many words that he could remember. Death must have given him a new personality.

"But after killing children, it takes something pretty special to top that again." Xavier stopped his mocking and sighed. "You really are as dull as the reports about you were to read."

Walking away, Xavier had a couple of the men with him make sure that Camden was securely bound and loaded onto a makeshift stretcher that was tied to the back of one of their pack horses.

"How are your friends these days?" Xavier asked as the group headed out. "I've been wondering quite a bit about them. I meant to send them a card or something, but wasn't sure if it was appropriate or not. Tell me. Would you have wanted to have been told about your child's death?"

"I wouldn't know," Camden said, trying to come up with any sort of plan that would end with his hands around Xavier's throat.

"How did you survive that night?" Xavier's voice turned serious. "I destroyed your ship. There were no survivors found."

Camden remembered the *Snow Break* being destroyed in the night darkness. It died, exploding fire down onto the edges of Courduff. He glared at Xavier. "How did you survive?"

"That was you then." Xavier said, ignoring his question as he pieced it together. "I didn't think much of it at the time, but after my little run in with that Falconcrest brat I wanted to make sure both of them died, but one went missing anyway."

Camden tried to remember that night they had rescued Alyssa. Suki had been trying to tell him something when he ran after Xavier. "That man took them," he said.

"The Guardian?" Xavier asked. "That much I had figured."

Camden nodded, remembering Mr. Eleazar showing up that night. "Someone else too."

Xavier closed his eyes for a moment remembering. "I think I know who. Very clever my old friend." Xavier changed the subject and lit himself a cigarette. "You never answered me yesterday. I'm curious to what would drive a man to abandon everything to chase me down?" Xavier's mocking tone returned. "I mean, there is the obvious. I am the bad guy."

"Isn't that enough?"

"For a Falconcrest it might be," Xavier admitted bitterly, exhaling the smoke. "It's written into their blood I think, but I know men like you Captain Arland. A noble cause is never going to be your motivation."

Camden refused to answer. He wasn't going to entertain Xavier.

"The silent treatment isn't advised. Your life span is directly related to your cooperation." Xavier smacked him and watched his reaction. "Oh please, don't tell me you're in this for love. Nothing ruins a man like a woman."

"You killed them."

"How unoriginally boring," Xavier said, rolling his eyes taking another drag from the cigarette. "At least they died."

Camden struggled against his bonds to no avail.

"You found the body. Didn't you?"

Camden cursed at Xavier. "I will kill you, I swear it."

"No you won't. I was going to kill you, but now I think I will let you live. That way you can go on living as a burden to those around you. A reminder to them of your failure." Xavier flicked the spent cigarette at him. It landed on his chest in a fold of his coat and smoldered. "Now that would be ironic," Xavier said, holding up his scarred hand. "Burned alive."

Suki kept her distance from Xavier and the group that had Camden. It had taken the wisp most of the morning to convince her not to flee the jungle never to return. Luckily they were making quite a bit of noise that allowed her to follow them without having to keep them in sight.

The wisp made a mournful sound.

"I know," Suki said. "I want to rescue him too. But there are too many of them."

The wisp flexed its little arms.

"I'm trying to be strong." Suki tried not to laugh when the wisp thumped its chest. Hiding behind the laugh were tears and enough self doubt that it took all of her willpower not to cripple her. "But I'm not Angela."

The wisp stopped its antics and looked like it was thinking hard about something.

"What?"

The wisp shook its head ignoring the question and took flight, heading after Camden and Xavier.

Suki scolded herself then reminded herself that she had been clinging to the wisp's company. It wouldn't do her any good by chasing it away or having it go off on its own and getting hurt or worse. She took a deep breath, pulling herself together to follow.

Chapter 41

SILVERTON

"I'll try my best to answer your questions, but there are many things that I don't have answers for." Alyssa looked at the faces of her parents and that of the Mastersons.

"What happened?" Kail asked. "What happened that night in Courduff?"

Taking a deep breath, Alyssa sat down next to Angela and set the rune staff on the table in the *Snow Break's* galley. Commander Bei had apparently seen all that he needed to and decided to return to Yunuan and report on what he had witnessed. She counted the number of the burned out runes that had returned to their silvery glow. "I'm actually really good with Enchantment," she said still thinking of the best way to answer her father's question. "When Bastiana died, the magic the staff had transferred to her to protect and heal her wounds returned to its original source," she said, patting the rune staff.

"All magic is like that," Kail said.

Alyssa nodded as she looked at the multitude of runic tattoos that covered her mother. "I can strip these, and the magic will return to the staff."

"But," Angela said, staring at her.

Alyssa nodded. "But, the wound will return. And it will return as if it had just been inflicted."

Kail frowned and looked at his wife.

"The ones you received today shouldn't be much of a problem, except for these here and here," Alyssa said, touching the hand that Bastiana had tried to incinerate and then the line of circular runes where she had been shot by one of the planes. "If Aunt Suki were here we could try. Her Necromancy, I mean healing, is far better than what I am capable of. The old one here." Alyssa indicated to the large tattoo on Angela's stomach from an earlier fight that Bastiana had inflicted in the Canyons of Cahir. "I'm afraid that one would be even beyond her ability," she finished.

Angela squeezed her hand. "Do it."

Alyssa nodded and tried to smile.

"I know it will hurt," Angela said, looking at Kail.

"Is there anything I can do to help?" Kail asked.

Alyssa shook her head. "No. Just listen and ask questions."

Kail nodded.

Alyssa started with the runes on her mother's face. She coaxed a small one to release its hold and return to the staff leaving a raw cut. "They came in the night. I don't remember how many of them there were, but I remember seeing the farm house burn." Alyssa softly rubbed her thumb across the wound as it slowly faded away. "After that we were taken to town and then onto the train to Courduff." She moved to another rune.

"How long until Camden and Suki arrived?" Kail asked.

Alyssa shook her head. "Days. Weeks. Months. I don't know, but it seemed like forever." She glanced at her father's face to judge his emotions. "Amaya was so strong and brave." She healed another revealed wound and took a deep breath. "She never cried, or even seemed scared. She knew."

Kail frowned and swallowed hard. "She knew? Explain."

Angela gave him a hard look.

"She said that it was time. She said that everything was going to be ok. That Uncle Camden was going to save us." Alyssa refused to look in her parents' eyes as she remembered and tried to focus on the runic tattoos. "She said these words every night." She paused. "Every night starting about a week before they took us."

It was Angela's turn to pull away. "Amaya knew you were going to be kidnapped?"

"Divination?" Kail asked.

Alyssa shrugged. "Probably, but I don't think it was just that. She *knew*." Alyssa looked at the Mastersons who could only hold her gaze for a moment before shifting uncomfortably.

"Suki said something similar about you," Kail mentioned.

Alyssa nodded. "After they took Amaya. Camden and Suki found me. She told me that she had to go and that she had to go back and save Uncle Camden. And that I had to go back too."

"To save Camden?" Angela asked.

"No, to save everyone else," Alyssa said. "Grandpa was waiting for me and," she held back before continuing. "And we went through The Eternal Gateway."

"Grandpa," Kail said. "Duke Falconcrest?"

Alyssa nodded. "Your father. He and Mr. Eleazar took care of me and taught me about magic and fighting." Alyssa removed the last of the runic tattoos from her mother's face and started on her arms.

She could tell that her father had a million follow up questions.

"I saw you. Twice through the gateway." Kail said. "Can you explain that?"

"No," Alyssa yelled, startling them. "I'm sorry," she reassured them. "There are rules."

Kail held up his hands confused.

"Like the swords," Angela said, understanding some of the problems with time travel. "There are three of them now."

Alyssa looked at her mother. "Kind of. There are still only two of them. This one is the same as the one you have." She pulled out the blade. "The other, I picked up in the canyon where you dropped it."

"When did you pick it up?" Angela asked.

Alyssa hesitated. "Not too long after you dropped it."

"You've been here for the better part of a year?" Kail burst out.

Alyssa nodded.

"Why didn't you say something? Why didn't you let us know you were alive and okay?" Kail demanded.

Rhonin stepped in. "Just let her explain Kail. Your questions will be answered."

Kail glared at Rhonin. "How much of this did you know about? Don't pretend that I don't know about you and Mr. Eleazar."

Rhonin shook his head, refusing to answer then nodded back to Alyssa.

"Kail. Let her continue, please," Angela said.

"It creates problems if you know too much about the future. Paradoxes, time eddies and loops get created. For example, let's say that you wanted to rescue Mom with Uncle Camden like you did years ago before I was born, but I travel back to tell you that you die or Camden gets killed, so you don't do it. Mom doesn't get rescued, and I don't get born," Alyssa said.

"But you were born," Kail said.

"I would be a paradox," Alyssa agreed. "It's dangerous, but only really becomes a factor if you go back in time. Going forward is not the same, because you simply are not part of the timeline during the gap."

"Is that why the Time Walker chose me?" Angela asked. "I only went forward, and I would have died in the past if not for him. So my mark on history was already finished."

Alyssa nodded. "You were what we classify as 'safe'. Your normal path through time was complete and had ended. You could be placed anywhere in time after that event and not cause a problem."

"But I have killed many people since arriving here. I have married, given birth, how does that not change the future?" Angela looked at her, trying to understand.

"It's not the same. It's relative to your point of view. That is how the people you killed died anyway," Alyssa said. "I don't want to get too deep into it. But the worst event is if you create a loop. You go back to do something, and then that is the cause of the reason you go back. You can become trapped in a segment of time reliving the same events over and over."

"But you could always just not go back the next time, right?" Kail asked.

Alyssa shook her head. "You will just have to trust me on this, but Mr. Eleazar explained how time is like a river. It flows and at best all we can do is guide it."

Everyone nodded. They all had heard Mr. Eleazar explain it that way.

Alyssa slid one of the war blades on the table in front of her. "Imagine this blade is time, and we move from one end to the other. This rune here could represent a war. Some of us will flow through that spot. Others will not and never know or be effected by the war." She put one finger of each hand on the blade. "Now, what happens if you continue on." She held up one finger. "And I go back?" She used her other finger to slide back on the blade.

"You meet us when we are younger, and you are older," Kail said. "That's what is going on right now."

Alyssa nodded. "You're right, but you are also very very wrong. You are up here in the timeline remember." She indicated with her finger that represented them. "Not back here. You have passed this."

"That doesn't make any sense," Kail said.

"Then who is back here with you?" Angela asked.

"You are, but not the same you that I left back here. And I don't have time to explain, but it's also possible that everyone here is someone else entirely. The river water is like people. It's still flowing down the river of time. If you look down river, you can see where you are going, and if you look back, you can see where you have been. But either way, there is still water. Just not you." Alyssa turned back to her mother. "We will need Aunt Suki to remove any more of these runes." Angela nodded and Alyssa could tell that everyone was confused with her explanation. "Don't worry about it. It took me years to get a real grasp of it, and I still find it confusing at times," she said.

"What matters is that you are safe and alright," Angela said warmly.

Alyssa smiled. "True, and there is still a lot of work for me to do."

"For us to do," Kail added.

Alyssa hesitated. "Yes, all of us."

Conrad Black entered, interrupting them. "The *Colossus* is here."

Alyssa nodded. "Thank you Mr. Black." Turning back to her parents she said, "That should be Mr. Eleazar."

COLOSSUS, SKIES ABOVE SILVERTON

"Not much of it left it appears," Vincent said, eyeing the burning ruins of Silverton. "Helm, put us down next to our *friends*." Vincent looked sideways at Mr. Eleazar, a broken man with his delicate house of cards fallen around him. Vincent could feel the cool brass of the golden pocket watch under his vest, a master key to The Eternal Gateway. It had taken decades to reach this point with this Guardian as well as centuries of patience before. Countless deals and favors given and called in, but soon he would be free of the prison he was forced to live. There was only one thing left to retrieve and that was Bastiana. "Cheer up Guardian. In a few more moments, all of this will be in the past, and you can continue on with your grand crusade."

"It will never work out the way you want it to Vincent," Mr. Eleazar said as the ship landed.

"That is where you are wrong. It already has, and that is the beauty of the matter."

Mr. Eleazar sighed. "We will always be after you."

Vincent smiled and shrugged. "But *you* won't." He turned, offering Mr. Eleazar the opportunity to go first. "Shall we?"

Mr. Eleazar set his teeth together and exited the bridge of the *Colossus*. With Vincent following, they made their way off of the ship. Alyssa along with Kail, Angela and the Mastersons were already outside waiting for them.

Alyssa started forward to meet them, but Mr. Eleazar gave her a slight shake of his head, stopping her.

"What's going on?" Kail asked her.

Alyssa frowned. "I don't know."

"Magic doesn't work against him," Kail said, eyeing Vincent. "What is he going to do when he finds out about Bastiana?" Kail asked, glancing at Angela.

Alyssa set her jaw and placed her hand on the hilt of her blade.

"Why is he even here?"

"We need him. That's all I can say. Mr. Eleazar and I can handle this." Alyssa could feel the pocket watch in her vest. Its arrival had been unexpected, but it reminded her that Suki was still in the jungles of Canyamar with the wisp and that their time table for taking back the gateway from Therion was quickly at hand.

"I don't like this," Kail continued to protest as Mr. Eleazar approached them.

Alyssa kept her thoughts to herself as Vincent walked over to Bastiana and knelt beside her body.

"What happened?" Alyssa asked Mr. Eleazar through clenched teeth.

"Plans have changed," Mr. Eleazar said.

"What does that mean? Plans have changed." She held her hand up, stopping her father.

Mr. Eleazar looked at Kail, Angela and the Mastersons before answering her. "There was always the possibility that this wouldn't work."

Alyssa cursed at him. "We didn't sacrifice everything for this not to work."

"I trust you got my gift?" Mr. Eleazar asked.

Alyssa reached into her vest, retrieving the pocket watch. "Yes, I got it. It nearly killed me when you sent it."

Mr. Eleazar pulled out a matching watch, showing her that he still had his own as well. "It's yours to keep." He looked back at Vincent who was still kneeling over Bastiana. "You're going to need it."

Alyssa frowned as Vincent picked up Bastiana, cradling her in his arms. "What did you do Mr. Eleazar?"

"What I had to do," he said softly, unable to look at Vincent and Bastiana any longer. "Someday you will understand."

Dread crawled up through Alyssa when she saw that Vincent also held a pocket watch in his hand. "What have you done?" she demanded as Vincent pressed his thumb onto the top release.

"Hang on," Kail said as the largest time quake so far washed over them. Her father threw his magic around them to help protect them, but the force of the disturbance from The Eternal Gateway still shook them to the ground.

Alyssa looked back towards Vincent and Bastiana, and her fears were confirmed. Both of them were gone. There were times in the past when she had been angry with Mr. Eleazar, but right now she wanted to kill him. "They're gone," she said, getting to her feet.

"Gone where?" Kail asked, helping Angela up from the ground.

"When is the correct question," Alyssa said, glaring at Mr. Eleazar. "How are we supposed to stop Therion now?"

Mr. Eleazar looked at everyone gathered. "If not us, then no one can. Vincent's role has come to an end. Now is the time of the Sentinel."

Chapter 42

SNOW BREAK

The *Snow Break* purred more than it vibrated beneath Kail's feet. According to Alyssa and Conrad Black it could go much faster, but they would have had to leave the *Odyssey* and the Masterson's behind. They were heading to The Eternal Gateway where everything was on the line.

"You have become a thorn in his side Kail," Mr. Eleazar stated. "You thwarted him when he tried to steal your powers. Then again when he held Angela prisoner. Even when he does destroy everything near you, you come back even stronger and more determined."

Kail wasn't convinced. Mr. Eleazar was understating the downside, the loss of so many friends and people who had expected him to keep them safe. His daughter, now only a handful of years younger than he, nodded her head in agreement. Her childhood lost to him as was her twin sister Amaya.

"We need your help father." Alyssa turned towards her mother. "We need all of your help."

Kail frowned. "We did this once before remember? A small group of us managed to get to the gateway, and I fought with Therion." He turned and faced Mr. Eleazar. "Do you want to *test* my powers again? Make sure I am up to the task, or do you have another agenda that involves Therion winning?" He pointed back and forth between Angela and himself. "You said our role in this is done. You also said you would find someone else, and I now see who that is," he finished, pointing at Alyssa.

"Kail, please," Angela asked.

"No, Angela. He comes clean." Kail turned to Alyssa. "As our daughter, I'm trusting you to see that he does."

Alyssa started to object, but Mr. Eleazar held up his hand, cutting her off. "He's right. I do owe you an explanation. I did test your magical powers before that assault. Part of it was for my own pride. I wanted to see how well I had taught you, but you exceeded every expectation I had. Exceeded is the wrong word. Your magical abilities put you into a class of mages that only handful have achieved in a lifetime of study and practice." Mr. Eleazar leaned forward. "Five years Kail. Five years after releasing your power from the bindings. That much, that fast, it's unheard of. Of course I weakened you before the assault. You would have been able to sweep Therion aside."

"I knew it," Kail said, nodding to Angela. "Then why did you stop me?"

"Because it wasn't time for Therion to be removed. The gateway locked, the timeline was preserved. This has to happen now. Only now can we change the course of time." Mr. Eleazar rubbed his face with his hands.

Alyssa nodded to let him know that the Guardian was being honest.

"Why now?   What's so important about now compared to then?"

Mr. Eleazar nodded at Alyssa.

"Because now Therion has unlocked the gateway. The earthquakes, the distortions coming from the gateway, are all effects of Therion changing time. As long as we were in control, certain events and histories remained locked in place. In order to set everything right, we had to give up that control. It erased our histories, our futures."

Kail was confused and looked to Angela for help, but she was frowning just the same as he. "And this is a good thing?"

Mr. Eleazar answered, "What your daughter is trying to tell you Kail, is that our future is one of darkness. Therion restores his full powers that were taken from him by your father. He returns magic users to a place above all other humans. Everyone else becomes slaves, or dies, or *food* for their growing powers."

Kail thought for a moment. "So the two of you have no idea what is going to happen?"

"We haven't known for a while. Six, maybe seven months now. Ever since Therion got past the final lock on the gateway," Alyssa answered.

"And has it worked?" Kail asked.

"What do you mean?" Alyssa asked.

"These last months. Are they any different this time than before?"

Alyssa hesitated before answering. "Some, but not much. Silverton was still destroyed, but Vincent."

"But Vincent what?"

"He was one of our greatest allies against Therion," Alyssa said obviously disappointed.

Kail scoffed at the idea. "Sounds more like this plan of yours hasn't worked out very well," he said, leaning away from the table everyone sat around.

Mr. Eleazar returned to the original topic. "Therion's hate for your father and for you, make the perfect distraction. You're strong enough to take him head on, draw him away from The Eternal Gateway which will allow us the time we need to ensure the future is put right."

Kail still felt like there was much more to their story, but he also knew there wasn't enough time for them to explain everything before they arrived. "What exactly do you want me to do?"

Alyssa sat up straighter. "Let him know we are coming. Use Divination, distract him from the gateway. He will react like a child on the night before their naming day."

Kail set his jaw and looked at his wife.

Angela nodded. "This is what we were brought together to do, my love."

"Alright," Kail said, getting up from his chair. "I'll do it." Holding out his hand to Angela, she took it and left the galley room with him.

Together they made their way to the *Snow Break's* bridge. "Watch over me," he asked her as he gathered his magic to push his mind towards The Eternal Gateway. Even knowing where The Eternal Gateway was located, the enchantments that surrounded the jungles of Canyamar still tried to hide it from him. He could feel them trying to distract him and persuade his attention to focus somewhere else.

He could see the gateway come into focus. A plain wooden door sat half open on a raised crop of stone. It looked absurd with an entire military outpost built up around it. He didn't sense Therion nearby. He could see Therion's airship, the *Inferno*, circling above. The *Lotus* was there as well, having left Silverton well ahead of them.

"See anything interesting?" Therion asked, materializing next to the gateway.

Therion looked exactly like he did all those years ago when Mr. Eleazar had taken him to the gateway. He was no longer bald, having let his hair grow out. He wore the same formal clothing as well. If Mr. Eleazar and Alyssa wanted things to change, so far they hadn't. Everything seemed to be playing out the same. "Nothing I haven't seen before," Kail said.

"I heard about the incident at your little town," Therion said. "I hope you had insurance."

Kail turned to face him. "You killed my daughter. For that alone I will see you dead, but know this; nothing, nothing will save you from Angela."

Therion stepped back, waving his hands. "There is a reason the Keratins are called a dead race."

Kail ignored the mocking and reached for the gateway. Even though he wasn't physically there it responded to his touch, and he shut it softly. He didn't try to lock it or attempt anything else and he honestly hadn't known if it would close, but he had felt that he could do it. He had even opened it once before when he was in Silverton.

Therion turned deadly serious. "Your power means nothing," he spat. "I've lived longer than your great grandparents, boy. I've killed more mages than you can even count." Therion held up his left arm. "See this?" He indicated the wristband with runes made of focusing stones. "Your father made it for me. Now there was a real mage with power, ambition, and a list of murder victims that put all my deeds to shame."

Kail refused to rise to the bait.

"You are nothing compared to what we accomplished," Therion continued and pointed at the gateway. "When I drain your soul, I will tear this world and all of time apart until I find your father. I will relish the look on his face when I present him your lifeless corpse." Therion paused, stepping closer to whisper. "It will go nicely along with your mother and daughter."

Kail had heard enough and started to withdraw his magic. "We will find out soon enough who is stronger," he said before returning to his body on the *Snow Break*.

Mr. Eleazar and Alyssa had come to the bridge while he was away.

"He knows we're coming," Kail said.

"Will he leave the gateway? Did you distract him enough?" Mr. Eleazar asked.

Kail nodded. "Yeah. I'm pretty sure he's pissed off." Kail turned to look at everyone. "I shut the gateway."

Alyssa's mouth fell open, and Mr. Eleazar looked confused.

"It was open. Therion wasn't impressed with any of us. He cared more about some jewelry that he claimed my father made for him, so I reached over and pulled the door shut."

"And that is all you did?" Mr. Eleazar asked.

Kail nodded. "I might have mentioned that Angela would kill him before I got the chance." He intentionally left out Therion's rant about Duke Falconcrest.

"You speak truth," Angela agreed.

"You have opened the gateway before," Mr. Eleazar admitted. "As long as that is all you did, I don't believe it will have any consequence on what we are trying to do."

"What was the jewelry?" Alyssa asked him.

"A bracelet." Kail held up his fingers. "About this large with some runes made from focusing stones."

Alyssa held up her arm and rolled back her sleeve. "Like this one?"

Kail nodded. "Just like that. What is it?"

Mr. Eleazar answered. "A war memento for mages. It does have focusing stones so be careful. Therion's magic will be stronger than when you last encountered him."

"So will mine."

"It's more than that," Alyssa said, earning her a frown from Mr. Eleazar. "While the stones do increase magical power, the runes they make protect him from corruption. Don't let him win, or he will steal your power."

Kail nodded. "He's tried once before, and he had a much larger stone that time, but it didn't work."

"Just be careful," Alyssa begged.

Kail assured her he would. "The *Lotus* is there as well. Let the Masterson's know," he added.

Chapter 43

CANYAMAR JUNGLE

"I don't remember that happening," Xavier said as he came up to Camden who was still lying on the ground. "Something has changed."

The time quake that had washed over sent all of the horses and pack animals running as the ground shook. Even trees had been uprooted. Camden had been dragged over a hundred yards before the makeshift sled he was strapped to, had broken free from the startled horse.

Xavier squatted down next to Camden and frowned as he looked him over. "I'm not a doctor, but I'm sure that's not supposed to bend or twist like that."

"Did you find him?" one of Xavier's men asked, bringing two more startled horses under control.

Xavier nodded as he stood. "What's left of him." He took the reins of one of the horses.

Camden could barely twist his head around to glare at Xavier. His back broken by Xavier earlier was now twisted around, and his legs were up near his shoulder. "Die," Camden spat through the pain.

Xavier shook his head. "Get in line Camden, get in line." He put one foot onto the stirrup, and started to haul himself up onto the horse. "I'm afraid this is where we must part ways. Time is running out, and I can't waste any more of it dragging you around. I have to say it has been quite entertaining."

Camden struggled managing to get his eyes on Xavier. "I know who you are."

Xavier paused then stepped back onto the ground from his horse. "Finally figured it all out have you?" he said slowly.

Camden hissed through the pain. "That's why you will never win," he announced. "You've already lost once. The power given up. The last to rule. Any of that sound familiar?"

"I still have revenge," Xavier said darkly, quoting the prophecy.

Camden winced as he chuckled. "No, you don't," he said. "You don't even have that."

"I can always start now," Xavier said, reaching across the back of his horse, pulling out a pistol. Cocked it. Pointed. And pulled the trigger.

Xavier's man jumped at the sudden gunshot. Camden writhed and twitched on the ground for a moment before laying still. "I think you killed him," the man said.

Xavier pointed the gun at his hired lackey who took a step back. "That *was* the general idea," he said before pulling the trigger again, shooting the man in the head as well.

He looked at the two dead bodies then scanned the jungle before putting his gun away. The Eternal Gateway was near, and there was a battle he needed to be at. He smiled, already knowing the outcome, but things could be changed, and he was going to be the one to do it.

Suki froze as she looked into the jungle. She had heard the two gunshots before everything fell deathly quiet. She now heard a piercing wail as the little blue wisp shot out of the undergrowth at her. Her first fear was that the wisp had somehow been injured, but that thought quickly passed as the wisp circled around her clearly agitated. "What is it? Is Xavier coming?" she asked, looking back into the jungle in the direction from which the gunshots had come.

The wisp cried and chattered as it flew forward.

Running after the wisp Suki replied. "I am hurrying." Several times the wisp circled back, and she was sure that if it had been bigger, it would have tried to pick her up to move her faster. "Wait. You know better than to run off like that."

Suki stumbled falling hard onto the ground. She stopped herself from crying out by placing her hand over her mouth. She didn't know who the man was that lay in front of her, but she knew he was dead. A bullet hole in his forehead with a surprised empty stare of his still open eyes on his face told her that much.

The wisp cried out again, snapping Suki's attention away from the corpse.

"No, no, no, no," she choked, scrambling over the top of the dead man's body after seeing Camden lying near. Her throat tightened, and her heart pounded so hard that it made it hard to breath. She flinched when she rolled Camden over and saw a head wound similar to the other dead man. She was too late. Her fears had kept her away too long, and now Camden had paid the ultimate price.

The wisp looked up to her, its eyes pleading.

Tears flowed down her cheeks as her trembling hands tenderly patted his body.

The wisp chattered at her and pointed.

Suki looked to where it pointed as one of Camden's hands tightened into a fist, then relaxed.

"He's not dead," she coughed, forcing back her sobs. "He's not dead yet!"

The gunshot to his head was her biggest concern so his twisted legs would have to wait. She took his hand that had moved into hers and held it tightly. "Don't leave me Cam." Kissing his hand, she cleaned away the blood matted hair from around the wound. "I need you," she whispered.

Closing her eyes, she found his heartbeat. It was irregular and growing fainter with each tired beat. Focusing on that spark, she willed her own heart to beat along with it. A strong beat to coax his weaker one to stay with her. "Come back to me Cam," she spoke. "Please, come back to me. You can't go. I need you."

She felt his heart give her one strong beat. It shook throughout her entire body and into her soul, then retreated. Again she focused, pouring her will for him to live into his fading heartbeat. His heart responded with thunder, causing her to gasp. She felt his hand tightening in her own. "Please. You can't die. I love you."

Fire raged through her as she poured every last bit of herself, her will, her love into that small point of life to which he still clung. She felt more than heard him gasp as his heart thundered and raced.

All of the smiles, the jokes and the memories she had of him swirled through her. She let him know how he made her feel when he had found and saved her all those years ago, not just from Xavier's betrayal but even before that when he asked her to join the crew of the *Snow Break*. She remembered when she had knocked him off of his horse, when he had made fun of her, to the lopsided grin when he heard her call him 'Cam' and lastly their kiss in the belly of the ship. "I love you so much," she cried, letting her magical power consume her as it flooded over the both of them.

The wisp clapped its little hands when Camden's eyes flew open, and he started breathing in deep heavy gasps.

He writhed underneath her as she continued to heal his wounds. "No, don't leave me," she cried out, holding him down. She could sense a dark spot inside his skull flare an angry red. *The bullet*, she thought. She caressed her hands against the sides of his face to focus on the dark spot, to make it smaller, to make it disappear and sooth away the angry colors she saw.

She could still feel there was something wrong with him. Only half of him seemed to be there. It reminded her of a tunnel or cave that had collapsed, blocking her from the rest of him. *His broken back,* she remembered. Her magic bore through the block. She could feel the broken bones reaching for each other through her magic. Torn muscle and nerve connections reattached and properly aligned themselves. "I love you," she whispered as her magic broke through, healing his spine and washing through to his legs.

Camden's body felt like he had been cast into a freezing lake of liquid fire, and Suki's magic was drowning him. He could see and feel her thoughts as she worked, and he knew without doubt that she meant every whisper he could hear. He should have felt shame for his actions that night when he had chased after Xavier, but breath stealing pain burst through his skull. Shame only seemed like a minor nuisance as his back started to heal causing the pain to double.

All he could do was force himself to focus on breathing as she worked. He found himself staring into a tiny set of blue eyes. Eyes he had not seen in many months. He wanted to tear his eyes away, but the wisp and Suki's healing held him in place. Memories, Suki's memories of the past few weeks flooded into him, and he saw Suki, Alyssa and the wisp. He hadn't seen Alyssa before, but he knew it was her because Suki did. The wisp was the same as both he and

Suki had remembered it. He felt like he hadn't slept in a month as exhaustion crashed over him. He still stared at the wisp. "I know who you are," he said before slipping into unconsciousness.

Chapter 44

CANYAMAR JUNGLE

Camden shot awake bolting upright. He caught movement from the corner of his eye as the little blue wisp came to land on the top of Suki's head. She was lying next to him and began to stir. "It wasn't a dream."

"What?" Suki said, lifting her head. "Camden, you're alright."

She filled his arms. "What's going on?" He looked around the jungle. "Where is Xavier?"

Suki looked up at him and shook her head. "I don't know, and I don't care."

Camden wiggled his toes inside his boots. "You healed me?"

Suki nodded as she brushed a blond lock of hair out of his face. "I thought you were dead. We found you lying here next to another man who had been shot in the head. I was so scared." Tears began to gather in her eyes.

"It's alright Suki. He should know by now that it takes a lot more than he's got to kill us."

Suki choked back a laugh as she wiped her eyes.

"We need to hurry. Xavier needs to be stopped."

Suki pulled back. "No. No Camden. Forget about him. Let's leave this place."

Camden looked at the wisp. "You have to believe me Suki. We have to do this." He nodded at the wisp. "Don't we?"

Suki looked at the wisp as it chirped at her.

"I know that he is a bad man," she said, and the wisp chirped again. "I, I can't lose you again Camden."

"I know. More than you can possibly imagine," he said, remembering her thoughts he experienced. He hugged her tightly keeping an eye on the wisp who nodded. "Come. Let's finish this. For all of us. For Amaya."

"For Amaya," she repeated.

THE ETERNAL GATEWAY

Kail stood on the outer deck of the *Snow Break* as the ship slowed on its approach to The Eternal Gateway. The *Lotus* and the *Inferno* hovered on the horizon.

"You have to keep him away from the gateway for as long as possible," Alyssa emphasized.

"I understand," Kail said. Moving over to Angela he put his hands on her shoulders. "You ready for this?" he asked her.

Angela nodded. She was ready with her war blade strapped to her back and the rune staff in her hand. "He will know my wrath." She dove off of the *Snow Break,* and he watched her disappear into the jungle below.

Kail focused his magic to teleport to the ground in front of the gateway. Therion wasn't there, but he wrapped his magic around him in a protective shield. The Eternal Gateway was as he had always seen it; a simple wooden doorway in the middle of the jungle. And like he had left it, it was shut. Therion hadn't bothered to reopen it.

He heard Therion's voice come from behind him. "When you think about it, the War of Antiquities has really never ended."

Kail turned to face him.

"The motivations are same, and even the players," Therion said referring to himself. "There won't be an escape for you this time."

In the sky above them, the *Snow Break* and *Odyssey* squared off with the *Lotus* and slower but heavily armed *Inferno*.

"This will end here," Kail said. "Only one of us will survive."

Therion teleported, and in an instant Kail was blasted away from the gateway. "You don't stand a chance," Therion taunted.

The attack was stronger than anything Kail had come across. Stronger than any of the sparing matches he had encountered with Mr. Eleazar or with Bastiana. "Is that the best you've got?" Kail asked, getting to his feet.

Therion smiled. "I plan to enjoy this for as long as I can."

Good, Kail thought. "I'm ready. Hope you enjoy disappointment." Kail opened himself up to the mix of

Chronomancy and Divination to try to predict where Therion would strike next but with The Eternal Gateway next to them, it was impossible.

"The stage has been set, and there is no better battlefield than here," Therion said, spreading his arms wide gathering his magic to him.

Kail blinked forward with enhanced speed and strength, swinging his fist now covered with magical energy. Therion grinned and leaned to the side easily dodging the blow. Kail followed up the attack with several punches that managed to keep Therion on the defensive while driving him back.

Therion brought up his knee and caught him in the chest, doubling him over. Kail barely got his arms up in front of him to block the backhand. Magic thundered and sparked between them as Kail was sent tumbling uncontrollably away from the gateway. Only a flicker warned him to teleport to safety when Therion came down exactly where he had just been. The attack left the ground charred as magic blasted outward from Therion.

Kail fired a bar of molten magic back at Therion.

Therion splayed his fingers, blocked the attack and sent it barreling through the outpost leaving a line of destruction.

Kail ran.

"Too much of a coward?" Therion shouted after him.

Kail used his magic to help him run through the outpost to put as much distance as he could between him and the gateway. He could have teleported, but he had to make sure Therion would follow him. A fist caught him squarely in the jaw, sending him off of his feet and onto his back.

Therion shook his head. "So inexperienced it's criminal."

Rolling backwards Kail brought up his foot, catching Therion under his ribs with a rewarding crunch and whoosh of air, knocking the breath out of the mage.

"That's more like it," Therion wheezed, getting to his feet.

Bringing up both hands, Kail fired a bar of energy.

Therion teleported out of the way, only to reappear right behind Kail with his own counter attack.

Kail blinked away before Therion was able to cut him in half but not before leaving behind a delayed explosion that caught Therion off guard. Kail kept an eye on Therion from the dark shadows as he wiped the blood away from his mouth.

Therion spun and magic flew at him. Kail barely managed to fire back as the energies collided between them. Jagged arcs of electricity and magic sprayed, leaving scorched lines on the ground and across the buildings. Weaker materials shattered and exploded while others caught fire.

"You're not going to win," Therion shouted, grabbing the bracelet on his wrist.

Kail was driven backwards as the force of Therion's magic flared and doubled. Even the Imaera hide armor started to smolder. Grunting he pushed to the side, redirecting the energy. The building next to him was instantly destroyed as both of their combined magic slammed into it.

The explosion washed over them. Kail forced his magic to shield him from the flames and debris. He could see Therion standing in the flames as his magic kept him from harm. Kail was slow getting to his feet.

"I should have known. The Falconcrests just get weaker and weaker with each generation," Therion taunted.

"But you have always been weaker than my father. Isn't that right?" Kail dusted himself off. "Even now you need his power to challenge me," he said, pointing to Therion's wrist.

"What is it you think you know?" Therion asked, holding up his arm. "You get a quick history lesson from the Guardian? He is even more pathetic than you are considering he's already dead. Think about it Falconcrest. How dangerous do I have to be for someone to scour all of time to find people to stop me?"

Kail moved closer to the edge of the outpost as Therion ranted.

"And you know what the best part is?" Therion mirrored his movements. "I must win, or he wouldn't be here."

"Then come win," Kail taunted, pulling his magic to his center and teleporting into the jungle.

ODYSSEY

"Fire," Rhonin shouted.

The *Snow Break* shot in front of them, cutting off the *Lotus* to give them a clear shot. The main cannons on the *Odyssey* fired in sequence. A line of explosions billowed out from the bow of the *Inferno* as the shells did their job. Twisted metal and flames fell from the wounded ship to the jungle below.

"Come around," he barked as a series of flashes came from the *Inferno* as it fired back. "Hang on it's going to be close."

The ship bucked, jostling everyone forward as the *Inferno's* attack missed wide, exploding behind them.

Rayne monitored the lights on the weapons board. "Reloaded," she called out when the lights turned green.

Rhonin acknowledged her update. "Brom, bring us up and over. Try to flank the *Lotus*."

"Aye sir," the pilot answered.

The *Inferno* was too slow to stop them as well as lacking the proper weapons placements. As the prototype of the Juggernaut class of ships, many of the flaws that had been corrected on the newer ships, still existed on the *Inferno*.

LOTUS

"Keep to the inside of them please," Admiral Bailon ordered. "They are faster, and they will get behind us if we let them."

"*Inferno* is taking fire. Minimal damage is being reported, a few casualties and minor fires that are being extinguished," Cid relayed the report.

Bailon eyed the *Odyssey* as it roared over the top of the *Inferno* to angle in front of them for a flanking maneuver. "Fire port cannons and dive," he called out. "Keep us along the *Inferno's* outer deck, and circle around between the port and starboard flanks. Here and here."

"Aye sir." The helmsman brought the ship around.

"The *Inferno* has the firepower, but not the mobility. As long as we cover their blind spots, the enemy will have to come to us. They can't flank us, and the *Inferno* will tear them apart from any other angle."

"Understood sir."

"Good." Bailon returned to his command chair, satisfied that the Silverton forces would either leave in a stalemate or make a mistake. And he was more than hoping they would do the latter.

Chapter 45

THE ETERNAL GATEWAY

Running past the destruction from Kail and Therion's fight, Xavier cursed when he found the vault like gateway closed and abandoned. "Where are they?" Holding his hands to his head, he tried to remember, but the information he could recall was full of holes. It won't matter he decided, shaking his head. The Guardian would be here soon and so would the Falconcrest brat he had failed to kill earlier.

All he had to do was wait. Then when they arrived, kill them.

CANYAMAR JUNGLE

Therion glanced down at Kail, still writhing at his feet. The Imaera hide armor Kail wore had taken the brunt of their last exchange. Therion was sure if he hadn't been wearing it Kail would not be alive, or if he had survived, at least not whole. "Fascinating material that armor of yours," he said. "Although, I think it has been ruined for good this time."

Kail groaned trying to get up.

Reaching down, Therion hauled Kail to his feet. "Let me help you with that." Lifting Duke's son off his feet by his throat, he pressed him against the trunk of a tree. "This will keep you from falling again." Magical bands formed around Kail's wrists, ankles and throat pinning him.

"Better make them tight," Kail said defiantly. "I've broken your bonds once before. Remember?"

"You just don't get it do you?" Therion stepped back, admiring Kail on display. He tightened the magic holding Kail as he had suggested, forcing a grunt from him. "I'm going to leave you hanging from this tree an empty husk." It had been decades since he had taken another mage's power. He had to restrain himself from rushing the moment. "This should have happened years ago." The runes on the bracelet made from focusing stones began to glow. He coaxed tendrils of Necromantic magic that hungered for Kail's power.

Kail flinched as the smoky magic touched his chest then caressed his face. Like a sticky spider web it pulled taut, and Kail screamed. It was worse than death. He could feel his soul being drained as it tore from his body. His magic was paralyzed while pain muddled his thoughts.

The blow drove Therion to the ground while the shockwave from exploding magic lifted him back up and tossed him through the air. The Keratin had ambushed him from above using Bastiana's rune staff. He was lucky to even be alive having been caught off guard like that. The ground where he had been standing while sucking away Kail's magic was cratered.

She didn't relent, and he rolled to the side as she stabbed down with her sword. Energy burst from where he had pinned Kail to the tree, and he knew Falconcrest had managed to break free of the enchantments that held him. His knack at being able to do that would normally have been a concern, but right now there was a more dangerous player to worry about.

"Women ruin everything," he said, trying to buy a moment to get centered and shake off the last attack.

Angela refused to take the bait and came at him through the air like a phantom banshee.

The staff might protect her from him killing her outright, but that would be about it. Bringing his hands up to channel his power through the focusing stones he fired a cone of magical energy that engulfed her. He called out in triumph as she disappeared inside his magic.

Only sheer reflex saved him, as his magic warned him of the attack. He managed to dodge the war blade, but Angela slammed into his back. It had all been a set-up. Kail had teleported the Keratin out of his attack's way and brought her back on the other side of him, allowing her to strike her blow.

They made for a deadly pair. Kail followed up her attack with a volley of magic that he was able to swat away, exploding harmlessly in the jungle. Now that they had lost the element of surprise, it was fairly easy for him to maintain a protective barrier that would keep the blade at bay. The rune staff could still cause problems, but he treated it the same as a magical attack from Kail.

"You better have more than this up your sleeves," Therion laughed, catching the rune staff with one hand, while sending a bolt of magic towards Kail that sent the mage ducking for cover. "Nice try," he said to Angela, forcing her to retreat as well.

She drew back to bring the war blade slicing around in a reverse grip while kicking off of a nearby tree to increase momentum. He could hear the air sing as it cut through the space he been moments ago. She was fast.

But his magic made him faster. Therion swung his fist as hard as he could, catching Angela on the side of the head. He missed the pleasure of seeing her go down as Kail teleported in next to him.

One blast, two, three, four. Kail's attacks came at him repeatedly, but Therion didn't pause as he deflected them. "Sacrificing each other is a weak plan," he mused. Again his magic warned him to duck as the rune staff swung wildly over his head.

"You killed her," Angela raged.

Keeping an eye on Kail, Therion shrugged as the three of them squared off. "Temper, temper now. If I said it wasn't personal, would you believe me?"

SNOW BREAK

"We don't have time for this," Alyssa complained. The *Lotus* and *Inferno* were keeping a tight defensive formation.   Magic erupted in the jungle below them. "Therion has left the gateway."   She turned towards Mr. Eleazar who wasn't paying attention to what she was saying. "Focus Mr. Eleazar. We need go now."

"What? Of course." He stood a little straighter as he eyed the battle.   "The *Lotus* can only partially protect the *Inferno*.   If we disable more of her, the Masterson's and Mr. Black should be able to handle things."

Alyssa looked to Conrad. "Take the controls." She looked at the time on her pocket watch and shook her head. "Mr. Eleazar, inform the Mastersons that as soon as I'm done, we secure the gateway."

Mr. Eleazar nodded. "Yes, of course."

She still wasn't sure what was going on with Mr. Eleazar, but it was starting to more than annoy her.   He hadn't explained what was going on with Vincent, but she did know that it had to be something serious.   She just hoped it wasn't anything that would keep him from doing what needed to be done.

She released herself to her magic to teleport onto the *Inferno*.   The wind rushed around her as she found a maintenance hatch that led inside.   Dropping inside, she drew her pistol and made her way to the engine room.

THE ETERNAL GATEWAY

Camden peeked around the corner. "Hurry Suki," he whispered, waving her over to him. The gateway outpost was like an angry hornets' nest, and if he could find Xavier without having to deal with any soldiers, all the better.

She kept her head low and made it to his side. "How much further?" she asked, taking hold of his hand. The wisp had chosen to ride along on her shoulder.

Camden gave her hand a squeeze. "Just past those buildings over there."

"The one that has a wall blown out?" she clarified.

He frowned. "Yes."

"And that doesn't just scream that we should get out of here as fast as we can?"

Camden faced Suki. "We have to do this Suki."

The wisp nodded in agreement.

She set her lips together to sigh, but didn't protest any further.

Together they circled around the back of the building to avoid being seen. The Eternal Gateway came into view. Two pillars of rock stood on a small uprising from the ground. One broken pillar leaned onto the other forming a crude arch.

Suki pulled back with a gasp. "Is that the gateway?"

"Yes," he said remembering that people saw the gateway differently. "What do you see?"

"I, I can't describe it. It's beautiful."

"Everyone's gateway is better than mine," he mumbled.

"What?" she replied still gazing at the gateway.

"Nothing." Camden looked around. "Where is he? Where's Xavier? He should be here. I know he should be here."

Now this is unexpected, Xavier thought as the blond brute he had left for dead stared at the gateway. However the girl with him reeked of Necromancy. The odds of Camden surviving being shot in the head were zero, but having a full blown Necromancer with enough skill to save him simply wandering around in the jungle was absurd.

He raised the rifle to point it at the girl. It was clearly her first time seeing the gateway as she just stood there gaping at it. If things had been different, or perhaps a different time, he wouldn't kill her. *Just bad timing girl*, he thought with irony. He pulled the trigger.

Suki jerked back to reality when a gun fired. The wisp that had been her companion and her source of strength through the jungle lay still on the ground. "No," she cried, looking for the source of the attack.

"Not again," she heard Camden yell, charging towards the ruined building they had passed. She saw Xavier fire a gun several times at him, but the bullets bounced harmlessly off of him.

She knelt down, picking up the wisp to cradle it.

"I see the hole in your head has healed," Xavier teased, slowly moving out of the rubble and around towards the gateway. His hands were held out wide in some attempt to feign that he was no longer armed. "Hasn't seemed to change your mind at all." He yelled to Suki. "Impressive work you've managed to do."

Camden, jaw set and fists transformed into iron, did not reply.

"I take it back. You can't fix his ability to hold a conversation."

"Kill him please," Camden heard Suki plea. It was the most defeated sound he had ever heard. He saw her trembling on her knees, holding the little blue wisp to her chest. "Please."

He looked back to Xavier, and he started to see red.

Xavier eyed Camden's hands. "Now you want this to be a fair fight. Kill me with one blow, and there won't be any satisfaction," Xavier remarked with a smirk. "Your hate demands it."

Camden stepped towards the gateway as well. He didn't want to fight Xavier too close to Suki. The traitor might turn on her just to get at him. "I'll make sure you survive the first blow," he promised.

Xavier made a move towards Suki, and Camden interceded. Xavier backed up, grinning to let him know that he would use Suki to handicap him as much as possible.

"Would you believe me if I said it wasn't personal?" Xavier asked, stepping forward to gauge Camden's reaction. "I told myself to kill both of those little girls."

Camden came in, then switched stances at the last second to swing a right cross, forcing the scarred man to jerk his head back to keep it attached to his shoulders.

"That's always been your problem," Xavier continued, unconcerned with the close call. "All caught up with the grand idea that you're somehow important. Distracted by loyalty and the itch between your legs you call love." Xavier charged at the end of the taunt, slipping past Camden's defenses to punch him twice in the ribs before knocking his head back with a fist to his jaw.

Camden staggered backwards and shook off the blows. Xavier was strong, abnormally strong like he was all those years ago when they fought on the *Snow Break*. Camden swung back, taking to the offense, driving the traitor back.

"Trust me, I still have plenty of power," Xavier explained. "Some things just can't be bound and locked away."

Camden wiped blood from his lip. "I don't know how you survived, but I won't let it happen again." Camden leapt forward savagely, swinging with his iron fists. Again Xavier backed up, staying out of range.

Camden stepped back as Xavier spun and kicked at his stomach. The traitor rolled ahead just out of the way as Camden came down, smashing his fist into the empty ground.

Xavier brought his foot up and caught him in the ribs and followed with a fist to the side of his head that sent him to the dirt in front of the gateway. "She is quite delicious, isn't she," Xavier said, stepping towards Suki. "All that magic, all that potential."

Camden yelled as he scrambled, tackling Xavier from behind. They fell back to the hard ground. Camden landed a punch to Xavier's mid-section with a satisfying crunch.

Xavier grunted, but got his arm up under Camden's, keeping him from landing another blow. "We could share," Xavier offered.

Camden spat in Xavier's face.

The scarred traitor smashed his forehead into Camden's nose and with a knee to the ribs forced Camden off. "I'll take that as a no." Xavier got to his feet and picked up a broken board.

The blood from his nose made it hard to breathe, but he managed to blink away the spinning in his head. Camden barely ducked out of the way as Xavier swung the board at his head. The traitor over extended letting Camden catch him squarely under the chin, sending the scarred man off of his feet and onto his back. "That's for my crew," Camden informed him.

INFERNO

The inside of the *Inferno* was exactly how Alyssa imagined it would be. Vast open areas supported by steel girders and suspended catwalks. All of it served only one function, to inflate the size of the ship making it appear larger and more intimidating. Locating the engine room wasn't going to be much of a problem. It turned out that there were several engine rooms for a ship this size. Destroying or disabling one wouldn't be enough to bring the ship down.

The sound of boots echoed on the catwalk from in front of her. A pair of soldiers on patrol emerged from a lower deck and were headed straight towards her. Before they noticed her, she used her ability to fly to hop over the safety rail. She held herself underneath the catwalk as they passed.

"I hate this. These walkways are too dangerous to be using in combat," one of the men above her complained.

"Would you rather nobody checks the ship for damage or fires and reports them? I'm not going to be the one responsible for the loss of the entire ship because you're afraid of heights or some turbulence," his companion retorted as they passed. "But, there isn't any reason to be up here any longer than we have to."

She waited for their complaining and footsteps to fade before returning back to the top of the catwalk. Alyssa stepped up her pace to make up for the lost time. By the time she arrived at the first engine room she had given up on any further attempts at stealth. She didn't bother putting on one of the sets of hearing protection that hung outside the engine room door. A small amount of magic would do the job just fine. She pulled on the securing latch, swinging the door inward and stepped inside.

The massive engine was at least twenty five feet long with pistons cycling along each side. Sabotaging the fuel intake she figured would be the simplest way to disable it.

An engineer spotted her, stepping around the far end of the engine. "Who are you? Get away from there."

Alyssa ignored him as she found one of the fuel lines. Using her magic she pinched it shut. Almost immediately the engine started to sputter.

The engineer pulled a pistol at her. "I said stop what you're doing," he ordered and fired a shot at her that ricochet off the wall.

Alyssa ducked pulling her own pistol and fired, dropping the man. Two more fuel lines and the engine stalled completely. A flashing red light told her that the crew knew there was a problem, and people would be arriving shortly. One more engine on this side of the ship should be enough to bring the *Inferno* down.

CANYAMAR JUNGLE

Angela tossed her war blade to Kail then gripped the rune staff with both hands. Kail spun the blade moving to flank Therion.

Therion smiled as the two of them positioned. "Useless," he said, teleporting behind Kail to attack with his magic.

Kail sidestepped the attack and brought Angela's sword to bear. Therion's magic protected him from the blade when he blocked with his forearm. Magic sparked and Kail fired a bolt of energy with his free hand.

Therion caught Kail's hand, forcing the attack to miss. He too went into a spinning rotation that brought Kail's arm up behind his back, pinning it. He was forced to release Kail when Angela tried to take his head off with the staff. Her attack missed high, but her follow up kick sent him back a few steps.

Kail began once more, attacking with both magic and sword. This time when Therion tried to block or counter, Angela was there to strike with the staff. Her ability to defy gravity let her attack from angles that no amount of training would have prepared him for. The Keratin came in high and fast, staff spinning from strike to strike. Each blow sending a ring of thunder into the jungle as the magic collided.

Therion laughed aloud. "Where were you during the war? This is a better fight than most ever managed to put up." A war blade sliced across in front of his face, reminding him that the couple was not fighting him for amusement.

Kail's expression was like focused death. Therion could feel the Duke's son's magic starting to build. It was time to stop playing around. Channeling his magic through the focusing stones he released an explosion above their heads.

The Keratin was knocked away as the blast sent the trees around them bowing backwards and away. The mage cried out after seeing his wife tumble into the underbrush. That is why Therion knew he would always win. Even with The Duke it had been simple enough to use those close to him to force him into doing what he had wanted. He never bought into any of the lectures Duke would give him about being alone or wanting more out of life. There was nothing that power, magic, and sheer force of will couldn't give him. Doing things for love was a cancer that led only to downfall.

Kail attacked erratically, clearly unfocused without the Keratin. It was easy enough to swat away the pitiful attacks. Motes of energy gathered around Therion's hands. He needed to knock him unconscious so he could drain Kail's magic and add it to his own.

Kail unleashed anew with his own magical attack. The strength and force of the magic surprised Therion, and he matched it with his own. Lightning arched through the jungle around them, setting parts of it ablaze where the cast off magics landed. The wind started to howl as it swirled around them.

THE ETERNAL GATEWAY

Xavier rolled over and rubbed his jaw. Nothing felt broken, but there was a click in the joint every time he moved it. That was all he managed to assess before he was hauled to his feet by Camden who proceeded to slug him in the stomach with those iron fists of his.

He blocked the next punch and pushed away. Kicking he caught Camden in the knee, sending both of them to the ground. He crawled towards the gateway but felt Camden grab him by his foot to drag him back. The big man's elbow slammed into his back knocking almost all of the air out of him. He managed to shove the man off and got a good kick to Camden's face.

The girl, he thought, glancing over at the Necromancer who was still sitting there crying over the little, whatever it was, that had intercepted the bullet meant for her. *What was it with the hero complex types that always made them bring their women to a fight?* Xavier drew a small blade and threw it at her as hard as he could. Unfortunately, it hit her in the head with the flat of the blade, knocking her over instead of sticking out of her like he had wished. *Something to practice on*, he thought.

"No," Camden roared, charging him.

Xavier cursed, he had intended for the brute to race to her side and lament, not to immediately come at him. Camden's shoulder slammed into him, picking him up before ramming him against the gateway. There was little he could do as iron fist after iron fist hit him in the ribs, the face, and the stomach. Human bone could withstand a lot of punishment. It flexed before it broke or shattered, but the skin surrounding it was easily split and smashed.

Camden continued to beat on him. Even when his legs gave out, Camden used one hand to hold him up so he could continue to beat the life out of him.

"Better check on her," Xavier whispered though a swollen face, earning him another punch. "She dies now when you could save her," he said, leaving the sentence unfinished.

Camden held off another blow as he looked at Suki lying on the ground. He let go of Xavier dropping him to the ground and scrambled to her side.

Xavier thanked whatever gods there were for the respite.

Camden rolled Suki over and sighed with relief that it was only a nasty cut on the side of her scalp and not something worse. "You're going to be ok Suki," he reassured her, helping her sit up.

"Did you finish it?" she asked, tenderly touching the cut. "Is he dead?"

"He's about to be," he said, turning back to where he had left Xavier beaten and bloody. The explosive wave of magic knocked both Suki and Camden back as if a giant hand tried to sweep them away.

The gateway stood open, and Xavier leaned against the entrance. "This isn't over," Xavier spat as the ground shook in response to the time energy flowing from the gateway.

"Stop him!" Suki shouted.

Camden tried. He put everything he had into reaching the gateway, but Xavier simply smirked, took a step backwards and disappeared. He was forced to shield his eyes as another explosion erupted from the gateway sending shockwaves through the outpost. Windows shattered and walls buckled. He could hear Suki's screams behind him, and he expected his own body to be blown away as well. But it never came. Everything fell silent. Not even a crackle of a fire or the whisperings of a breeze. Everything was frozen in place. The gateway was still open, and light poured through. He no longer saw it as a broken pillar, but now two carved columns standing proud and tall, topped with a detailed arch. Camden bolted towards the gateway. He would hunt down and kill Xavier Ross no matter where or when the scarred traitor tried to hide.

"Stop," a little girl's voice shattered the silence.

Camden froze as his heart thundered in his chest. He had lost count of how many times he had wished to hear that voice again, or the endless sacrifices he would have performed to have it back. His throat tightened as he felt tears start to sting his eyes as he turned around.

Suki was on her knees sobbing as she stared.

"Hello Uncle Camden," Amaya said with a smile.

Camden couldn't keep back the tears. "I knew it," his voice cracked. "When I saw you in the jungle."

Amaya stepped forward. Her body cast a faint blue light around her. The same blue light of the tiny wisp. "You cannot travel after the bad man," she said.

Camden looked away. "I have to," he insisted. "I have to kill him for what he's done. What he did to you, to all of us."

Amaya stopped next to Suki. "I know. But this is not your destiny." She helped her get to her feet then held her hand like she used to do.

"How is this possible?" Suki asked. It all came rushing back on her as she remembered the last few weeks talking with Alyssa and traveling through the jungle with the wisp. She always understood what the wisp had said even though words were never spoken.

"Mr. Eleazar," Camden answered. "It was him, wasn't it? He came and said I couldn't be there."

Amaya nodded. "And my grandpa."

"He saved you," Camden said.

Amaya walked over to take his hand looking up at him. "No. You saved me. You always have and always will. Never forget that. Both of you."

Camden wanted to argue, but Amaya's smiling face prevented it.

The Eternal Gateway groaned.

"I cannot hold this time stop for much longer," Amaya said. "I have to go now." She took both of their hands and put them together then stepped in front of the gateway.

"Please don't go," Suki tearfully begged as Camden held her close to him.

"I have to. It's my turn to save you from the bad man."

"You always will," Camden repeated, understanding now that Amaya would chase Xavier through time and do as she promised. He knew because he had seen her do it all those years ago in the engine room of the *Snow Break*. And Amaya knew she would too. He tried not to think about how many times before the little girl might have repeated this exact moment. But he was satisfied with how Xavier would meet his end. If he wasn't to be the one to kill him then Amaya deserved to.

"Good-bye Aunt Suki. Good-bye Uncle Camden," Amaya said, stepping through the The Eternal Gateway's light.

Chapter 46

INFERNO

The entire airship rocked and bucked as warning klaxons echoed throughout the ship. Alyssa held on as the *Inferno* began to list. Her skin tingled from the release of magical energy that swept through the ship. It had to have been The Eternal Gateway. The *Inferno* was going down so further sabotage was no longer required. She tried to teleport herself off of the ship but was unable. That confirmed that it was the gateway and she cursed. It was throwing her Chronomancy magic awry. Unfortunately that meant she would quickly have to find another way off of the ship if she didn't want to experience firsthand a Juggernaut class airship colliding with the ground.

Support beams throughout the ship began to groan as the weight of the ship shifted, reminding her that she needed to escape. The weapon's deck would be her best chance. The hull there would be open to the outside where the cannons were housed.

The railing started to give out, and the catwalk lost its use as the angle of the ship steepened. Relying on her ability to fly, she soared through the ship dodging debris that filled the air. She was quickly approaching one of the giant doorways to the weapon's deck. She fired off a round, aiming at chain that was suspended across the empty hold that was used to help load munitions and equipment through the *Inferno*. The chain severed, and she caught the end with her free hand as it fell. Her arm was nearly yanked from its socket, but she held on as it changed her decent by pulling her towards the doorway at a sharper angle than she could have flown by herself.

Alyssa prayed there would be a clear shot through the next room, or this ride would end with her smashing into a wall or cannon. If it did, at least the *Inferno* would bury her leaving no trace of her folly. Luck was with her as she let go of the chain to shoot through the weapons deck and outside to the sky.

The front bow of the *Inferno* crumpled as the ship ran into the ground. The rest of the *Inferno* followed as if the ground had not even been there until nothing was left but a cloud of dirt and smoke billowing into the sky above the jungle.

She spared only a moment to appreciate how close she had come to being a part of the wreckage. Turning towards the gateway she flew as fast as she could.

CANYAMAR JUNGLE

The time disturbance from The Eternal Gateway ended the stalemate with Kail. Anger rose inside Therion as he pointed at Kail. "You think you can deceive me? I control

The Eternal Gateway. I am its master. I write history. I decide the future."

"I am tired of the sound of your voice," Kail retorted.

Therion rolled his eyes. "I take it all back, Falconcrest. If that is the best you have then I understand why your father left you behind. I wouldn't be able to stand the disappointment either." He released his amplified magic at the Duke's son. Kail used the indestructible war blade to help deflect part of the attack to either side of him causing the magic to burn away the jungle behind him. It was only a matter of time however before Kail would be incinerated.

Kail braced to send a sliver of magic along the ground towards Therion. He couldn't spare enough to kill him, but he hoped it would put an end to the current assault.

The ground at Therion's feet erupted in front of him, sending part of the jungle floor into the air around him. He lashed out, striking Kail back with his magic. Another temblor emanated from the gateway. Therion couldn't waste anymore time. He knew that someone had used the gateway, and now someone else had used it a second time. He could eventually kill Kail, but the gateway was more important. He launched another attack where Kail had fallen. It should delay him while he secured the gateway.

SNOW BREAK

Mr. Eleazar frowned. "Mr. Black, I am afraid that I am going to have to ask you to withdraw from the fight and land so I may depart."

"Are you crazy?" Conrad asked, piloting the *Snow Break* as best he could. "I'm not leaving the *Odyssey* now. Alyssa just took down the *Inferno*."

"I assure you, the Mastersons are more than capable of handling themselves. Normally I would teleport off of this ship, but The Eternal Gateway is preventing my doing so," he explained. "Now I ask you again to land. I assure you the rest of my magic is not being hindered," he threatened.

Conrad mumbled a curse and for the first time appreciated why the Mastersons acted the way they did whenever Mr. Eleazar showed up. "You're a bad man Mr. Eleazar," he said.

"I have been called worse Mr. Black."

THE ETERNAL GATEWAY

"Aunt Suki, Camden," Alyssa said, landing at the gateway. "What are you doing here?" she asked, eyeing the open gateway.

Suki answered, "Amaya... She's, she's gone."

"She went after Xavier," Camden added.

Alyssa focused on the ground. "She always said she had to save you." She turned to face Camden and Suki. "When she insisted on staying in the jungle, I thought that was what she meant." Alyssa pulled the gateway shut, not voicing that they were likely to never see Amaya again.

Camden stepped forward, sensing her loss. "She's going to be fine."

Alyssa hesitated then nodded. "You two need to leave."

"What?" Suki protested. "Why?"

"Therion is coming, and I need to secure the gateway."

"We can help," Camden insisted.

"No," Alyssa shouted, causing them to flinch. "No. I can't fight Therion or secure the gateway knowing you might be killed."

Camden wasn't going to let that excuse stop him. "There is more to Xavier and Therion than you know."

"Please Uncle Camden," she begged, cutting him off. "Mr. Eleazar should be here. I need the two of you with the *Snow Break*." Mentioning the *Snow Break* got their attention. "When this is over, we *all* are going to need to escape."

Camden frowned, and Suki looked desperate.

Alyssa could see that they were warring against her judgment and their desire to stay to help. "Please."

Camden relented. "We will wait for you. No matter what."

Suki nodded.

"Thank you. Both of you," Alyssa said as the *Snow Break* passed over the outpost.

CANYAMAR JUNGLE

Kail found Angela lying in the jungle with a nasty bruise on her forehead. Helping her sit up he asked, "Are you alright?"

Angela nodded with a wince. "Where is Therion?"

"He's going to the gateway. We need to hurry. Can you move?"

"You let him get away?" Angela got to her feet with his help.

"Not exactly. He's a lot stronger than last time, and The Eternal Gateway caused another one of those time quakes."

"Alyssa?" Angela asked, looking around for the rune staff.

He shrugged. "I hope so. I tried to use my magic to get there, but something is blocking it," Kail said. The *Snow Break* flew in low over the tree tops above them. "It's landing. Come on."

THE ETERNAL GATEWAY

"And just who might you be?" Therion asked, approaching the gateway.

Alyssa held her ground. "I am the Sentinel of The Eternal Gateway." She drew both of her mother's war blades.

Therion squinted at hearing the word sentinel and eyed the swords. "Just how many of those are there? Was there a giveaway for indestructible weapons that I missed?" He smoothed out his dress uniform and brushed away some of the ash that had gotten onto it. "There is a familiarity here that I can't quite place."

"I'm sure it will come to you."

"Half witted insults. I should have known. First Kail and his wife, and now I have to dispose of his daughter." Therion paused. "Again," he added. "You're the one that got away. You seem to have grown up rather quickly."

"War does that," she answered.

That confirmed what Therion had already suspected, and it brought a smile to his lips. "I've already won," he said, lifting his arms in victory over his head.

"If you believe that, fall onto my blade and prove it."

Therion waved his hand to sweep her away with magic.

Alyssa smiled at his attempt to cast her aside. Her own magic protected her. "Half witted attempt," she mocked. "I expected better." Channeling her magic through her own focusing stones she pointed one of the war blades at Therion, pouring every ounce of magic she had at him. Lightning struck from the end of the blade at Therion.

The searing force of the blast slammed Therion in the chest sending him flying back, his breath forced from his lungs, and his magic almost failing. He borrowed strength from the focusing stones to shield himself as he struck the ground then bounced through the far wall of a ruined building.

Therion almost wished he had taken her up on the offer to fall on her sword. His whole body felt burned and crispy from her attack, and stabs of pain ran down his back from the impact. He shook his head, forcing away the pain to keep from passing out. Looking back to where he had been standing he saw her, guarding the gateway, breathing heavily. *She spent everything she had*, he realized.

Therion's head was still cloudy as he tried to understand how she could have summoned that much power so quickly. Without the focusing stones, it would have taken him several minutes to generate an attack of that force, and there wasn't a mage alive that could match him.

Apparently there was, he corrected. As soon as he started to move her sword shot up again pointed in his direction. Therion barely brought his magic up in time to absorb the lightning that forked and danced towards his body.

She then stepped forward, her magic still channeling down the sword. Therion had a hard time believing what he was seeing. That much magic, and she was still coming after him. It was impossible for the sword to be helping her that much. Now he understood, she had to have a focusing stone of her own, it was the only explanation. He feigned an attempt to flee when she took another step moving the lightning off of him. He brought up his hand and aimed towards her center, using his magic he fired a bar of hot energy that hurled her back towards the gateway.

Therion was on his feet, sprinting towards the gateway. But the girl was just as fast; foregoing her magic in favor of the twin war blades. He saw the glint of the silvery runes slicing towards him as the girl leapt through the air. He spun away and kicked with the same follow through. She grunted as his boot landed against her ribs and underneath her deadly blades.

A sword hilt came swinging over the top of his leg, driving hard into his temple. He couldn't help but cry out as spots of color blurred his vision. He blindly lashed out with his magic to keep her away while he tried to recover, but she made him pay for each second with a painful kick or strike.

He knew that sooner or later one of her strikes could be fatal. He also knew she must be as drained as he was, her from attacking with magic, and he defending from it. Therion took a quick look around for anything he could use against her blades until his magic returned. Her pistol was the only thing in reach.

She punished him for the respite. Thankfully it didn't take much magic to deflect the war blade from stabbing his insides. Therion countered by going for the gun. She tried to side step him when she saw what he was reaching for. The opening was all he needed as he rolled through her arm, pulling her along against the gateway. The war blade came free, and he caught it. It was now simple for him to parry and back away, putting space between them.

Therion took the pause to catch his breath. "We shouldn't be doing this. There aren't enough of us left," he said, buying time.

Alyssa paced in front of the gateway. "Is this where you try to buy time by trying to convince me to join your cause?"

Therion sighed and nodded. "Yeah, it is."

"I'm listening."

It was one of the few times in his life he was truly left speechless. "Okay, what is it that you want?"

"I've seen your vision of the future. It is a return to the old ways and like the War of Antiquities it leaves the world in ruin," she told him.

"It is our destiny to rule. Our role in this world is to lord over our lessers. Mages have ruled for thousands of years. That is proof enough of our right. The weak serve to enrich the strong. Even insects know this."

She shrugged. "And how long before you turn on me, my family, or any other mage? I know all about the war. I know what you did to your so called equals."

He pointed the sword at her and snarled. "You have no idea what you're talking about. Your grandfather did worse by a hundred fold."

"That may be true, but at least he realized what he had done and put a stop to it." She raised her hands to include the outpost and the destruction. "You never did Therion. He tried to start over, to make amends, but you wouldn't let him. In the end it was all about you and your games."

"Enough of this. After I kill you, I will send each part of your drained corpse through the gateway. A reminder for all of history," Therion promised.

"Now that would create a rather large mess for me to clean up," Mr. Eleazar said, stepping forward from behind the gateway. "It would be much appreciated if you refrained."

Therion felt his anger rise even more having been played for a fool. She needed to rest more than he did, and all of this talk had been nothing more than a ruse until her reinforcements arrived. That meant that Kail, and his pet wife would soon follow.

Therion opened himself fully to his magic, pulling it in through the focusing stones on his wrist. The magic poured in from all around him, overflowing and consuming him with a roaring torrent of power.

"Look out Alyssa," Mr. Eleazar shouted.

Therion raised his hand towards the two of them, releasing his fury. The girl shot into the sky, dodging out of the way, but the old man wasn't as quick. The Guardian caught a glancing blow before he retreated behind the closed gateway. Hiding wasn't going to do the Guardian any good.

Thrusting out his arms, he split his attack causing the magic to circle wide around the far side of the gateway and explode.

The Eternal Gateway swung open, and Therion halted his attack. Kail stood on the other side looking at him. *They were like rats*, he thought. *A Falconcrest at every turn.* It would take only a heartbeat to kill the younger version here and now.

Alyssa shot from the sky and slammed the gateway shut rolling out of the way as Therion's magic slammed into The Eternal Gateway. Therion cursed as the ground bucked and groaned in protest as the gateway absorbed his magic, releasing another earthquake.

SNOW BREAK

Camden didn't spare any time to admire the ship as he ran up the boarding ramp and sprinted to the bridge. "Get everything ready to take off," he ordered.

Conrad Black spun around. "Who are you?" he demanded.

"Camden Arland, and this is my ship."

Suki burst onto the bridge out of breath.

"Who's all out there?" Camden asked.

Conrad gave up trying to understand what was going on. He jerked his thumb towards the door. "The strange guy, Mr. Eleazar just left. Alyssa took down the *Inferno,* and her parents jumped off when we first got here."

"Kail and Angela are here too?" Suki asked.

Conrad busied himself with getting the engines back to full power. "That's what I said isn't it? We need to get back up there. The Mastersons need us."

"No," Camden ordered.

Conrad started to protest.

"I said no. We're not leaving until we have everyone." He looked at Suki and nodded. "We all make it or none of us do."

Conrad threw up his hands.

"There," Suki shouted, pointing out to the side of the ship.

Kail and Angela came running out of the jungle. Camden and Suki left the bridge to meet them while Conrad was still yelling at them.

"Camden, Suki, you're here?" Kail asked, skidding to a halt. "Is it over? Did they do it?"

Angela and Suki embraced each other.

Camden shook his head. "I tried Kail. I swear I tried, but Xavier got away."

"That burned rat was here? At The Eternal Gateway?" Angela asked.

Camden nodded, and Suki confirmed it.

"That last disturbance, it was Xavier? Not Alyssa?" Kail realized.

Camden hung his head down. "I'm sorry Kail. Amaya went after him. I'm so sorry."

Kail staggered back. "Amaya?" he asked, looking at Suki. "She's alive?"

Suki couldn't meet his gaze.

"I don't understand," Kail said.

Angela asked. "You were with her? Was she well?" Her stoic demeanor started to crack.

Suki halfheartedly nodded. "She was the same as I remembered."

Angela nodded. For now it was enough for her, and she turned towards the gateway. "Therion is still alive then, and our daughter fights him."

"Wait," Suki begged. "Alyssa said not to help."

Angela stopped and turned her head.

"She begged us, made us promise to stay here to make sure everyone escapes," Suki explained.

Kail rounded on them. "You want us to just stay here and do nothing? We already lost one child, and the other is now an adult, raised by someone we've never met."

"I, I just know we can't go. Amaya was the same way Kail. You have to believe us," Suki cried.

The ground shook from the release at The Eternal Gateway.

"No, there has to be something we can do. I won't see my family torn apart again," Kail insisted.

"There is something," Angela said with a distant look to her eyes.

Kail grew suspicious. "What are you thinking Angela?"

She walked over to Suki and held out her hand. "The bindings. Do you still have them?"

It took a moment for Suki to understand was she was asking. "I, I do." She took off her pack, opening it. "They are right here." She pulled out the three silvery rings and handed them to Angela.

"She said that Vincent was an ally," Angela repeated what Alyssa had said earlier. "A man we did not understand."

Kail stopped her. "What are you thinking?"

"The old plan. Bind Therion's magic away."

Kail reached for the bindings, but Angela jerked away stepping back.

"Angela," he said carefully, "what are you doing?"

"You cannot get them to her. They block your magic." She looked at the others. "You are too slow. But I can get them there."

Kail tried to come up with a different plan. "No, Angela," he said, but he knew she was right. Only Angela's ability to fly would get the bindings to Alyssa in time.

Suki stepped forward. "Go, go now Angela," she shouted.

"No." Kail reached for his wife, but she was already gone. Camden had his hand on Kail, holding him back. "Let go of me," he shouted.

"Let her do this Kail," Camden said, easing up once Kail quit fighting him. "They need you here, we need you here with the ship so we can all leave together."

Kail knew they were right. "Then why do I feel like I will never see her again?"

Suki came over to hug him. "They will both be here, I promise. Therion doesn't stand a chance with two female Keratins after him."

Kail hoped that it was true.

THE ETERNAL GATEWAY

"You've got to stop him," Mr. Eleazar shouted to Alyssa as both of them were being pushed back from the gateway by Therion's magic.

Alyssa grunted her answer as she shot into the sky, trying to split Therion's attention and hopefully the power of his attack. He simply had too much experience, too much command over magic for even the two of them to fight him head on.

Therion's eyes were wild, drunk with power as he allowed his magic to follow her into the sky.

Mr. Eleazar turned to the gateway to get to work when it opened again. Kail once again stood there. "I am more sorry than you can ever know Kail. But this is not your time or your fight," he said, shutting the door with a shake of his head. Kail's connection with The Eternal Gateway was a mystery to be solved another day. Again the gateway opened without his doing. "Oh my," was all he said as a heavy boot kicked him in the head.

Alyssa dodged around Therion's assault. She sent her own magic raining back down on him. Their best hope was for Mr. Eleazar to secure the gateway and for them to regroup later with her father and maybe the others for another chance at eliminating Therion.

Suddenly Therion stopped his attack, and she saw why.

"You will not touch my daughter," Angela growled.

Therion whirled with fury and magic bleeding from his eyes, but Angela held her ground with her sword pointed at him. The runes on its blade reflected the light from the magic that emanated from him. "That won't save you this time," he promised as he unleashed his rage on the elder Keratin.

Therion's magic hit her like an airship, but she held her ground. She pressed the sword and the staff in front of her, blocking the brunt of the attack. Her Imaera armor and the bindings in her possession did the rest as she stepped forward.

It wasn't possible, Therion's mind screamed. *How could she still be standing? How could she even survive? What gods saw fit that she could advance on him?* He poured everything he had at the red-headed Keratin. Magic flowed off of him and through the focusing stones on his wrist. "How?" he screamed at her. "You should be dead."

Angela held as his power increased. "I died a thousand years ago." Her eyes betrayed her when she glanced past him.

Therion spun, keeping one arm on Angela as he fired at Alyssa coming down on him from above. His blast caught her square in the stomach, swatting her from the sky.

It was the opening Angela needed. As soon as he split his magic, all of the resistance let up. Her strike was true to its mark as the end of her blade stabbed behind his hand and through the wrist band of focusing stones.

Therion's head jerked back towards her as he screamed. The magic, no longer focused rebounded with an explosion that sent Angela spinning through the air, and the world went dark.

Chapter 47

THE ETERNAL GATEWAY

Mr. Eleazar was the first to her side. She could hear screaming, the kind someone would make if they were being burned alive. "Angela, are you okay?" he asked.

She could see Therion lying in front of the gateway, writhing in agony as erratic magic lashed out around him. "Now," she said hoarsely, getting up as she pulled the bindings from her vest. "We bind him."

Mr. Eleazar nodded and helped her up as Alyssa scrambled over, clutching her wounded stomach. He took one of the loops and handed it to Alyssa and another for himself. "Just get them on," he instructed. "They will do the rest on their own."

Therion was gruesome. His arm from the elbow down where she had severed the stones was burned to the bone in some places. The smell of charred hair and flesh filled her nostrils. Burns covered the rest of his left side. The explosion had destroyed much of his face and chest. His eyes however poured pain and hate at her as she set the bindings around his neck.

His screams renewed as Mr. Eleazar and Alyssa secured the rest of the binding runes. The magic instantly ceased, leaving him with only his pain and screams.

"Look out!" Mr. Eleazar shouted, catching both of the Keratins in his arms and knocking them away.

The *Lotus* screamed overhead cannons firing. Explosions erupted around them and against the gateway as it passed. It only got one pass at them before the *Odyssey* gave chase.

Mr. Eleazar cursed when he looked back. The Eternal Gateway shuddered as light flashed from the open gateway.

"It's damaged," Alyssa shouted over the noise of the gateway. "We need to get out of here."

"Where is Therion?" Angela shouted, shielding her eyes from the wind.

Mr. Eleazar shook his head. "You two need to leave. It's not safe anymore. The gateway is going to reset." He looked at Alyssa. "It's your time now. I have to go back."

"No," she protested.

"When I go, you won't have much time. You have to take control. It's the only way."

"What about Therion?" Alyssa demanded.

Mr. Eleazar shook his head. "Doesn't matter, he's dead and done either way. You knew this had to happen. If I stay, the paradox won't be complete." He turned to Angela. "I have delivered on my promise Angela. Make this world a place worth living for."

Angela looked at her daughter then nodded. "I promise."

Mr. Eleazar stood in front of the gateway, straightened his jacket, then pulled out his pocket watch to adjusted the time. He looked back and smiled before stepping through time.

The Eternal Gateway Book Two:

Guardian, Chapter 8

THE ETERNAL GATEWAY

If this is death, then the living have it easy. . . .

Pain layered upon pain disjointed his thoughts. Darkness clouded his vision between each breath he managed to gasp through the burning pain. There were even new definitions of pain being created here. *I can see the bones in my hand*, he thought lying on his back. Ash drifted through the sky in a grey blizzard. The movement brought a wave of dizziness that threatened his consciousness.

Willpower alone isn't going to be enough this time. Fighting through the pain he blinked in rhythm with each forced breath pushing the pain further and further from his mind. It was easier than he expected. His brain had no objections to retreat from the suffering. He could feel the adrenalin start to fade from his system. *No, shock will kill me if I don't fight.* The pain was beginning to fade only to be replaced by the duller ebbing away of his life. Of all the desires and seductions he had faced in his life, none had been as sweet or as comforting as the thought of drifting to sleep, succumbing to the relief of the darkness.

It was the smell that brought him back from the abyss of death. *I will not sleep with the stench of burnt flesh. My flesh*, he chided himself. The pain returned, but this time he welcomed it, used it to fire his desire to live. He could feel the jungle floor beneath him in every detail. Every nerve ending screamed to let him know that death was not an option. Sound returned as well, and the storm of ash highlighted the roar of nearby jungle dying to fire. Again he looked at his left hand, burned, melted and useless as he pushed himself up onto his knees with the other.

Faint shouts were coming from all directions as he took in his surroundings. *I know this place*, he thought as recognition began to creep into the back of his mind, *I know... this time*.

"Over here!" someone shouted.

Through the smoke and ash a soldier ran over to where he had managed to kneel.

"Another survivor?" a second voice called out through the haze.

Courduff's uniform. The Gateway. He recognized the insignia on the soldier's uniform.

"Try not to move, sir. Stay still, you are badly burned. Are you a commander from the *Inferno*?" the soldier asked after seeing the remains of his formal clothing.

He couldn't speak, so he waved the soldier closer signaling he could whisper. As the soldier leaned in closer, he wrapped his good arm around the back of the soldier's neck, cupped his chin and with a hard jerk, spun the man's head until it faced the wrong direction. He needed to hurry, more soldiers were coming.   Peeling off his clothing, he nearly fainted again from the pain. Cloth was melted into where his skin caught fire in the battle at the Gateway. His left hand was useless as he traded his clothing for the dead soldier's uniform. The last bit was to loop the man's identification tags around his neck.

He needed to get away from the dead body. Shock set in, and the loss of blood took its toll as he crawled away. He could see a medic head his way against the silhouette of the flaming jungle. Darkness slid over him, and his final thought was, *revenge*.

Chapter 48

THE ETERNAL GATEWAY, THE PRESENT

The entire outpost started to rumble. "We need to go," Angela shouted. "It destroyed half the jungle last time."

Alyssa shook her head. "I know, but not yet." She pulled out the pocket watch that Mr. Eleazar had made for her and synchronized it before snapping it shut and pressing the plunger. She pointed. "Grab the staff," she shouted as she picked up two of the war blades. The third blade, the one Therion had taken from her she couldn't find.

The *Snow Break* hovered above them. Kail stood at the bottom of the open boarding ramp. "Come on," he yelled, waving at them.

Angela and Alyssa didn't need to be told twice as they flew into the air together.

"Go, go, go," he yelled once the two women were aboard. The *Snow Break* banked as it accelerated away from The Eternal Gateway.

Kail, Angela and Alyssa stormed onto the bridge. "Punch it Camden," Alyssa said, eyeing the cleared jungle in front of them.

"What is that?" Camden asked as trees, rocks and the jungle tore free flying up at them.

"The gateway. It's resetting, finishing the paradox," Alyssa answered.

Camden had experienced the gateway reset once before, and he had no desire to be anywhere near when it happened again. He pushed the throttle to the engines as far as they would go.

"Where are the Mastersons?" Angela asked.

"They're clear," Camden answered, focusing on getting them out of there. "The *Lotus* escaped, and the *Odyssey* is waiting for us about five miles out."

"It's happening," Alyssa informed them.

The outpost surrounding The Eternal Gateway came apart as it was sucked into a tornado of swirling debris. A wave of light shot past them, rocking the *Snow Break*. The airship shot forward, released from the gateway's pull.

"There's nothing left," Kail said. "It's like it was never there."

Alyssa nodded. "It's complete. There is no going back now, only forward."

The jungle that had been destroyed, and the clearing for the outpost was restored. All trace of Therion's control, wiped clean.

"It's still there isn't it?" Kail asked.

Alyssa nodded. "It is. But the enchantments are restored as well. No one will find it unless one of us shows them where it is."

Suki held her hand to her mouth. Only pristine jungle spread around them. "Mr. Eleazar?" she asked.

Angela hung her head and Alyssa said, "He's gone. He went back, to see the rest of you safe, to finish training you. Gathering heroes."

Camden growled, "He doesn't know then. He never knew."

"Camden," Suki said softly.

"Therion wasn't defeated at all," Camden continued.

"What are you saying?" Alyssa insisted on knowing.

"You bound him. Don't you get it?" Camden looked at all of them in turn. "Therion *is* Xavier. They are the same person."

"What?" Kail couldn't believe what he was hearing. "Angela?"

Angela shook her head. "I do not know. He was wounded, severely burned and dying." She remembered his face and his hand as they bound away his magic. Wounds that would leave horrible and disfiguring scars if he managed to survive. "We have created him," she whispered.

"And he punished us for it. He knew from the beginning who we were, and he punished us for it. Played us all for fools," Camden said. He turned to Angela and smiled. "Amaya gets her revenge. And the door shall open for revenge yet taken," he quoted. "The childless one."

"It's over then," Suki said. "We won."

Alyssa started to tremble and nodded. "It's over."

"Let's get you two to the infirmary," Suki suggested, leading Alyssa and her mother off of the bridge.

"*Odyssey* to *Snow Break*. Camden, tell us some good news," Rhonin's voice squawked from the radio.

Kail sat back at one of the consoles, and Camden picked up the radio. "Mr. Eleazar is gone. Everyone else is alive and on board. We did it. Therion's dead."

Rhonin sounded relieved. "Roger *Snow Break*. Where to now?"

Camden released the transmit button and caught Kail's eye. "Where to dirt farmer?"

Kail thought about it for a moment. Therion was gone and with him most of Courduff's power and aggression. Cahir no longer had Vincent or Bastiana influencing people against them either. There were a lot of good people who had helped and followed them. People who they needed to repay, and to help rebuild a city that his daughter had only seen as ruin. "Silverton," he decided then he added. "A place with a beach wouldn't be bad either."

Camden shook his head smiling as he pressed the transmitter. "Let's head home *Odyssey*."

"Copy that *Snow Break*. See you all on the ground."

End.

Extra Chapter

SILVERTON, SEVERAL YEARS LATER

Kail sat at his desk frowning at the pile of papers in front of him. Outside his window a large crane swung a palate of building material to the top of an unfinished sky tower. An airship also unloaded material for the project as well. Angela massaged his shoulders. "That feels good," he sighed.

She leaned forward to rub her cheek against his ear and hugged him. "Are you ready for this?" she asked.

Kail sighed and nodded. "I think it's too soon. She's too young. In fact they both are to be doing this."

"We were younger," Angela pointed out, stepping around to sit on his lap while resting against his chest. "Well, you were."

He would never get over being surprised at how light Angela was. "Things were different back then. And they fight a lot," he reminded her.

Angela had to admit that. "It is how they express their feelings for each other."

"I'm not sure I agree with her insistence that Courduff be allowed to attend."

Angela walked her fingers across his arm. "It is Suki's wedding, and Bailon is her brother. There is still a lot of mistrust between Silverton and the rest of the world, but having the leader of Courduff attend will go a long way to clear up that old misunderstanding."

It was the same argument that Suki had presented to him earlier when she wanted Wilhelm and Ari on the guest list. "You know, I grew up with Bailon's wife in Aldervale. It's amazing how things have changed since I used to sell turnips at the market there."

The door to the study burst open and slammed against the wall as Camden marched in. "It's off. The whole thing is off."

Kail sighed and Angela buried her face to keep Camden from seeing her laugh. "What is it this time Camden?"

"Have you seen these?" Camden asked, holding long strips of cloth.

Kail shook his head not recognizing them. "What about them?"

Camden shook them as if he were choking the life out of deadly snakes. "They're socks," he announced, throwing them onto the floor.

"So what?"

Camden pointed at them. "They are purple, that's what."

Kail threw his head back. "Get out of my study Camden," he yelled. "Get out right now."

Angela got up to shoo Camden out of the room and shut the door. The purple socks lay on the floor between them. Angela picked them up and wrapped them around her hands smiling. "These might be useful later," she said with a wink.

Kail smiled. "Wait till Camden finds out what we used them for."

Angela laughed and pulled him up from his chair. "Come, Alyssa and Suki are waiting for us with lunch."

He let her pull him up as he caught her around her waist and spun her around, holding her hand at arms length.

"You are looking forward to this," she said, dancing back to him and giving him a kiss.

"Don't tell Camden." He opened the door.

"Hello Kail," a man in dirt torn clothes said.

Kail shoved Angela behind him and wrapped the both of them in protective magic. On the other side of the door was not the rest of their house, but instead thick jungle. He recognized it as The Eternal Gateway. Kail held up his hand. "Who are you?"

"I need your help to rescue someone very dear to us," the man said. "I need your help to rescue my granddaughter."

Kail slowly lowered his hand and felt Angela step around to his side.

"I need both of your help," Duke Falconcrest said. "Your daughter, Amaya, needs us."

End End.